THE
MIDWIFE

Tricia Cresswell is a retired public health doctor. She temporarily returned to work in spring 2020 in response to the COVID-19 pandemic, and in 2021 volunteered as a vaccinator. She achieved a Distinction in her Creative Writing MA at Newcastle University in 2017. Creative response to the climate emergency has now taken priority in her writing though, like everything, this has been disrupted by the pandemic. *The Midwife* is her first novel and was the winner of the 2020 *Mslexia* debut novel award.

By Tricia Cresswell

The Midwife

THE
MIDWIFE

~⦿~

Tricia Cresswell

MANTLE

First published 2022 by Mantle
an imprint of Pan Macmillan
The Smithson, 6 Briset Street, London EC1M 5NR
EU representative: Macmillan Publishers Ireland Ltd, 1st Floor,
The Liffey Trust Centre, 117–126 Sheriff Street Upper,
Dublin 1, D01 YC43
Associated companies throughout the world
www.panmacmillan.com

ISBN 978-1-5290-9368-1

1 3 5 7 9 8 6 4 2

A CIP catalogue record for this book is available from the British Library.

Typeset in Fairfield LT Std by Jouve (UK), Milton Keynes
Printed and bound by CPI Group (UK) Ltd, Croydon, CR0 4YY

MIX
Paper from
responsible sources
FSC® C116313

Visit **www.panmacmillan.com** to read more about all our books
and to buy them. You will also find features, author interviews and
news of any author events, and you can sign up for e-newsletters
so that you're always first to hear about our new releases.

For Hugh, Simon and Becky

Part One

1

A Beginning

The woman lay curled in the heather, her skin blue-white against the frost. She was so cold to John Elliott's first touch; so certainly dead, that the sound of her breathing was shocking. He stood up, perhaps to run away, but she moved and cried out, one single, formless shout. He took her arm and shook her gently, but she lay still again, folded up like a child. Too heavy for him to lift, he left her wrapped in his plaid and ran down the moor past the crags to the farm.

2

London, February 1841

D r Borthwick looked critically at his reflection, turning his head from side to side. The long mirror was high quality, expensive and new compared with the well-used wardrobe and chest and the dented pewter candelabra on the bedside table. The image looked back, dressed in a sober grey waist-coat and trousers with a starched white shirt and dark cravat, reflecting a respectable professional man of modest means. Checking that the drawers in the chest were locked and the keys in his pocket, he turned to go downstairs where he would exchange a morning greeting with Betty, as she served his ritual porridge then eggs.

3

Unknown

She woke into dark silence, her tongue so dry and swollen that she retched. The noise and movement hurt her head, the throbbing pain worsening then ebbing again. Images flitted by but she could not catch them, dreams of rain with her hair wet and cold on her neck.

Perhaps time passed. She was lying on a hard surface with something over her body and there were nameless smells. A dim light appeared which became a small window in a bare wall and then the smells developed names: smoke, animal dung, mould. She lifted her hands and moved her fingers across her face; her hair was damp and her skin was cold. Her face, but she couldn't make a picture of it in her mind.

Later, she was woken by a touch on her shoulder; the animal smell was stronger, underpinned by stale human sweat. Someone leaned over her, and a female voice spoke, but she couldn't understand what was being said. Her own tongue was clumsy, but she forced a whisper: 'What happened to me?'

She felt her head being lifted and the woman put a cup to her mouth. The pain was terrible, but her thirst was suddenly overwhelming and she managed to sip the liquid and swallow a little, coughing. It tasted of warm milk but sharper. The woman helped her to drink more, saying nothing, and then eased her back down.

She lay motionless, trying to remember. She was in this small bare room. But where was she? Who was she?

London, February 1841

It was the first time Dr Borthwick had been to Belgrave Square; the first time a footman in a periwig and satin breeches had opened a front door for him and shown him soundlessly past tall double doors and marquetry side tables and gas lamps on the walls, all alight. Dr Borthwick inhaled with pleasure as the smell of polish and lavender displaced the acrid smokiness of the fog outside.

He had received the elegantly written card requesting him to call on Sir Jeremy Gasgoine with surprise: he had no patients in this part of London and did not think any of his current ones moved in the same elevated circles as Sir Jeremy and his wife. He was intrigued, though, by the opportunity to see inside a recently built house already renowned for its extravagant decoration and paintings, and its conservatory reportedly filled with fruits and flowers, even in the winter.

The morning room was warm and well lit against the gloom at the windows, a side lamp illuminating the bleached face of a heavily pregnant woman lying on a day bed. As she turned to nod at Dr Borthwick's greeting and bow, her pale lips stretched in the memory of a lovely smile.

Sir Jeremy was polite but brisk. 'Lady Gasgoine is carrying twins according to Dr Preston and Dr James,' he said, naming two eminent physicians who provided advice on childbirth to the very rich. 'There is some disagreement as to how best she can be helped. My wife wishes for a further opinion.'

He sat down by the fire, gesturing Dr Borthwick towards his wife, but Dr Borthwick knew he was being carefully observed.

'Lady Gasgoine, would you be kind enough to tell me how you are feeling and perhaps respond to my questions?' Dr Borthwick said, pulling a chair beside the bed so he could sit and face her.

'Yes. But I tell you now, I will not be bled again.' The voice was quiet, but each word was clear and decisive.

Leaning forward, he felt her pulse and then turned over her arms, gently pushing back the loose silk sleeves of her robe. The skin was translucent white, patterned with the livid marks of multiple lancet wounds.

'How often have you been bled?'

'Every day for weeks,' she said.

He looked up and hesitated, then: 'For my own part, I would not recommend any further bloodletting at this late stage, but perhaps there are other ways I could help.'

He was crossing a line: he knew of Dr Preston's reputation for vicious professional jealousy; he had heard of Dr Preston's ridiculing of the work of the *accoucheur*, the man-midwife, as disgustingly Frenchified and an insult to English modesty.

5

Northumberland, March 1838

Joanna woke at Mary Elliott's call feeling the usual bone-deep cold; she was always cold. The window was just visible as a pale grey patch in the black darkness. They started work with the first dawn light then went to bed as soon as the short day ended. She would lie awake, white dots dancing in front of her eyes as she strained to see something, anything, then fall asleep only to awaken to Mary's voice and the cold and the darkness, again.

Trying not to think, she sat up and dragged the shawl from under the bedcover, wrapping it over her dress, across her shoulders and chest and tying it behind. Then she took out her pair of wool stockings and pulled them up over her socks, stifling a groan when the keens on her chapped fingers opened and bled as she fastened the ties. One morning she had woken to find the stockings frozen to the floor: now, she did as Mary had told her and kept all her clothes in bed. She waited a moment, the cover pulled back over her, until the ever-present hunger won.

She held an arm over her head as she stood: the room was in the roof space, the rough-hewn beams touching the floor on two sides, and she could only stand up straight in the centre where the ladder stair disappeared through the hole. Feeling her way, she went down to the kitchen, which was as cold as the loft and filled with brown smoke from the peat fire, the only light.

Mary was leaning over the hanging pot, stirring, her dress pulled tight across her pregnant belly. Smiling, she straightened up with one hand supporting the small of her back, and handed Joanna a cup of thin gruel which she took, swallowing it quickly.

The door crashed open and John came in, rain dripping from his hat and cape. He sat down and looked at the table as Mary put a cup of gruel and a bowl of stew in front of him and then he started to eat. Joanna watched, envying him the stew, the floating lumps of fat and gristle. Perhaps that's why she spoke. 'Good morning to you, John.'

He looked at her briefly, picked up the bowl and drank the rest, wiping his mouth on his sleeve as he finished and then, standing up slowly, he coughed and spat past her into the fire. She looked away, disgust vying with something she thought might be pity.

She was indebted to him, to them both: he had told her how he found her on the high moor and, with Mary, carried her down to the farm. That was all he would say. He rarely spoke. She knew from Mary that she was covered only by his plaid, that he had found her all but naked and thought her dead. She also knew that Mary fed her and cared for her when she was too weak even to climb down the stairs, and that there was little food but Mary always shared her portion. She owed them her life, but this life here seemed not to be hers.

She could understand them now and already her speech was filled with their words for the farm and the work they did, but each day she would say things they did not understand and use words for things they did not seem to have any experience of; then those words would disappear again. She didn't know where they came from, the words just floated in and out of her head, but they related to what she could remember of her 'other place'. She couldn't make the other place real; she couldn't remember it or who she was in it.

She only knew for certain that she was Joanna now, the name Mary had given her.

As the days passed, she became less clumsy, more able to do some of the tasks that filled Mary's day, taking on some of her work. None of it seemed right at first, even chopping potatoes for the stew pot, though she recognized the feel and smell of the potato, knowing its name and that it needed to be cooked. Some things were harder: Mary had slowly and patiently taught her how to milk the two ewes, how to keep the peat fire alight and make it hotter to boil water, even how to tie up her stockings.

Some nights she dreamed but as she woke the fragments drifted away even as she tried to keep hold of them. There were bright colours, glimpses of sunlight. Then the sea and movement that she could feel and, sometimes, the sound of waves. And the salt taste of her tears.

She heard Mary's cry late in the afternoon and found her bent over, arms braced against the barn wall, fluid pooling at her feet.

'We need to go inside,' she said, putting her arm round Mary's shoulders and pulling her gently away from the wall.

Mary looked at her in terror and for the first time Joanna realized how young she was, a girl with a woman's red weather-beaten face.

'Come inside. I'll look after you.' Joanna repeated her words slower still and Mary nodded.

John arrived from the fields at dusk, the wind blowing in with him. She was ladling water from the big hanging kettle into the one metal bowl; she had stoked up the fire to boil the water and the room was almost warm. He looked at her and nodded as he heard Mary moan behind the bed curtain, and went to the stew pot and served himself. A silent statement, Joanna thought, that he understood that the women were busy with other work.

As the darkness thickened, Mary walked round and round the kitchen holding Joanna's arm tightly and moaning long and hard with each contraction. As each one subsided, Joanna tried to explain to Mary what was happening to her and the baby, using words which came easily into her head and which she understood but which Mary did not seem to. These words stayed, they didn't float away, they were words she had used many times before.

She took Mary over to the bed and settled her on the blanket. 'Mary,' she said, 'I know how to help you. I need to feel for the baby.'

Mary's eyes were wide, pupils huge, and her hair was plastered down with sweat. Her fingers were digging into both of

Joanna's hands as she shook her head, shouting as the next contraction started: 'No. Make it gan away. Make it not be.'

'I can't. The baby has to be born.' She held the sobbing girl until the pain passed.

Her hands were certain as they examined Mary. She let the certainty fill her mind. She had done this many times before, in the other place, wherever it may be. There should be more, she thought, than hands, hot water, a cloth, boiled string, a knife, a single candle. But she was here, and this was all there was.

The candle was only half-burned by the time it was done; Mary was undamaged, and the baby looked a good weight. He was to be called James, Mary said, after old Farmer Elliott. As was tradition: James to son John to son James.

As Joanna came back in from dumping the soiled blanket in the outhouse for washing tomorrow, John pointed to a pan of water and a cloth. 'Ee gan on wash, and I'll heat up milk,' he said.

She smiled at him, understanding the thank-you he was making in the gesture, and carried the water up the stairs. For the first time since being found, she knew some part of herself.

Joanna woke with the sky bright at the window. She pulled on her clothes, fastening the stocking ties with a grunt of exasperation, then slid down the ladder stair to the kitchen and smiled: the fire was well stoked and the bed curtain was pulled back. Mary was sleeping, her baby against her. There was no sign of John but there was water in the kettle and gruel in the pan. She stirred it and ladled out a cupful for her and one for Mary and then drank hers slowly, drowsy as she watched the smouldering peat.

There was one flickering red flame which grew until she was somewhere else, watching the red sun drop below the horizon; then back, eyes filled with peat smoke, not remembering. She blinked to clear away the tears, picked up Mary's cup and went over to the bed.

The day passed very quickly. In the fading light, as she was spreading the last of the fresh straw inside the dilapidated shed, she felt a weary contentment. The two milk ewes, seemingly incapable of learning, kept wandering in front of the pitchfork; she knew them both well now from the daily milking and pushed them out of the way amiably enough. Any job that was out of the wind was a bonus and she had saved this one for the afternoon, knowing it would thaw out her fingers after washing the blanket in ice-cold water. She was pushing the sheep back into the pen, lifting the broken hurdle into place, when she felt a hand on her shoulder and she turned her head, thinking it must be Mary, outdoors far too soon.

It was John. She started to speak but he shoved her forwards, bending her over the top of the hurdle, his weight pinning her there as he pulled up her skirts. She fought then, trying to straighten up and turn round, but he was heavy and strong. When he had finished, she stood up tall and smoothed down her skirts and walked out past him, ignoring him as he fumbled with his breeches.

She went into the kitchen and filled the bowl with water from the kettle and vinegar from the almost empty store cupboard, ignoring Mary who sat silent by the fire, feeding the baby, watching her. Joanna climbed the stairs and pulled up her skirts and washed as best she could with the hot acidic water. Her hands started to tremble then, and she sat down heavily on the hard bed. She must not get pregnant, not here, not in this place, but the words in her head that had made her wash with vinegar had gone again.

Mary came awkwardly up the ladder stair, baby James in one arm, then she put the other round Joanna. They sat, not speaking.

There was no colour except grey in the yard at dawn. She had slept little; had dreamed and woken and dreamed: trying to push him away from her again, but he had been stronger again. She looked around her at the gates, hanging off their hinges, tied with string; at the collapsed end of the barn and the sagging roof; at the piles of stones up against the crumbling walls.

Flexing and stretching her cracked fingers before grasping the pump handle, she pushed hard until water spat then glugged from the spout, bitter cold on her hand. She stooped to pick up the heavy pail, lifting it painfully, and walked to the door, clogs slipping on the ice and mud.

John was in the kitchen and took the pail from her, silent as he filled the big kettle, not looking at her. She stood for a moment until he turned, meeting her gaze. 'I will pay my keep, but not that way,' she said.

He dropped his eyes and she took back the pail and walked out, back rigid.

6

London, April 1841

D r Borthwick resisted straightening his cravat as they were shown into the large sitting room. There were two women seated by the fire to whom he bowed as he introduced himself and Mrs Bates, the midwife. After a long pause, the older woman, tightly contained in a voluminous black bombazine gown, rose majestically to introduce first herself, Mrs Westwood, and then her daughter, Mrs Davies. Mrs Davies, young and very pregnant, looked up from her sewing with a small smile and half-rose awkwardly then sat again, a blush spreading over her cheeks. Dr Borthwick pulled round a chair to face her: she was the one who mattered.

Mr Davies had called on him the day before and after the usual exchanges had begun abruptly and with some agitation: 'You have been recommended to me by Sir Jeremy Gasgoine. You attended his wife and she, and both her twins, survived and indeed he says are all very well. He lays credit for this with your care. He says there is no doubt that you saved her.'

'How very kind of Sir Jeremy,' said Dr Borthwick.

'My wife is in need of attendance. The baby must be only a month or two away.'

Dr Borthwick bowed and smiled: 'I would be very pleased to call on Mrs Davies tomorrow.' He paused then asked, 'Is this your and Mrs Davies's first baby?'

'Her first. She is young, my second wife. Very young. Very innocent.'

'You are concerned for her in childbirth?'

Mr Davies nodded.

'There is always danger, for the mother and her baby, but with care and attention we can help the mother to deliver and lessen the chance of injury to them both. We can increase the prospect of a living child and an undamaged mother. But I can give no guarantees,' said Dr Borthwick, his voice calm and measured.

Mr Davies looked down at the floor and then back to him. 'It took my first wife three days to die. The baby with her.'

Dr Borthwick was used to pregnant women's mothers, whom, certainly in London, he had found mostly to be either ignorant but helpful or ignorant and obstructive. He did realize that this was unfair: he had occasionally chided Mrs Bates, the midwife, for her pithy comments about grandmothers-in-waiting, and then felt that he was a hypocrite.

Mr Davies, however, had made it clear that his mother-in-law, Mrs Westwood, was going to be difficult and that he had been forced to override her voluble objections both to the place of birth and to seeking the advice of an *accoucheur*. Mrs Westwood wanted her daughter to be confined in her own family house in the country, attended by a local woman, as she herself had been seventeen years earlier. She certainly did not want her dearest Emily to be attended by 'some gin-soaked harridan and a likely lecherous, so-called man midwife in the filthy city'. Dr Borthwick and Mr Davies had agreed that the London newspapers were not always helpful on such matters, though the comment about the city was only too true. The stench of human effluent from the Thames last summer had been vile.

Mr Davies had added rather sadly that his young wife had been sheltered by her mother from any knowledge of childbirth, indeed had even been prevented from seeing the whelping of puppies.

It was becoming evident to Dr Borthwick that Mrs Davies would do nothing other than blush and nod whilst her mother, when not actively interrupting, was fidgeting with irritation at his questions. He turned to Mrs Westwood: 'It would be helpful for Mrs Bates, the midwife, and I to see the lying-in room. Perhaps we could visit the room now?'

He stood up, catching Mrs Bates's eye. She, with the practised demeanour of a valued upper servant, was already standing, waiting in the background. They all went upstairs, Dr Borthwick commenting on the fine wooden balustrade as they climbed in procession: Mrs Davies first; then her mother, skirts bunched and rustling, holding his arm; Mrs Bates silently behind.

As Mrs Bates steered Mrs Davies over to the window to check for light and air, Dr Borthwick placed himself firmly in front of Mrs Westwood. 'I have always found it useful to speak with the lady in private in the lying-in room – chaperoned, of course, by Mrs Bates – so that we are all understanding of what will happen on the day. I think you know Lady Gasgoine who indeed commented only last week on how useful she had found the approach.'

He assumed that quoting his success from a higher social tier would be persuasive, and the Gasgoines were very elevated indeed, but Mrs Westwood surprised him.

'I should stay. I do not want Emily to be frightened. I think she knows what happened to the first Mrs Davies. The servants have been gossiping,' she said.

Dr Borthwick took her hand. 'We both want the best for your dear daughter. Please will you trust Mrs Bates and myself, as Mr Davies has, and as I hope your Emily will?'

Mrs Emily Davies lay in the bed in her shift, covers firmly tucked under her chin, having been undressed by Mrs Bates whilst he waited outside. Pulling up a chair beside her, he asked her what she expected would happen when the baby was due to be born.

He decided she was not as entirely ignorant as her mother may have wanted, but she was embarrassed by his description of how her body would work to deliver her baby. Once or twice she turned to Mrs Bates for confirmation of his seemingly outlandish comments and Mrs Bates nodded composedly. In a grey dress with starched white cuffs and linen cap, Mrs Bates radiated nun-like calm and respectability. It was an image which fitted her very well: she was as she looked, a sober and competent midwife.

He decided that he had given Emily enough to think about. 'It is likely, Mrs Davies, that your baby will be arriving perhaps rather earlier than Mr Davies thought. I need to examine you. Mrs Bates will just sort out the covers,' he said.

He turned away and then back again at Mrs Bates's discreet cough. The sheet was folded down and Emily's shift turned up so just the pregnant belly was uncovered. Ludicrously – and he still resented it every time – Mrs Bates was holding another sheet up across Emily's body so that he could no longer see Emily's face and she could not see what he was doing; could not see her own body being touched; could not be allowed to understand. He could, however, see Mrs Bates and he raised his eyebrows, and, as usual, she ignored him. He palpated the belly carefully, then turned away again until modesty was restored.

'I think your baby is going to be here soon, perhaps in the next fortnight. We will call on you again next week and then you and Mrs Bates will probably manage having the baby very well between you. Mrs Bates has helped many hundreds of babies into the world. I will go to speak with Mrs Westwood whilst you dress.'

The welcome the following week was different: both women stood up as soon as Dr Borthwick and Mrs Bates were shown into the sitting room. Mrs Westwood reported with some enthusiasm that 'dear Emily' was feeling much better after following his advice on diet and had taken the air in the garden every day, with Mr Davies escorting her. Emily looked straight at Dr Borthwick and smiled her agreement. He nodded briefly, pleased he had freed her from being caged with her mother since the first frosts.

They took tea amicably, Mrs Westwood even deigning to

pass a cup to Mrs Bates. Then they all trooped upstairs again, although this time Mrs Westwood left them at the door, saying she would be in her own room.

Later, after he had examined Emily and the sheet was pulled up firmly to her chin, he placed the chair beside the bed again.

'So, as we thought, your baby will be wanting to see the world in the next week or so.' He was watching her, waiting.

She turned her head and the sobbing started. Mrs Bates, standing on the other side of the bed, bent over to take her hand. He sat quiet, unspeaking, until the sobs subsided. 'Tell me,' he said, his voice very gentle.

'Mrs Davies, the first Mrs Davies, I mean Mr Davies's first wife . . .' She stopped, struggling to say the words. 'They say she screamed for three days. Then she died. The baby stuck inside her.'

Dr Borthwick thought that 'they' were unkind, cruel even, but probably not intentionally so. He spoke calmly. 'Sometimes childbirth is difficult. But you are young and healthy and Mrs Bates will help you and I will too, if you need me. But I can make you one promise: you will not scream for three days. I have medicine I can give you that will help.'

Dr Borthwick rarely permitted himself to be angry, but he could be about this. There was no need in the modern world for women to die screaming. When he had arrived in London, he had followed his former mentor's wry advice to find a decent apothecary, one who was both properly licensed and did not consume too many of his own potions. Dr Borthwick administered tincture of laudanum if forceps were needed but used much stronger opium resin for women when the baby was dead and had to be removed. Women still sometimes died, and he was deeply distressed by his inability to save them, but at least he could dull their pain and blunt their fear with opium.

He was eating lunch when the note came, two days later, in Mrs Bates's neat script: *'Mrs Davies is tiring. No progress after 15 hours. Mrs Margaret Bates.'*

Betty, the maid, said that Mr Davies's carriage was waiting outside. He picked up his instrument bags, collected his coat from Betty in the hall and left.

Mr Davies himself opened the door to his house and took Dr Borthwick upstairs, pausing outside the room, unable to speak.

'I'll see how Mrs Davies is progressing. Where is Mrs Westwood?' said Dr Borthwick.

'She's in there. Emily asked for her,' said Mr Davies and turned away.

Dr Borthwick opened the door and closed it quietly behind him, watching the scene: Mrs Bates supporting Emily as the contraction subsided; the girl's head lolling forwards, sweat or tears running down her cheeks; Mrs Westwood sitting by the bed sobbing loudly. Mrs Bates looked up and shook her head, then grimaced in Mrs Westwood's direction.

'Mrs Westwood,' he said, taking her arm. 'I need to examine Emily, so please could you wait outside.'

As he leaned forward to help Mrs Westwood up, he was engulfed in a miasma of eau de cologne, alcohol and laudanum. After closing the door firmly behind her, he spoke to Emily as he removed his coat and washed his hands in one of the bowls laid out on a table by the bed. 'Mrs Davies, Mrs Bates is going to help you get in position so I can examine you before the next pain. It will be uncomfortable, I'm afraid, but it will be quick.'

She barely opened her eyes, but she nodded. No modesty sheets now, just the sweat-soaked shift pulled up, one knee resting against Mrs Bates, the other against him. Emily made soft mewling cries as he examined her. Finishing, he carefully lowered the girl's knees and pulled down her shift. He looked at Mrs Bates who nodded towards the instrument bag.

'Hopefully not. Let us have one more try,' he said to Mrs Bates, then, 'Mrs Davies, I know you are very tired. We are going to help you change position again. You need to squat on the floor. It is time you had this baby. I want you to concentrate very hard on what Mrs Bates says.'

They supported her as she squatted down through the next contractions. He felt the increase in energy as Emily, perhaps for the first time in her life, took control. She breathed and pushed and panted in rhythm with Mrs Bates's firm instructions, until with final loud and triumphant cries, she gave birth to a healthy baby girl.

A little later, Emily lay half-dozing with her baby close against her as Mrs Bates tucked a clean sheet over them and Dr Borthwick finished packing his bag. Straightening up, he stretched for a moment, back arched, then turned to find Emily looking at him with a slight frown, as if to ask a question. As he moved to the bed her eyes drifted closed. He smiled as he gently felt her pulse which was strong and steady as she slept.

*

Dr Borthwick, leaving the house with Mrs Bates, was delayed yet again by Mr Davies thanking him and shaking his hand. He was used to the relief of husbands that their wives had survived but was finding Mr Davies's frank and open delight in his wife and baby daughter to be very touching in a man he had thought to be rather dour. He smiled when Mr Davies turned to Mrs Bates, pressing a whole crown into her hand.

'You'll be able to charge him a good amount then,' murmured Mrs Bates as they got into the carriage and she carefully fastened the money into her pocket. Dr Borthwick said nothing but smiled again and nodded. He knew that she struggled with him charging a variable amount, based on what he thought the family could afford to pay, which was sometimes surprisingly little. He paid her a generous hourly rate regardless and she kept any extras.

She settled back on the cushioned seat and closed her eyes, as she always did. Mrs Bates was not interested in general conversation: they spoke only about work, which to a large extent suited him. He looked at her now with affection.

His first landlady had introduced him to the widowed midwife who had a room in a house run by her friend. The landlady had been keen to tell him that only respectable widows lodged there, no men or children allowed.

At their first meeting, Mrs Bates had been cold and suspicious. 'What are you then? One of them man-midwives?'

'I do not claim to be a midwife and certainly do not have your years of experience. I am a physician, but I am also an *accoucheur*, with training in the use of forceps and other instruments. But I use them only when needed,' he said.

'So, what do you want?

'I have a number of ladies now who need the attention of a good midwife. But I have some requirements about how the work is done.'

'What might they be?' Her voice was hard.

He knew she had complied at first for the money and then later the status: as his practice had grown, she worked more and more in the smart new streets and squares where well-dressed servants opened the front door to her. Their relationship had changed when Mrs Bates sent him a note asking for help with one of her own mothers, as she called them, a local woman living in her street. He had gone immediately.

'Her third but a big one, too big,' Mrs Bates had told him as he entered the small, cold room.

He nodded and then focused on the pale woman who was barely responding to Mrs Bates's encouragement to push.

It was the first time Mrs Bates had watched him use forceps. He delivered the baby with difficulty but to his surprise and pleasure the little girl was alive. In the everyday miracle which still moved him, the exhausted mother reached out for her daughter and held her tenderly.

Later, as he left, Mrs Bates turned to him: 'I'd have lost her. Babe also. What you did, it was well done.'

Dr Borthwick had gone home and toasted victory with a hot bath and a small glass of port.

The carriage stopped at her lodgings. Mrs Bates opened her eyes and caught him looking at her, smiling in recollection.

'What?' she said.

'We have been working together for a year.'

'That's all right then,' she said.

He took her arm and helped her out of the carriage.

The doctor's house was warm: Betty knew to keep the fires going if he was called out. He handed his coat to her and agreed that a chop and gravy would be required in half an hour and then walked up to his bedroom to wash, locking the door behind him.

7

Northumberland, April 1838

John had kept away, not speaking to Joanna at all for weeks, so she was surprised when he looked up from his stew. 'Jack Turnbull's wife at Broome Farm is for a baby soon and I told'm as you would act midwife. Her from village is gone away, not that her was any use as they say. I told'm as you did a good job for Mary.'

These were the most words he had ever said to her.

She nodded. 'You should make them pay something – not much, but something.'

'Aye. Two laying hens.'

Farmer Turnbull came for her early that Sunday afternoon with no information except that his wife had sent him to fetch her as it was time. Pulling her shawl over her head, Joanna followed him outside and then stopped, looking up at the huge horse and then back at the farmer who, shaking his head slightly, pulled himself easily up into the saddle. John bent and cupped his hands, telling her to step up, and then the farmer leaned down from the saddle and hauled her on to the horse in front of him. To make it worse he unconcernedly pulled her right leg across until she was sitting legs astride. Knowing she was blushing, she pulled her bunched skirt as far down as it would go over her filthy stockings and tied-on clogs. He took the reins in one hand and kept his other arm casually round her waist.

It was the first time she had been beyond the yard and home field. The horse walked down the path and turned into the valley and then the sun was behind them. She could see for miles: rolling moorland rising to the left with bright green patches of early grass; woodland falling away to the right, some in spring leaf, some still winter dark; patchwork fields ahead, where far away on the horizon was a line of darker blue. The sea – she knew it was the sea – eastwards to the sea.

She was content to watch, treasuring this certainty as the view unfolded, but the horse's back was wide, and her thighs started to ache. 'How long will it be to your farm?' she said, turning her head as far as she could towards the farmer.

'Not long, another quarter-hour.'

He did not speak again but she was very aware of his arm heavy round her each time she tried to move to lessen the pain, now worst in her buttocks.

Farmer Turnbull got off the horse at the field gate, leaving her clinging to the reins until he lifted her down on to her shaking legs, handling her without comment. As she leaned heavily on the gate, he methodically tied up the horse next to a water trough and then walked across the yard to the farmhouse, gesturing at her to follow him.

The Turnbulls were not like Mary and John, not always hungry and always cold, not starving poor. Their kitchen was warm with a coal fire burning in a big metal range. As well as a table with benches there were three wooden chairs round the hearth and two spinning wheels, but above all there was a lovely smell which Joanna immediately recognized as baking bread. She stood, waiting; aware her dress was dirty, hanging loose, shapeless and too short; aware the farmer was looking at her with seeming distaste. Then she heard the low moaning and she felt the certainty come into her head with relief.

'I'll need hot water and soap to wash my hands and then more water boiling, a knife and string both cleaned and boiled, and clean linen. Now, is Mrs Turnbull through that door?' Her voice was calm. She could feel rather than see Farmer Turnbull's surprise.

'Aye,' he said. 'Her mam's with her.'

She delivered Ellen Turnbull's baby girl two hours later. It was an easy birth, third baby to this big-hipped young woman who moaned loudly with each contraction and then leaned back against her mother with a wide smile. She pushed and panted with muscular enthusiasm when Joanna told her and laughed through her tears as Joanna lifted the baby girl on to her belly.

Joanna realized that she was smiling too and that it felt both forgotten and remembered.

An hour later, Joanna left Ellen clean and comfortable, nursing her baby, with her husband and two young sons sitting round the bed in a silent but admiring circle. The kitchen was still warm, the coals glowing, and Ellen's mother gave her a big bowl full of thick stew with plenty of meat and turnip and a slice of soft and fragrant bread. She was a lined and heavier version of her daughter, but her smile was marred by blackened, broken teeth. Ready to laugh and talk, pleased with her new granddaughter, she sat spinning as she watched Joanna gulp down the stew.

'There's more bread on table,' she said.

'I'll take it home for Mary, please,' said Joanna.

'That bad, is it?'

'There's been me to feed as well.'

'Looks from eez hands that ee been doing plenty work in return. Eat more bread. I'll give ee some for Mary.' Ellen's mother paused the wheel to join the thread. Then she nodded, settling back in her chair, the wheel spinning again. 'That were a good farm in old James Elliott's time,' she said.

'What happened?'

Joanna finished the stew, wiping the bowl clean with a second and then a third slice of bread, as the story was told at length, with great relish but also some sympathy. The Elliott farm, high up on the moor, had suffered more than most from the drop in the price of wool after the war and old Farmer Elliott's death had left his widow to cope with only two daughters to help. John, their much older brother, had gone away to sea years before. After Widow Elliott died, John came back to claim his inheritance but found no money, a sickly flock, ten years of repairs not done and two sisters to feed. He rapidly made himself unpopular with his neighbours by endless carping about being cheated out of prize money in the Navy. Worse, though, when drunk, he would accuse them of having stolen from his mother.

Joanna, warm and full of food, interrupted when Ellen's mother next paused. 'Where are the two sisters?'

'Older girl, Joanna her name too, her died that first winter John were back. Were a bad year, Edlingham Burn frozen solid for a two-month. Me man Billy went too, God rest his soul, and old man Johnson, allus death in threes.' She paused, joined the thread again, and continued in a lowered voice, 'So that left just John and Mary.'

'Mary? But Mary . . . I thought Mary was . . . ?' Joanna stopped.

So it was that. Not poverty that stopped Mary going with John to the village. Not his angry pride that kept visitors away after the baby was born. A deeper shame.

''Ee not know then? Mary's the youngest sister, born after John went to sea. They never met 'til him came back. Still a mortal sin. Best her's kept hidden, her and child.'

Joanna felt angry, the strongest feeling since she had awakened in the small dark room. She knew enough of John's sin. Then she looked down at the wiped-clean bowl, and thought of the remorseless, grinding work John and Mary did every day, just to eat, and of Mary's tenderness with her baby. Tears filled her eyes, quickly squeezed away.

Ellen's mother stopped spinning and leaned forwards, whispering now: 'Is it well formed? Or monster?'

'Little James is a healthy baby,' she said. So far.

Farmer Turnbull took her back in the evening light in his cart, two hens squawking in a box behind. He didn't speak at all in the thirty-minute journey but he handed her down from the cart gently enough.

'I'll carry hens, but you go indoors quick-like with this. Ellen said it's for you and Mary,' he said, handing her a bundle.

He took the hens round the back, calling out for John, and

Joanna went in to the kitchen and opened the bundle with Mary: a piece of soft flannel to make baby clothes; a bobbin of thread with a needle; a fresh white loaf. Riches.

A week later Joanna delivered another big fat baby, a boy and a first child, for Ellen's sister, much to his grandmother's delight. This time Farmer Turnbull took her in both directions in his cart, to and from his brother-in-law's farm on the hillside at the end of the track. On the way back with the flitch of bacon which John had required for her services, Farmer Turnbull took her hand and pressed a thrupenny piece into it: 'From brother-in-law and me. For you. Not for John Elliott.'

The week after that she was called to Blacksmith Weddell's wife, a first venture into Edlingham village. The cottage stood alone at the end of the lane, opposite the forge, surrounded by a low wall with yellow primroses massed against the honey-coloured stone. Inside, she had only a fleeting impression of the sheen of the polished table and dresser and the blue-patterned plates as the blacksmith hurried her through to the bedroom and left her with his wife.

Mrs Weddell moved her head and started to smile but, turning away, coughed again and again. Joanna waited until the deep rasping sound stopped and passed the young woman a cloth from the neatly folded pile on the little table by the bed.

'Would you like a drink?'

Mrs Weddell nodded.

Joanna helped her forward, arm round the thin shoulders, and put the cup to the white lips. Mrs Weddell sipped and leaned back.

'Thank you. Farmer Turnbull said to send for you.' Her voice was quiet but clear, different from any Joanna had heard on the farms.

She stood by the bed, aware of her rags in this clean room, not wanting to sit on the pale blue quilt. Then Mrs Weddell moved slightly in the bed.

'Are you having any pain?' Joanna said.

'Not yet. The bleeding started this morning. Same as the last two.'

'When was your last monthly?'

'Christmas. The others . . .' Mrs Weddell closed her eyes and one small tear ran down her cheek. 'The same. Four months.'

Joanna looked at Mrs Weddell's pale face, the shadows under her eyes dark as bruises, the fair hair damp with sweat. Again, the certainty, the knowledge, came to her, but this time touched with pity.

'Mrs Weddell, I need to examine you but first I must wash my hands and –' she gestured at her skirt – 'I need to borrow a clean apron.'

'Jane, please call me Jane.' Jane Weddell opened her eyes and smiled. 'There'll be warm water in the copper through the back, and aprons on the drying rack.'

In the scullery there was a small square mirror on a hook over the big enamel sink. Joanna looked at the speckled surface; the first time she had seen herself, the bone-thin face with hollow eyes and lank, dirty hair. She looked away as other pictures appeared in her head of the face: fuller, smiling, framed with thick brown hair. Then the pictures faded and were lost. She shook her head.

Joanna sat with pale, coughing Jane Weddell as she miscarried for the third time, holding her hand until the cramps had stopped and then washing and changing her.

Blacksmith Weddell towered over her as she came out of the bedroom with a large bowl covered in a bloody cloth. A massive man but his voice was quiet and slow.

'How's my Jane?'

'She's lost a lot of blood. She may bleed more. But go in now. She wants to see you.'

'Will she live?' Tears were running down his furnace-reddened cheeks.

'I don't know. But if she does, she won't survive another pregnancy.' She paused, but he deserved the truth. 'Or another winter, I doubt. I think she has a sickness on her lungs.'

They both knew what she meant.

He nodded and went in, to be with his dying wife.

It was warm in the spring sunshine as she went outside to empty the blood-filled bowl into the privy and wash it out under the pump. The yard was tidy, a few hens pecking round her feet and two metal troughs planted with more primroses. She left the bowl to dry and went over and carefully picked a few, stroking the pale yellow petals, and took them inside and found a blue vase on the dresser. As she arranged them, she knew she had done this before; had put flowers in a pot; had seen primroses growing. But there was nothing more, not where or when.

Putting down the flowers, she ran out to the pump and pushed the handle hard up and down, forcing her head under the cold water and scrubbing one-handed at her face and hair.

The blacksmith said nothing as he came out, but he handed her a dry cloth and later wrapped a blanket round her before he lifted her on to his cart and took her back to the Elliotts' farm.

But not, she was sure, to home.

Blacksmith Weddell arrived at the farm again the next day with nails and newly forged hinges, the required price for her services, and then helped John fit them as an unexpected extra payment. She looked up from milking the ewe as he effortlessly lifted up the shed door, holding it as John hammered in the long nails. The smith's forearms were bare, and she could see the scars where hot metal had splattered and then the thick corded muscles. She felt a flash of something remembered then forgotten, but enough to make her smile and bury her face against the sheep's greasy flank. The ewe, sensing her lack of concentration, pulled away and she only just caught the pail before it tipped over. There was little enough milk now with the ewe almost dried off, she thought, irritated with herself as she carried the milk through to the kitchen.

Blacksmith Weddell came to see her before he left and pushed a package into her hands.

'This is for you, not him. From my Jane. She said as you were very kind. I thank you for that and for your honesty,' he said, then looked away, clenching his massive hands.

'Thank you both,' she said.

'I'll ask for you again when she needs you. For the coughing, I mean. I'll not risk the other.' He looked at her, desolate.

'Whenever she needs me, I'll come,' she said.

He left then, so tall he had to bend his back to go through the doorway. In the package was a woollen shawl and a starched white apron. Folded inside was a shilling. She gave the shawl to Mary, for baby James, but she hid the shilling behind the loose plank upstairs, along with the thrupenny piece.

Two weeks passed and the extra food, eggs from the hens and the flitch of bacon, made a huge difference to how they felt and how they lived. John was doing more repair work ready for lambing and, as Mary picked up the household tasks again, Joanna worked companionably enough outside with him. He never touched her but sometimes she could feel him watching as she moved across the yard.

Then, one morning, she woke and realized that, for the first time in this room, she did not feel cold. It was early and very quiet, with only the faintest of light at the window. She ran her fingers over her face and tried to picture herself, but the only image was of the thin white face and filthy hair in Jane Weddell's mirror. Not her. It couldn't be how she had looked before, when she had learned to be a midwife and more. She tried to remember: she knew that Jane would die from the disease in her lungs but what was its name? It had a name, but it was lost. Lost. The tears started to well up, but she wiped them away and sat up. She needed to think, to plan. She had to leave the farm, find a safe place to live, find work. Maybe set up as a midwife in the village. Perhaps then she would find herself.

There was movement below, Mary raking the fire and then the clang of the gruel pot on its chain over the hearth. Her debts to Mary were paid off: she had cared for her and baby James; the farm was in a better state than when she arrived. But she would be leaving Mary to him.

The dead lamb was very small and malformed and already foul smelling. John had hold of the mother, inspecting its bloodied rear end.

'Yow's well enough,' he said as he let the ewe go, not ungently. The second miscarried lamb this week, two the week before, and he did not need to explain to her what the losses meant: another poor lambing would lead to another half-starving winter and there was a baby now to be fed. They walked on in silence, Joanna thinking through what she needed to say, wary of his quick temper. She was worth something: she had earned again last week, a half-bag of oatmeal for splinting the broken arm of one of the quarrymen's sons (and a penny for herself). She needed him to listen, though, for Mary's sake.

'Have the other farms lost lambs?'

'Not my business,' said John.

'But perhaps there's something could be done. You could ask Farmer Turnbull?'

'I'll do as I see fit. And ee not be speaking my business with any else.'

He strode away, driving his crook hard into the ground with each step, and she felt both sadness and a small sense of release, a hardening of her resolve to leave them.

She worked it out in the wakeful nights: she would offer her services as a nurse to poor dying Jane Weddell, the black-smith's wife, and make herself indispensable. She would be safe there, safe with Blacksmith Weddell, safe from John. She would escape next week on market day, whilst John was away. Take her few coins and the white apron and the clothes she was wearing and walk away up and across the moor. Then, one day, she would try to look for the other place, for the woman she may have once been.

8

London, May 1841

D r Borthwick very rarely accepted luncheon or dinner engagements and never evening parties, his excuse of being always too busy only enhancing his reputation. However, the invitation to dinner with Mr Robert Brown, a well-known man of science, could not be refused, particularly when hand-delivered by Mr Swan. With considerable excitement and some trepidation, he had accepted.

He had met the Swans in the winter, recommended by the Gasgoines, he assumed. It was Mrs Swan's first pregnancy. On Dr Borthwick's second visit, as he and Mrs Bates were ushered in by the footman to await their patient, he had noticed three botanical drawings on the wall of the morning room. They were very fine and similar he thought to some on display at the botanical gardens at Kew, a place he visited frequently. Mrs Swan arrived, slightly short of breath, a couple of moments later. She looked robustly healthy: clear blue eyes and fine skin and her pregnancy clearly visible in a loosely fitted chintz morning gown.

'Dr Borthwick and Mrs Bates, please forgive me for keeping

you waiting. My dear mama has arrived early for luncheon but Mr Swan has kindly taken her for a tour of the garden. He feels she must see the cherry tree which is just now come into flower.'

She caught his eye and he smiled as he bowed; both of them, he felt, being very grateful to the cherry blossom and Mr Swan.

'We have been here but a moment and I am entertained completely by seeing these most beautiful botanical drawings,' he said, turning back to look at them.

'Oh, I am pleased you like them; they are a double favourite of ours. They were given to Mr Swan by his godfather, Mr Robert Brown, and to add to our pleasure, were drawn by my own second cousin, Mr Charles Darrow,' she replied cheerfully.

'Mr Robert Brown the illustrious botanist?' he said and stopped, realizing he was breaking the rules: never state a fact unless certain where it came from; never engage unprepared in conversations on specific topics; always avoid wider conversation about individuals.

'You are kind to say so but yes, Mr Brown is indeed well known in scientific circles.'

He gave a polite nod and turned back to the pictures, deliberately slowing his breathing.

In the following weeks he made sure he knew about Robert Brown's position as Keeper of Botany at the British Museum and about his travels to Australia, and he read Mr Brown's published paper to the Linnean Society on the orchid cell.

Mrs Swan's baby remained persistently breech in late pregnancy. At Dr Borthwick's second attempt to turn the baby, she managed to fluster Mrs Bates by refusing the modesty sheet between them as he examined her and continuing to make comments and queries whilst his hand was on her naked belly. He had explained the possible serious problems of breech birth in detail. He enjoyed her intelligent questions: she was well educated and had a better understanding of the mechanics of childbirth than any of his previous patients.

After they left the house, Mrs Bates stated that women could be over-educated, a remark he had chosen to let pass.

Two weeks later, in response to Mrs Bates's note, he arrived at the house and was escorted rapidly upstairs by the footman. Even he was surprised to find Mr Swan, jacket off, walking his wife round the bedroom. Mrs Bates's stiffened back radiated disapproval as she straightened the bowls and cloths on the white linen-covered table.

'Good evening, Mrs Swan, Mr Swan. Mrs Bates, how is the baby?'

'Still breech and well down.'

He allowed himself a raised eyebrow at a comment which, even by Mrs Bates's standards, was unusually brusque. 'I'll examine Mrs Swan when this next pain is finished,' he said. 'Mr Swan, if you could help Mrs Swan on to the bed when she is ready?'

Mr Swan looked up and nodded, about to speak, and then stopped as his wife gripped his arm, making a strangled cry. Mrs Bates turned round towards her, but Mr Swan was in control. 'Breathe, my dear, breathe.'

He held her, breathing with her, intimate and loving, and then she got on to the bed with little fuss or need for help.

'Ah, Dr Borthwick. This is now quite unpleasant. Too late

to change my mind, I suppose?' She managed a wry smile as her husband wiped her forehead with a damp cloth.

'Yes, but not much longer to go,' he said, smiling back. Then, 'Mr Swan, you are very welcome to stay but could I ask you to turn away while I attend to Mrs Swan?'

Mrs Bates was opposite now and glared at him. She held up the modesty sheet somewhat defiantly before he felt Mrs Swan's belly.

'Your baby is still breech and I need to know exactly what is happening. I want you to breathe through the next pain and then I'll examine you further,' he said.

Not very much later, Mrs Swan, concentrating and intense, was supported on the edge of the bed by Mr Swan behind her and Mrs Bates holding her legs, as Dr Borthwick very slowly extracted her son, bottom first. As his head was finally delivered, the baby cried loudly but was almost surpassed by Mr Swan, who wept noisily and managed to kiss not only his wife but also Mrs Bates. She appeared to be better pleased with the gold sovereign he gave her later.

The invitation to dinner with Mr Robert Brown was clearly in reward for the safe outcome for both mother and son. Mr Swan delivered the invitation from his godfather in person, adding that he would escort Dr Bates and that, 'The evening party will be small. My godfather has a fear of mixed dinners so it will be all scientific men and most of them quite, indeed some very, old.'

On the evening of the dinner, he dressed with care in his best white linen cravat and black tailcoat. His clothes were more expensive now, both a mark and an advertisement of his professional success, but still discreet. Mr Swan arrived promptly and spoke amiably about his wife and child in response to Dr Borthwick's enquiries as they travelled in his carriage to the more fashionable part of the city. As they approached Mr Brown's impressive house in Soho Square, Dr Borthwick was aware of his increased heart rate.

There were no preliminaries: they were relieved of their hats by an aged and unsmiling manservant and ushered straight through a dark panelled hall into the dining room. There, light from several huge candelabra reflected from shining silver and faceted glassware on the massive rectangular table, making the room much brighter than he had expected. There were, as far as he could count quickly, twenty place settings, each with an elaborate display of cutlery.

As they sat down, Mr Swan introduced him briefly to the man on his left: as expected, it was Mr Charles Darrow, second cousin to Mrs Swan and a botanist and illustrator who worked for Mr Brown. The three of them were at least a generation younger than the other guests, and Dr Borthwick thought that Mr Swan had arranged for them to sit together as a form of defence against what was undoubtedly a collection of some of the finest minds in natural sciences. From time to time rather tetchy exchanges could be heard rising above, and then submerging back into, the pool of ritual chatter required during the meal.

He was gently quizzed over the soup by Mr Swan about his past, forcing him to focus.

'Mrs Swan tells me that you have spent time in India?'

'Yes indeed, as a child. I was born there. My father travelled extensively in his youth, as far even as China. My travels have been modest in comparison with his and certainly nothing compared to those of your godfather.' Dr Borthwick nodded politely in the direction of their host.

This led to the intended exchange about Mr Brown's travels to Australia, moving away from any detail about his own past and with Mr Swan providing all the information. Dr Borthwick was now very experienced in this: it was not usually difficult to move men to discussion of factual issues, though women were more persistently inquisitive in social situations. As the meat was served, he turned slightly, as etiquette required, to Mr Darrow on his left, who nodded and spoke first.

'It is a great pleasure to have an opportunity to speak to you, Dr Borthwick. My dear cousin Mrs Swan speaks most highly of you and more importantly says you have admired three of my drawings,' he said.

Dr Borthwick looked fully at him for the first time, polite smile in place. And was lost. He looked quickly down again, away from the brown eyes and beautiful mouth, the top lip moving against the fine hairs of the dark moustache. He stared then at the hand, almost touching his, long fingers resting on the table, and could not breathe. Feeling the warm flush rise up his cheeks, he turned away, coughing into his napkin.

Somehow, he managed the next hour: apologizing for no doubt having over-peppered his soup, responding as briefly as was polite to Mr Darrow's further comments, turning with relief back to Mr Swan as soon as he could. He knew, though, that the young illustrator continued to watch him during the wider scientific debate, led by Mr Brown, of which Dr Borthwick would remember nothing at all.

Later, safe at home behind the locked bedroom door, he examined his face carefully in the long mirror. The light in the dining room had been very bright and Charles Darrow must have seen the blush.

The next morning Betty appeared at his study door smoothing her dress, rushing her words. 'Dr Borthwick, there's a gentleman, Mr Charles Darrow, called to leave his card and parcel but I said as you might be available, but then there's no fire in the morning room. Oh, shall I light one?'

She gave him the visiting card then stood wringing her hands: any change to routine upset her.

'Bring Mr Darrow in here then. And could you ask Mrs Hayward for some coffee? Thank you, Betty,' he said.

'But it isn't coffee time yet, doctor . . .' Her voice trailed off miserably.

'Perhaps if you were to say that I asked her as a special favour? That should help.'

He watched her as she left the room, rehearsing the words under her breath. Turning the card over and over in his hand, he walked across the room and stood by the fireplace. He closed his eyes for a moment, breathing slowly. In and out.

Betty opened the door and announced his guest, this time spacing her words carefully as he had taught her: 'Mr Charles Darrow to see Dr Borthwick.'

'Mr Darrow, so kind of you to call. Please sit down here by

the fire. There is still a cold wind outside, I think. Will you take some coffee?' Dr Borthwick kept his voice level and calm.

'Please forgive me for calling unannounced but I had business in the square and was hoping to leave you this book. You expressed an interest in Mr Dickens's works . . .' He handed Dr Borthwick a carefully wrapped and labelled parcel.

Dr Borthwick looked up into the brown eyes and said his thanks with measured politeness. There was a slight pause as they both sat down.

'You are well, I hope. I feared last night that you may be developing a chill or even a fever,' Mr Darrow said.

'I am very well, thank you. Just too much pepper causing sneezing. My own fault. I think I must have developed a taste for spiced food in my childhood in India. Which takes me to a better topic for conversation than my over-indulgence. Please would you tell me more about your planned travels? You said you are setting off in the autumn of next year?' He felt more in control now, comfortable in his own study surrounded by his books and certificates, the recognizable paraphernalia of a medical man.

Conversation became easy, Mr Darrow describing his route: he was to travel through South America drawing plants in their native habitat and bringing back seeds where possible. He was travelling with William Lobb, a renowned plant collector, and they aimed to send back certain live specimens which Mr Robert Brown had specified. They were to leave in about seventeen months' time, in October 1842, arriving in the southern hemisphere's early summer, with a planned return a year later.

Dr Borthwick was of necessity an excellent listener: he never tried to impose his own stories or memories, never interrupted, never commented other than by timely questions. He started to relax, enjoying Mr Darrow's enthusiasm, and was surprised by the clock chiming, surprised that so much time had passed.

'Dr Borthwick, my apologies. I have been going on about myself for too long. Do you have plans to travel again?'

'No, alas, not at present. I need to further my professional interests, to establish myself here in London.'

'Sometimes I think it is only when travelling that I can be fully myself. Outside the constraints of our London society. Perhaps you feel the same?'

Dr Borthwick made himself look directly at his guest as he replied. 'I do find London very different, more formal. But it is easier here to find interesting and lively intellectual conversation with men and indeed with educated women such as your cousin.'

'I thought perhaps you might be interested then in joining a club for men with a taste for travel and such things?'

Dr Borthwick looked at his hands, away from the brown eyes. Charles Darrow was taking a serious risk and deserved some sort of honest answer. 'I socialize very little. My working hours are unpredictable and often long and that can make me poor company.' He paused, seeking words which could not be misinterpreted, then said, 'But I prefer either a scientific meeting or a very small mixed gathering. I have never been one for gentlemen's clubs.' He paused again. 'Not of any type.'

He glanced up, expressionless, watching the slight frown as Charles Darrow nodded and looked quickly away.

After a few more polite exchanges, Mr Darrow made his

farewells and Dr Borthwick escorted him to the front door and then stood for a moment before going back into his study.

Later he sat by the fire and slowly unwrapped the parcel: it was a bound volume of *The Life and Adventures of Nicholas Nickleby*, recently published. How apt a title. He looked round his study: the small collection of medical books, the two framed certificates, the new desk and leather chair, the trappings of his hard work. He rented this house and kept the cook and maid and coachman warm, well fed and well paid. There were women and babies alive who would have been dead without him. It had to be enough. What else could he do?

It was a long time since he had allowed himself to think beyond his London life and there could be no place in it for Charles Darrow. He opened the book and turned a few pages, unseeing, as the undisciplined tears filled his eyes.

Northumberland, May 1838

Joanna woke with a red-hot fever and a throbbing pain in her head with every movement. She got dressed slowly, sitting on the bed, fingers aching as she fumbled with the ties on her stockings and pain spreading to every joint as she moved. She tried to stand, head swimming, and then willingly fell into darkness.

Mary was leaning over her again, helping her drink, but this time she could understand the words. 'Likely be the lambing sickness. Just lie abed. It passes.'

It did pass, but only after days of fever, of being so weak she could barely lift her head. Market day, the day of her planned escape, came and went and she was only just able to get out of bed, incarcerated once more by weakness, indebted once more to Mary.

Joanna stood over the fire, scraping the last of the bacon into the stew pot; her shoulders ached with the effort and her nose was full of the smell of the now rancid fat. Resting her head on the hearth, she closed her eyes against the smoke and the sight of the bubbles rising slowly up through the grease, and then there were flames flickering faster and faster and she could smell woodsmoke and salt and hear something familiar. Waves . . . the sea. For a moment she was back there, and she could feel her hand held tight in his. Who? And then gone.

She fell back on to the low stool, trying to hold the memory, but it drifted away and she was here: the stone walls, the few remaining patches of whitewash, the remnants of crumbling mortar with the chinks plugged with mud and straw. The dark wooden dresser on the back wall, once polished, was scratched and battered now, and the table and stools were just crude chunks of wood nailed together. There was no other furniture except the bed behind the curtain and the wooden cradle.

This was her life.

Lambing proper was at its peak and she stayed with baby James and hand-fed the kitchen lambs and fetched the water and made the gruel and the stew, whilst Mary and John worked outside with the sheep, coming in for food and sleep, turn-and-turn-about, exhausted. John, though, was slightly less morose as the days passed: the full-term lambs were healthy enough, he said, and there had been some twins.

She dropped her head into her hands, pressing her fingers against her temples: she had to think, to plan, but she was so very tired. Mary had said John was going to market again to sell two ewes with their suckling lambs; they desperately needed money for food, even the oatmeal sack was nearly empty, just fine powder left in the folds. Perhaps she could escape then, across the moor to the Blacksmith and Jane Weddell.

*

In the end John took her with him to Alnwick the following week. He told Joanna that he was going to borrow Farmer Turnbull's cart, which would cost him, but then Farmer Turnbull said he could have use of the cart for free if he would take six of his old dry yows in to Butcher Black for slaughter. So John drove the cart with the two ewes and their suckling lambs and Joanna walked behind with the old ewes, women's work.

It was the first time she had been beyond the village, eastwards towards the sea, and she felt the beginning of excitement as they reached the Alnwick Road, but the rutted surface was hard underfoot and the cart seemed always to be going just too fast for her to keep up. Each step became harder and slower and John started to shout at her to come on, so she barely noticed when the cobbles started.

The cart stopped and she looked around at buildings swaying above her and then voices shouting, animals grunting, black spots dancing.

'Here, drink.' John's voice and cold water to swallow. She held on to him, the dizziness starting to fade, and he half-lifted her into the cart.

'Watch lambs whilst I hand over old yows to Butcher Black.' He pushed a piece of bread into her hand and their eyes met; she saw some sympathy there but looked away. She owed him nothing.

Sitting, chewing on the bread and warm in the sunshine, the feeling of excitement started again: she was surrounded by men with reddened cheeks in rough smocks, and sheep and cows and wooden cages of hens and ducks. Farmer Turnbull's huge but placid horse, which she knew a little better now, was standing head down and munching slowly. She smiled then, knowing that John must have put down hay for the horse before he gave her water. That was the order of things here: men, then horses, then sheep, then women.

On the cart, she was higher than the crowd and she watched it move apart as three men came across the square. Two were older, in breeches and coats and tall hats, and the younger one, bare-headed, was leather-aproned with a belt of long knives; he must, she thought, be Butcher Black. As they passed by, one of the older men looked up at her and then away. She felt shame then for her matted hair and ragged dress, for being starving poor, but the younger man, strong and handsome and clearly knowing it, gave her a sudden big smile, showing his good white teeth. She could not help but smile back and feel a moment of pleasure and she knew that he saw it too.

She was watching with enjoyment as the farmers showed off their sheep and cows to Butcher Black, so she had a good view when it happened. One of the farmers' boys was struggling with a big sheep and it pulled free. As it leapt forwards it barged into the butcher who slipped and fell, rolling over. It should have been nothing, but she saw him try to stand then fall on to his back, blood spurting, the crowd pulling away.

Without thinking, she was on the ground shouting and running, and the bystanders let her through as she pushed past and stood back as she lifted the leather apron. She forced her hands down hard, left on top of right, pressing on the artery in the butcher's groin as blood splattered across her chest and arms. She could see where the knife point had gone through the leather.

'Get me a cloth, now!' Her fingers were slicked with blood and slipping. Someone pushed a neck cloth against her hands and she moved her left hand to grab it and push it under her right, pressing harder as the blood spurted up and then stopped again.

She looked then at the man's face, ashen and sweating now, curly hair plastered down.

'The knife has nicked the big artery to your leg. If we keep the pressure on, it might seal up. Lie very still. You're Butcher Black?'

He nodded slowly, confirming his name and that he understood the injury, knew it was bad, very bad.

'Send to my wife, send to Alice,' he said, his words no more than a faint exhalation.

There was movement behind Joanna, but she didn't look. She knew only this: she must press with all her weight for ten minutes.

'Should we move'm on to cart, take'm home?' A voice behind her was concerned, unsure.

'No. He'll bleed to death if I stop pressing,' Joanna said, filled with calm certainty.

'Her be midwife, her'll be right on this. Leave'm be.' John's voice, her ally now.

'John, get the doctor,' Joanna said.

'Dr Soames is coming.' Another voice from the crowd.

Her arms were shaking already with the strain of taking all her upper-body weight as she pressed. She could feel sweat running down her cheeks and under her arms and smell the metallic tang of the butcher's blood. All the time she counted the seconds, the slow seconds.

The low muttering in the crowd became silence and she sensed movement beside her, someone else kneeling down. She kept her eyes on the butcher's white face, his eyelids closed now, but he was still breathing.

'I'm Dr Soames. Wound to the groin?' An educated male voice, the words clear.

'Yes. One of his knives. Femoral artery.' Her answer came crisply. The words were from the other place, but she knew they were right.

'How long have you been pressing?'

'Four hundred and twenty seconds, needs six hundred,' she said as she counted, arms weakening and her head beginning to swim.

'I'm going to put my hand on top of yours and start pressing. When I say, "Now," I want you to pull your left hand away, but keep your right hard on the cloth . . . Now . . . Good. I am going to keep pressing on your right hand and the cloth. It will hurt your hand, but you can rest your arm. Keep counting and tell me at six hundred.'

That is how they continued: Joanna trapped by his hand on hers; kneeling, leaning against his strong, solid body; the pain in her hand worsening; the butcher still breathing.

'Six hundred,' she said.

He relaxed the pressure and very gently released her.

Dr Soames supervised the careful lifting of Butcher Black on to the cart. She watched, still kneeling, blood coagulating all around her, as the townspeople edged away. John reappeared and said something but the words were distant. She shook her head as he grabbed her arm and started to pull her up.

'John Elliott, bring her over here. I'll need her to help with nursing Butcher Black,' said Dr Soames.

She stood up then, swaying. She was drenched in blood, all clotted down her front, but she smiled, feeling the dried blood on her face crack.

'Hurry up, John,' said Dr Soames with the absolute authority of someone who is always obeyed.

John helped her climb on to the cart. 'I'll come for her next week. Her be needed on farm.'

'She may be needed more here. Move on slowly, very slowly,' said Dr Soames, turning away to speak to the undertaker whose strongly built cart, she later learned, was used for moving Dr Soames's living as well as dead patients.

Dr Soames had a large room devoted to surgery and those patients who survived the ordeal were sometimes also nursed there for a day or so. As well as the scrubbed table there was a bed, and the men carried in Butcher Black and laid him down, slowly, helped by a man called Peter who seemed to be part of the household. Joanna followed and stood by the bed, focused on the butcher's face. He was becoming conscious and Dr Soames leaned over him.

'Arthur, you are at my house. You have bled a very great amount from the artery in the groin. The wound is sealed for now, but you must lie still. Very still.'

He watched the white face as the eyes fluttered open for a moment and the head nodded slightly.

'Good man,' said Dr Soames.

Joanna reached out and squeezed Arthur's hand and realized that Dr Soames was now looking at her. She felt ashamed again: she was filthy with blood and months of dirt; her dress was ragged and she was wearing clogs fastened on with string. She looked away from Arthur's face and directly at Dr Soames.

'I'm half-starved and filthy but I know how to care for the sick. I can nurse him. I'll work hard,' she said.

He smiled briefly. 'We will need to cut off his clothes and wash him but best let him lie undisturbed for a while now. First you need bathing, clean garments and some food. I'll sit with him until then.'

He made it sound commonplace, a casual politeness to offer cleansing and clothing.

If his servants were surprised at being asked to fill a bath for a strange and blood-drenched woman, they didn't show it. She was taken through the scullery to a small bathhouse by the manservant, Peter, and a young girl in a clean striped dress and apron carried in bucket after bucket of hot water. There was a sink and a pump as well as the metal hip bath, so Joanna stripped off and sluiced her arms and face and hair under the pump, gasping at the cold. The bloody water stung her eyes, but she carried on until it started to run clear and then climbed into the hot bath, immersing herself as far as possible with real pleasure. The girl came in with towels and another bucket which she put down with a groan and then came over to the bath, taking something from the pocket of her apron, all the while trying not to look directly at Joanna.

'Cook said to give ee the good soap,' she said.

Joanna took it and smiled. 'Thank you for the soap and for carrying all that water. I'm Joanna.'

The girl half-bobbed a curtsey then stopped, blushing. 'Jenny,' she managed, then, 'Cook, Mrs Godwin that is, her's finding a dress,' as she backed out, head down.

Properly clean, smelling of lavender, and demurely clothed, albeit in an ill-fitting black dress, Joanna walked into the room. She saw Dr Soames's surprise, quickly covered, as he glanced up at her. He was sitting beside Arthur, writing in a small book.

'Have you eaten?' he said.

'Far too much,' she said and noticed the flicker of amusement on his face. 'The best food I can remember. Thank you.'

'I think Mrs Godwin deserves the thanks for that,' he said.

'And for the dress. I have thanked her. But I'll always be most grateful for the lavender soap.'

'Well, if you would care to put on an apron, I think we should have another look at Arthur Black, make sure he is clean and comfortable before his poor wife comes back.' He stopped and looked at her again and stood up. 'I apologize. We have not been properly introduced. I am Dr Albert Soames,' he said with a polite bow.

'Joanna. It's the name Mary Elliott gave me.'

He waited.

'It's the only name I have,' she said.

'Where are you from? Your family?'

'I don't know.'

They worked together, cutting the clothes away but leaving the blood-hardened wedge of cloth over the injury. She knew to leave that, to keep Arthur Black's leg still, to keep him warm as she washed him where the blood had soaked through his clothes. He lay silent, barely conscious, but she spoke to him softly as she worked, explaining what she was doing. After a while Dr Soames left them, returning with a jug and cup with a spout which he gave to her.

'He needs to drink frequently in small amounts. If I'm not here Peter will help you to move him or deal with any other necessaries,' he said.

She nodded, then, 'What is it?'

'Water boiled with honey and camomile. Mrs Godwin is making beef tea for him to have later.'

He was interrupted by Peter coming to tell him that Mrs Black and Old Mrs Black had arrived and were in the sitting room. Dr Soames looked at Joanna and raised his eyebrows as he went out to speak to them.

Joanna bundled up the blood-drenched clothing and Peter carried it away, returning quickly to take the bowls and bloody wash cloths. She spoke quietly to Arthur as she gave him a drink and wiped his mouth, then straightened the covers over him and placed two chairs by the bed. She called a calm, 'Come in,' to the knock on the door. Dr Soames brought them in: Mrs Black, almost as pale as her husband, hanging on to Dr Soames's arm, and Old Mrs Black grim-faced, thin lips in a tight line as she marched behind, straight-backed. Arthur Black showed his mettle, rousing enough to manage a faint smile for his wife and a whispered, 'Soon be up working,' to his mother.

To Joanna's surprise it was old Mrs Black who then broke down and wept, and her daughter-in-law, Alice, who sat staunchly by her husband, fiercely intent, holding his hand as if she could anchor him to life. Dr Soames left Joanna with them and she sat across the room, only disturbing them to give Arthur drinks. After a while Peter came and offered to drive both Mrs Blacks home in the doctor's carriage but young Alice Black wouldn't go, fixed beside Arthur, still holding his hand.

Joanna and Alice nursed him together as the long day darkened, beginning a muted conversation as he drifted in and out of sleep. Peter returned and lit the lamps and later brought the beef tea for Arthur and bread and cheese for Joanna and Alice. Eventually Alice's eyelids drifted closed and Joanna sat alone in the darkness, just the one lamp left on, Arthur lying as white as his sheet in a pool of faint light. She knew, but could not remember, that she had sat many times before, somewhere, watching and waiting like this, half-asleep but listening. She stood up and checked Arthur and then moved silently round the bed to put a rug over his wife.

Dr Soames came in not so much later. The lamp by the bed was burning low and the dawn light of early summer was just visible through the big window. He took Arthur's pulse then nodded to her and she followed him to the far side of the room.

Joanna stood composedly in front of the doctor, her voice low: 'He has had two jugs of honey water and one pan of beef tea. He passed a very small amount of dark urine three hours ago. He seems not to be in pain and has spoken rationally with his wife.'

She waited then, slowing her breathing, aware she was being assessed.

'Do you know what this is, what it is for?' he said, handing her a small wooden tube, highly polished and hollow.

She held it, turning it towards the light, uncertain, but a word appeared in her head. 'A type of stethoscope, for listening to the heart and lungs.' As she spoke, she knew for certain.

He said something else then, but in a language she didn't understand, and she shook her head.

'I asked if you have studied Latin?' he said.

She shook her head again but kept her gaze steady, looking slightly upwards, eyes on his; he was very tall, almost as tall as Blacksmith Weddell.

He paused, looking back at her, then shrugged slightly. 'I'll watch Arthur for a while. You go and take some rest. Jenny will wake you for breakfast at nine o'clock.'

'Where shall I go to rest?'

'There's a bed made for you. Upstairs, the second door on the left. Mrs Godwin has put out what you need.'

Joanna nodded and started to turn away as she felt the tears prickling, but swallowed and then, 'How long will I stay here?'

'Let us say two weeks to nurse Arthur Black.' He paused. 'To start with.'

Joanna looked across at her patient, motionless beside his sleeping wife. 'And what will happen to me if he dies before then?'

'Do you think he will?' he said.

'If the wound becomes putrid he'll bleed again and die immediately or die of fever. But with careful nursing there is a chance. A small one, I think, but better with me here than not,' she said.

He smiled briefly. 'Two weeks then. To start with.'

'Thank you,' she said and then turned back as she opened the door, 'Thank you. You won't be disappointed in me.'

10

London, June 1841

D r Borthwick was only a little surprised to receive the invitation to a 'family dinner, no formality' from Mrs Swan. She was close to Charles Darrow, her cousin, who appeared to be a regular visitor to the Swans' house. Would he be there? More importantly, did the Swans know about Charles's private life and were they seeking to protect him?

He dressed carefully and arrived exactly on time.

The Swans were charming and welcoming as ever. Mr Swan came himself into the hall to greet him and take him straight through to the dining room. There was one other guest, a woman, sitting opposite Mrs Swan. Dr Borthwick bowed politely to them both.

'Dr Borthwick, do come and sit by me,' said his hostess, gesturing to the place next to her. 'I have been very keen for you to meet my dearest friend, Mrs Eleanor Johnson, who is staying with us a while. I think you will find she shares many of your opinions on health and education for women.'

Mrs Johnson was looking openly at him and smiled with marginally raised eyebrows at her friend's comments. Her dress was unadorned grey, but her cap was white lace. A widow, but not recent, Dr Borthwick thought. He bowed again to her, rather formally.

'Mrs Johnson may perhaps feel more entitled to such opinions and even permit me to share hers?'

'Well said indeed, Dr Borthwick,' said Mr Swan, clearly amused, as he sat down.

As they were served the soup, Mrs Swan responded cheerfully to Dr Borthwick's questions about her infant son. She had recovered quickly, as he had both hoped and expected, and was feeding her baby herself, which he had strongly recommended.

She seemed very keen, though, to change the topic to her friend. She discreetly made it clear to him that Mrs Johnson was highly educated and that 'dear Reverend Johnson, sadly departed last year, may he rest in peace' had left her very comfortably provided for, very comfortable indeed, including a substantial house in Winchester. To his suppressed amusement, she moved on, almost without a breath, to describe Mrs Johnson's charitable work.

'Not just money, though she is most generous. She teaches reading in two of the poor schools and has fought to provide reading lessons for the laundry women in Winchester.' Mrs Swan paused and laughed, but ruefully. 'She says that she buys the menfolk off with free bread and soup.'

Dr Borthwick smiled and nodded and then looked across the table. The paragon was engaged in animated conversation with Mr Swan. He waited for a pause, deciding he must reward Mrs Swan's efforts.

'Mrs Johnson, our hostess has been telling me about your work to improve the literacy of women in Winchester.'

She looked directly at him and he briefly met the hazel eyes. Her gaze was steady, no girlish looking down, no affectation at all.

'It is my firm belief that every man and woman should be able to read and write,' she said.

He picked up the gauntlet without a pause.

'Well said indeed, Mrs Johnson. I could not agree more.'

She smiled, a quick movement of her lips, and continued: 'All young children should go to school.'

'Of course.'

'And older girls should have the opportunity to study widely, to learn mathematics and history at proper schools in each town, as boys do.'

'Only some boys learn those things. Not the poor. Not, indeed, most boys.'

She paused, then looked directly at him again. 'So how would you resolve that?'

'All boys and girls should go to school, at least until they are twelve years old, perhaps older. All. Town and country, gentry and pauper. All.'

There was a short silence.

Mr Swan leaned forward. 'You are an enlightened man, I know, Dr Borthwick. Some would say you are even a radical.' He smiled as he spoke, meaning a compliment and not an insult.

'I am no politician. I am a doctor. I see the results of poverty and lack of education in my work. I see suffering that could be avoided,' Dr Borthwick said.

Mrs Johnson spoke quickly, her cheeks now slightly flushed. 'You do not confine your work to the smart squares then?'

'No, I attend women even by the river when my midwife seeks my help.' He paused, realizing he was becoming too open, too animated. That he was not following his rules. He made his voice calm and measured.

'But lack of education affects some of my patients in the smart squares too. I see very few ladies with the education and sense of a Mrs Swan,' he said with a gentle inclination of his head to his hostess.

Mrs Swan smiled her acknowledgement and expertly turned the conversation to the weather as the servants brought in the meat. The required comments were made about the day being warm but certainly not hot and the light breeze being most pleasant. But after the food was served, Mr Swan deftly introduced the question of suffrage. Dr Borthwick was amused: he knew the Swans quite well now and was sure that they had prearranged the topics of conversation to show off both his and Mrs Johnson's views and virtues.

Suffrage did not last long as a topic: they were all in agreement that the Reform Act of '32 was only a first step and that full enfranchisement of the working man was the desired goal. No mention of women, which did not surprise Dr Borthwick at all. Some ideas were perhaps too radical even in this company.

The Swans had adopted the new habit of taking a cup of coffee at the end of dinner and this was served in the drawing room. The beverage at the Swans' was excellent. Dr Borthwick had very few complaints about the food prepared by Mrs

Hayward, his cook, but his coffee at home was often gritty. He sat back, savouring each mouthful from the fine china cup. The Swans were interesting: their wealth was in no way ostentatiously displayed, their house nowhere near as grand as Sir Jeremy Gasgoine's, but Mr Swan seemed to be very influential. There was talk of him standing as a London MP, which needed both money and powerful backers to succeed.

Dr Borthwick looked up as Mr Swan stopped speaking. They were grouped round the fireplace, seated on elegant high-backed chairs; he and Mrs Swan on one side with Mr Swan and Mrs Johnson opposite. The room was pleasantly cool and scented by a large bowl of pink roses in the fire grate.

He commented on the flowers which led to a discussion on where roses had originated and then an easy mention by Mr Swan of Mr Darrow's planned trip. Dr Borthwick immediately expressed admiration for Mr Darrow's adventurous spirit and admitted to some envy of the trip even though travelling in South America was considered risky and uncomfortable.

'So, do you see travel in itself as virtuous?' asked Mrs Johnson, her face expressionless.

'That is an interesting question,' he said, giving himself time to think why it seemed so filled with intent.

Mrs Johnson nodded, expressionless.

Dr Borthwick was aware of Mr and Mrs Swan watching each of them in turn. 'I see the travel that Mr Darrow is undertaking more as a scientific venture: the seeking of important new information. And perhaps more laudable in involving him in some discomfort. But I see no objection to travel for pleasure be it visiting friends or family or a place of beauty,' he said.

'But that travel would not be virtuous in itself. It is the reason which is the virtue, surely?' said Mr Swan.

'And what if travel leads to a wrong, an unvirtuous thing, an injury to the people or place?' said Mrs Johnson, still watching Dr Borthwick.

He paused and looked directly into the hazel eyes. 'Do you speak of slavery?'

Mrs Johnson nodded; her lips firmly compressed in distaste.

Dr Borthwick thought again for a moment before he answered, his voice gentle. 'I see your abhorrence even of the word. I share it completely. There is no place for enslavement of any man, woman or child in any place, any country. Nor any action which supports or promotes it. Never.'

'Bravo, Dr Borthwick,' said Mrs Swan very quietly.

He heard her murmured comment, but he did not respond. To his surprise Mrs Johnson seemed genuinely upset, struggling for composure, looking downwards. After a moment she looked up.

'Forgive me, Dr Borthwick. It is a topic about which I have the strongest feelings. I fear they overwhelm me. My late husband, Reverend Stephen Johnson, gave so much, at terrible cost to his health. He gave his life to the cause of abolition.' She looked away, blinking back her tears.

Mr Swan spoke for her then. 'We were fortunate indeed to count Reverend Johnson among our friends. He died soon after the Anti-Slavery Convention. Only his faith in God, and Eleanor's devotion, kept him alive in those last few months.'

Dr Borthwick thought carefully again before he spoke.

'You must forgive me, Mrs Johnson. I had not realized that

your husband was the man who gave such inspiration to so many over the years. I had the very great pleasure of hearing him speak last summer. It was clear he was unwell, but the strength of his argument and his conviction could not have been resisted by anyone in the room.'

She looked at him intently as he spoke and then she smiled, a frank and open gesture. He smiled back.

Mrs Swan commented again on the weather and she and her husband began a quiet conversation about the need for rain to clear the pavements.

Dr Borthwick listened and nodded as more coffee was poured and then Mrs Swan and Eleanor returned to the question of roses. Eleanor. When had he begun to think of her as that? She looked to be a similar age to Mrs Swan, whom he knew to be twenty-eight. Her husband must have been very much older. When he saw the Reverend Johnson at the anti-slavery meeting, he would have guessed his age at near sixty, though he looked extremely ill, probably with consumption.

He watched Eleanor as she got up and then bent and picked one of the blooms from the bowl to settle some question of Mr Swan's about how thorns were arranged on the stem. She moved neatly, perhaps even gracefully. Perhaps slightly for his benefit. Another complexity.

He realized that Mrs Swan was watching him watching Eleanor. He turned back to her. 'I do not remember more interesting dinner conversation,' he said and was rewarded by her generous smile.

'Indeed, Dr Borthwick, I am not sure that I do either!'

'It is a real pleasure to be in company which is so enlightened in its views,' he said.

Mrs Swan replied, dropping her voice slightly. 'Indeed. I knew you would enjoy Mrs Johnson's company. She is truly my closest friend. A person with whom we can speak with openness, with candour.'

'Candour in general is to be greatly admired as long as it is not misunderstood,' he replied, nodding.

He felt Mrs Swan's sudden tension.

'Misunderstood?' she said after a brief pause.

'Perhaps I should better have said does not lead unintentionally to misunderstanding. Does not lead to a well-meant mistake. I was involved in such a conversation quite recently, but the mistake caused no lasting offence. No offence at all. Indeed, already forgotten.'

She looked directly at him as she spoke. 'Charles was afraid he had spoken too frankly. Been perhaps indiscreet?'

'No, indeed not. As I said, it is forgotten.'

She started to speak but the Swans' butler appeared at Dr Borthwick's shoulder and gave him a note, murmuring to him, 'Your man is outside with your carriage.'

As he read, Mrs Swan looked away but turned back when he spoke.

'Please forgive me, Mrs Swan, but I have a note from Mrs Bates. A patient requires my immediate attention. I am very sorry to leave such an excellent party, but I must go at once.'

'Of course you must go.' Mrs Swan smiled very warmly and took his hand briefly.

Mr Swan stood as Dr Borthwick bowed to the women.

'It has been a great pleasure to meet you, Mrs Johnson,' he said, and she gave him her hand.

As always, he thought only about his patient as Hayward drove the carriage over the cobbles and then turned on to the smooth road of the new square. Lady Florence was a small and very slender woman, so it was no bad thing she was in labour at around eight months, but Mrs Bates's note had expressed concern about a report of bleeding earlier in the day.

Lady Florence Stephenson, as Mrs Bates had told him in detail, was titled; not aristocracy but the wife of a man made very rich by his business in the Midlands potteries. Sir Alfred Stephenson was recently made a baronet and they lived in considerable style in a newly built house. It was said that he had bought his very young wife, the third daughter of an impoverished northern landowner of impeccable Norman lineage, for the cost of her eldest brother's substantial gambling debts and urgent and considerable repairs to her family's huge and decaying house.

On their first meeting Dr Borthwick had no difficulty in deciding that Sir Alfred fell into the category of objectionable husband: too old, too possessive and with the red face of a drinker. He knew he was being judgemental and that his opinion was influenced by the way Sir Alfred had spoken to him, requiring his services as if he were a wine merchant and the expected baby a case of expensive claret. After his second visit to Lady Florence he had left her with Mrs Bates and sought out Sir Alfred in his study.

The room was in the new style with dark wooden panelling

and heavy furniture, its cost shown by its bulk rather than its beauty. He reassured Sir Alfred that all seemed to be well but was careful to explain again the risks to both mother and child. He found Sir Alfred to be more sympathetic than expected. Slowly he realized why he had not sought one of the fashionable older physicians who attended the rich. Sir Alfred told Dr Borthwick that he had listened in his club to the men who recommended instead a young doctor, a man-midwife some called him. Others disapproved, not wanting a man to touch their wives. However, it had seemed to Sir Alfred that those who cared for their wives were the ones who recommended him. Dr Borthwick listened: Sir Alfred, it appeared, did indeed love his wife.

As his carriage pulled up at the imposing entrance, Dr Borthwick was concerned to see Sir Alfred himself at the door with his butler.

'Thank God you are here. I have just sent out another note from Mrs Bates. My wife is losing blood. Heavily.'

He followed Sir Alfred up the wide curving stairs; the only sound in the listening house was that of their rapid footsteps.

He was mentally rehearsing what to do as they entered the room. But the girl was lying flat on the bed, already unmoving. Mrs Bates was holding a cloth between her legs: there was a lot of blood.

He pulled off his jacket and started washing his hands, asking Mrs Bates, 'How long has she been bleeding?'

'A trickle at first and then very heavily for ten minutes,' she said, looking quickly across at the clock on the mantelpiece.

'Pain?'

'She started regular heavy pains just before the bleeding.'

'How long has she been unconscious?'

'About five minutes.'

He turned to Sir Alfred who was standing grim-faced at the door. 'I need to examine Lady Florence. Do you want to wait outside?'

Sir Alfred said nothing but turned and walked out.

There was no pulse at the girl's bleached throat.

He gently took away the blood-sodden cloths and examined her. Mrs Bates stood unmoving beside him. When he shook his head, she sighed and started to whisper the Lord's Prayer.

Mrs Bates passed him a small roll of white felt and he carefully pushed it into place. Then they washed the dead girl. They worked quickly together, the silence interrupted only by Mrs Bates's prayers; they had done this before. Finally, Mrs Bates rolled up the blood-drenched linen. They washed their hands and then covered the still figure with clean sheets.

He went out into the wide corridor to do the hardest thing.

'I am deeply sorry, but your wife has not survived the loss of blood. She has passed away.'

Sir Alfred was leaning against the wall, impassive.

'The baby?'

'Never born. They are together.' He paused a while, then, 'Do you want to go in?'

The room was quiet: the girl's face translucent, white on the white pillow; Mrs Bates waiting, her lips still moving in prayer.

'They will say I should have had Dr Preston or one of the

others like him. One of the ones the aristos use,' said Sir Alfred, his voice harsh and distorted.

'Perhaps. But they could not have saved her,' said Dr Borthwick.

'Why did this happen? Why is she dead?'

'The afterbirth was in the way of the baby being born and came away too soon. I have seen this a number of times, with the same sad loss of life. There is nothing that can be done. I am very sorry,' said Dr Borthwick.

He glanced at Mrs Bates and they left the room, left Sir Alfred with his dead wife and never-born child. They walked down into the hall where the butler was waiting with three servants.

'Is it bad news, doctor?' the butler asked.

'I regret so. Lady Florence has sadly died with her unborn child. Sir Alfred is with her –' Dr Borthwick paused – 'may she rest in peace.'

'Amen. A sad day for us all,' murmured the butler. 'Should I send up her maid to start . . . to . . .' He stopped, uncertain.

'Perhaps it would be better to give Sir Alfred a while longer. All is left seemly for now but . . .' He looked at the dark-uniformed maid who was staring at him wide-eyed as tears poured down her cheeks.

Dr Borthwick moved further down the hall with the butler. 'There was severe loss of blood. It would be better to bring in an experienced older woman to do the laying-out. Kinder.' He looked towards the now sobbing maid.

'Yes, yes. I will go and speak with Cook. She'll know of someone.'

*

Mrs Bates didn't speak until Hayward turned the carriage into the streets near her lodgings.

'He'll be angry, Sir Alfred. He's that sort. Expects to get what he wants,' she said, her voice hard.

'He was very fond of her, I think,' said Dr Borthwick.

'Oh, I don't doubt he decided that he loved her well enough. But he'll have expected at least one baby and for her to be around a year or two. He paid a lot for her. Over five thousand pounds, they say. That's a lot even for a man like him.'

Dr Borthwick shrugged but said nothing. He was never sure of Mrs Bates's sources of information but they were usually accurate.

The carriage stopped under the one gas light on the narrow street.

'He'll as like blame you,' she said as he helped her down from the carriage.

'Perhaps. But there was nothing you or I could have done. We both know that. That's what matters,' he said. And then, 'Goodnight.'

He climbed back in with a nod to Hayward and closed his eyes, trying not to think, until the carriage stopped again at his own house. He stepped down and went, suddenly very tired, to the door, waving goodnight to Hayward as he drove off in the carriage into the mews.

Betty took his coat, telling him in her night-time whisper that Mrs Hayward had left him some cocoa on the stove and there was bread and cheese laid out in the pantry. He smiled and told her to lock up and then go and have the cocoa and food herself, if she wanted, and then get off to bed. He turned away and walked slowly up to his bedroom. He stopped at the curve of the stairs and, looking back, saw her watching him. He called, 'Goodnight,' but quietly.

Dr Borthwick locked the bedroom door behind him and sat down heavily on the bed. He heard Betty pull the heavy bolt across the front door and imagined her snuffing out the big candles and carrying her lamp through to the kitchen. She would drink the cocoa furtively and carry the bread and cheese upstairs to her attic room. At least she would have some pleasure from the day.

He went through the ritual of undressing and washing behind the closed curtains and then, decent in his nightgown, he opened the curtains again. It was near midsummer and there was still some faint light in the sky to the west. And the moon was high and huge, full and silver-gold. There were even a few stars but never as many here as in the wide-open skies of the north.

Smiling, self-mocking, he turned away and began his nightly struggle with the feather mattress. He knew sleep would be skittish.

Mrs Bates was right about Sir Alfred; he would be angry and he would remember the men who had spoken against *accoucheurs*, the men who were rich enough to pay for a physician to visit and to stand outside the bedroom door, advising the midwife but never touching the patient. The physicians who leeched pregnant women, advised nothing but rest and seclusion, and charged in guineas for each visit; then blamed the midwife if the woman died.

Dr Preston would be the first to comment, not to criticize

directly but to insinuate, to speak sadly of what might have been with a more experienced doctor, a physician, to advise. But not to his peers. No, Dr Preston would speak to his own patients and their families, knowing that was the best way to start the gossip in the Pall Mall clubs.

The thoughts rattled round and round and he forced himself to think of something pleasant. The azaleas at Kew had been magnificent on his last visit. He had ridden out west early in the morning, in the cool air. Dr Atkins had agreed to attend his patients, if Mrs Bates had need of an *accoucheur*. It worked well, he and Atkins occasionally helping each other; Atkins was sound. Not like most of the London quacks, Dr Preston and his cronies.

He turned over again and thought determinedly about the plants, bushes covered in big pink and white flowers. The gardener had surprised him, telling him the whole bed had been made just five years ago with azaleas from the United States, not from Persia as he had thought. Which led to roses and then pink roses and to Eleanor. Eleanor, so neat and graceful and fierce.

Later, sleep claimed him and then he woke from the old dream with tears on his cheeks. He squeezed his eyes tight closed: the past was over, finished.

Later still, he lay awake watching the moon as it faded against the brightening sky.

11

Northumberland, June 1838

In the first few days Arthur's life hung poised, balanced still on the sharp point of his butcher's knife, and Joanna left him only if Dr Soames was beside him. He drifted in and out of consciousness and each time he opened his eyes she made him drink the honey water or beef tea and helped him to shift position a little, then checked the pulses in his feet and the dressing on his groin.

In the mornings she talked softly with Alice Black who sat all day beside her husband's bed, hands always busy stitching or knitting. In the afternoons, when Dr Soames was there, Joanna would go upstairs to sleep. But at night she watched Arthur alone, learning each feature in the lamplight – like a lover, she thought.

It was easy to talk to Alice in the cool, quiet room and Joanna knew she had done this before, heard stories of a life whilst another life was watched, the ebb and the flow. But not what or where.

Over the days, shyly at first, Alice told her about having feelings for handsome, smiling Arthur since they were children and that she could not even now believe her good fortune in being married to him. Her parents and old Mrs Black had encouraged the match: the butcher had a good income and she had a small dowry from her grandfather. The draper's daughter, she still helped her now widowed father in his shop. She measured and did fittings on the ladies and dealt with the sale of ladies' items, and – in a whisper – 'undergarments'. Alice also said, artlessly, that this left old Mrs Black to run the butcher's shop and keep his accounts without distraction.

It wasn't until the third day that Alice asked any questions back.

'They say as you came in town with John Elliott?'

'Yes.'

'That you was living with him and Mary?'

'Yes,' Joanna nodded and smiled a little, to lessen the brevity of her answers.

'John Elliott is not a man well spoken-of,' Alice said.

Joanna had expected the questions to come first from Dr Soames but he had asked her nothing more about her past, not yet. She looked at Alice, at the strong-featured face with the dark eyebrows frowning now. Some part of the truth, then.

'He is not a kind man but he and Mary saved me. He found me lost on the moor. They took me in.'

Alice looked straight at her.

'Some say as you was his doxy, come in on a boat.'

'No. He found me and Mary looked after me. I was extremely sick.'

'Blacksmith Weddell has spoken for you. His word counts a great deal,' Alice said and nodded briskly as she turned to her sewing.

As Joanna watched the quick fingers stitching a buttonhole in a piece of grey cloth, she realized that she knew what Alice was doing and how to do it. She could remember the feeling of silk cloth in her fingers and a gossamer thread, white not grey. As the picture drifted away, Arthur stirred and she got up and gave him honey water and wiped his lips. He half-smiled, then his eyes drifted closed again. Alice took his hand and held it and Joanna saw his fingers tighten on hers. They would not easily let each other go, she thought.

Alice waited until he was asleep again and carefully let go of his hand before picking up her sewing. She spoke again, head bent. 'We know what you did for him, Mother Black and me. That he would have died in the square if you had not been there. Dr Soames told us so. He says as Arthur would have been well dead afore he got to him.'

'I did what I could but he is still in danger. The wound might putrefy—'

Alice looked up, interrupting her. 'I know. But at least I'll have had chance to sit with him, to hold his hand.'

The tears, so long held back, came then and Joanna went round and held Alice as she sobbed.

Later, when Peter brought in a tray with fresh beef tea for Arthur and soup and bread for them, Alice was showing her how to bind the edges of a white lace collar, both of them busy together.

Arthur woke early on the fourth morning and smiled at her as she leaned over with the cup.

'Good strong ale this time, is it?' he whispered through cracked lips.

'Better than ale. Honey water and then Mrs Godwin's excellent beef tea,' she said, lifting his head.

He drank obediently and sighed as she settled him down again. He lay still for a moment then turned to her with a stronger voice. 'How long since it happened?'

'It's Saturday now, so nearly four days ago,' said Joanna.

'How's my Alice? I know she's been here.'

'She was here all the first day and night but Dr Soames persuaded her to go home to sleep on the nights since. She'll be here soon.'

He turned away, looking up at the ceiling in the dawn light, and she sat hands folded in her lap, waiting for him to speak again.

'Will I live?'

'Probably. But we must be sure the wound heals over. The cloth is still stuck on it. We won't know for sure until the cloth is shed.'

He looked directly at her: 'If it goes putrid, then I'll die?'

'Yes,' she said, holding his gaze. 'But you're young and strong and have survived the blood loss. You have a good chance.'

To her surprise, he laughed.

'Best do as I'm told then. And I need a piss.'

Over the next few days Arthur did as he was told without complaint, moving only with Joanna and Peter's help, eating and drinking whatever he was given, still sleeping much of the time unless Alice was with him, reading to him or stitching busily as they talked. Dr Soames appeared morning, noon and evening, listened attentively to Joanna's report and spoke to

80

Arthur if he was awake. Joanna and Peter shared the evening and night-time care and she slept well and ate three good meals a day. She knew she was getting stronger, more herself, and let the days pass.

On the seventh day after the accident, she came down from the bedroom, which now seemed not only safe but familiar, to find Arthur already sitting propped up in bed. He was clean-shaven, and the blonde curls were neatly brushed. Peter gave her a quick nod as he carried away the washing bowl and towel. Although they had worked together caring for Arthur, Peter barely spoke to her, answering her questions very briefly but always doing as she asked and always gentle with Arthur. She thought that he must not approve of her – and why should he?

Later, Arthur, who was less subdued now as each day passed, announced firmly that he would only eat blood pudding, again, and greens, again, for dinner if she would read to him, as Alice was away, busy on market day, and he was bored. They settled on *The Pilgrim's Progress,* a book strongly recommended by Reverend MacPherson, who took his duties to all his flock very seriously. Joanna felt the recommendation may have been made more for her benefit than for Arthur Black. The reverend, whom she had now met twice, treated her with a wary politeness seemingly tinged with anxiety that she might have too unpleasant a past for his limited experience in redeeming.

They were quiet, Arthur beginning to doze, when the door was pushed open hard, banging back against the hinges, and John Elliott walked in unannounced, trailed by a protesting and tearful Jenny.

'I'm here to take ee home,' he said as he stopped by the bed, expressionless.

She didn't move. Arthur Black opened his eyes and looked up with his widest smile.

'Good day to you, John Elliott,' he said. 'Nice of you to visit. Joanna works for Dr Soames now.'

'Er works for me. Owes me rent an all,' John said.

'Maybe so, but she's nursing me today so you'd best wait on Dr Soames.'

Joanna stood up then, still in her borrowed dress, using her height. Her voice was crisp and measured. 'Indeed, Dr Soames will want to speak to you. Jenny, please take Mr Elliott to the kitchen to await Dr Soames's return from the dispensary. And ask Peter to come and help me with Mr Black.'

She felt pity then through her fear: pity for John Elliott's filthy hands and rank, unwashed smell; pity for the life he lived. He looked at her, hesitating.

'Aye, that'll be for best,' Arthur Black said in his warm, friendly voice. 'I'm needing Peter to help me lie down flat again. Off you go, John.'

She turned back to Arthur and pulled the sheet neatly across him, keeping her face hidden. The door closed and she sank back into the chair, trying to stop the tears. Arthur reached across and took her hand and stayed silent until her breathing settled.

'Did he hurt you?'

She nodded.

'Are you . . . ?'

She shook her head then looked straight at him. The shame was not hers.

'No, I'm not.'

'For the best that. You can start afresh here. Folk need a midwife. Blacksmith Weddell has spoken for you. People listen to him and Dr Soames.'

Peter arrived then, short of breath.

'Jenny said as you need help,' he said, looking at Arthur.

Joanna watched some sort of soundless exchange between the two men and felt a wave of unexpected irritation at being excluded. Arthur shrugged.

'So you hit him?' Arthur said.

'Yes. Broke his nose, I reckon.'

'Good.'

Joanna said nothing but went and filled a bowl with water and bathed Peter's bruised and bleeding knuckles. When she had finished she looked up at him but he turned quickly away.

She didn't know what John Elliott said to Dr Soames, or the doctor's response, only that he told her in the evening she need have no more concerns. She assumed Dr Soames had given John Elliott money. Another debt she must repay.

On the tenth day, she was awakened by a soft knocking.

'What is it? Is he bleeding?' she asked through the door as she pulled on her dress, fingers fumbling on the buttons.

'No, but I've just helped him sit up and he says the wound feels wrong. He asked me to get you,' said Peter.

Joanna felt her stomach tighten and then calmness came from the other place and she followed Peter who held the lamp to light the stairs.

Arthur was sitting very still and his smile was forced so she took his hand and squeezed it.

'Is the wound hurting?'

'No. Feels different. Scratchy,' Arthur said, his voice shaking just a little.

'We need to have a look. Peter, can you bring another lamp, please?'

She washed her hands and collected a bowl and clean cloths. She felt in control, her fingers remembering. Once the light was good enough, they helped Arthur lie down and she nodded to Peter who pulled back the covers. There was no bleeding.

Joanna very gently lifted the edge of the thick lump of material, layers matted with dried clotted blood, and it moved freely away. The small dry puncture wound was just visible in the skin over purple-green bruising. She covered it with a clean cloth.

'Well, Arthur Black, I think your good chance came through! We'll prop up your head and shoulders, then I want you to keep still until Dr Soames comes,' she said.

It was Arthur who gave her another name. She knew that he more than anyone watched her change day by day: saw the deep hollows in her face fill out; witnessed the birth of the respectable nurse and midwife. She in turn came to like and admire him for his stoicism and good humour, his love for his childless wife and his benign tolerance of his dour mother.

The eleventh day was her naming day. Alice was already there when she came down in the early morning and sat quietly as Joanna spoke to Arthur and checked his pulse. Then, to Joanna's surprise, Alice jumped up.

'We have something for you,' she said.

Arthur smiled with deep affection at his wife. 'Be truer to say Alice made something for you.'

Alice came round the bed with a large bundle which she shook out with some ceremony, handing it to Joanna.

'It should fit. I'm good at judging size but you try it on and I'll alter it as needed and there's three sets of white cuffs as I thought you'd want white and . . .' The words ran together and Alice stopped.

The tears were pouring down Joanna's cheeks as she looked at the pale grey dress, the rows of pin tucks and pearl buttons, and then she felt Alice's arms around her and then her own arms round Alice's broad shoulders.

Joanna squeezed her eyes tight to stop the tears and swallowed her sobs.

'Oh, Alice, thank you. It looks so . . . so neat, so elegant.'

'Aye, and clean and long enough,' Arthur said, making it easier for her to smile.

She came downstairs again, clothed in soft grey, and did a twirl. Alice came over to her and straightened the sleeves, folding back the white cuffs more neatly, and then pinched in a little fabric at the waist; Alice, the draper's daughter, frowned with concentration.

'It could be tighter but Arthur reckons you still need to fatten up a bit,' she said seriously then blushed. 'I mean, we know as you were ill and . . .'

'Indeed I was but I am much better now,' said Joanna.

'There's something from Mother Black too,' said Alice, pushing a small parcel into Joanna's hand.

It was two white cotton caps trimmed with lace, like Alice's. She put one on, pushing her hair underneath, and

Alice reached up, shy again, and pulled some loose wisps of brown hair forwards at the front.

Joanna went over to the glass-fronted cabinet filled with Dr Soames's instruments and looked at herself; so strange, this tall woman dressed like Alice but with white cuffs. Who was she? Who had she been?

As if he had heard her thoughts, Arthur said, 'So what will we call you now?'

'Joanna,' she replied, still looking at the image, her shadow self.

'No. That won't do. You're a respectable woman now. Mrs . . . ?'

'I don't know,' Joanna turned, shrugging.

'Aye, Dr Soames said as much. So, choose a name then.'

There was nothing in her head; no words drifted by. Just the now, here with Arthur Black who would live and Alice Black who had made her a dress, a camouflage, a suit of armour.

'I know,' Arthur said, 'I know!'

'What?'

'Mrs Sharp, on account of how we met and you became Dr Soames's nurse,' he said, laughing.

She caught Alice's appalled look and then they both laughed too.

That evening, Dr Soames came in after Alice had gone home to bed and Arthur was sleeping. She stood up, eyes lowered, feeling his calm gaze, and then she looked at him. He bowed politely.

'Good evening. I think we need to be introduced again. I'm Dr Soames.'

She smiled then. 'Good evening, Dr Soames. I am Mrs Sharp, nurse and midwife.'

12

London, July 1841

Dr Borthwick had seen squalor before but nothing like the alleys leading off Duck Lane.

They left the carriage and walked along a dark passage between the houses fronting the street. Those houses were in poor enough repair but behind them was a grey and tumbling otherworld. The buildings were slumped together, the narrow gaps between them unpaved and slicked with foul mud. Everything was broken: fractured doorways and windows blocked with jagged planks, piles of ash and rubbish against the walls. The stench was terrible.

And everywhere there were children, thin and ragged and pale. They looked up at him, some dull-eyed, some wary, eyes darting, ready for flight.

Eleanor had written to him, asking him to visit the refuge there for fallen women. Her husband had been involved with its establishment and she was supporting it now she was staying in London with the Swans. As well as giving money, she went twice a week to teach reading and writing, as she had done in Winchester. She had warned him that the area behind Duck Lane and Old Pye Street was the worst in London, that it was a dangerous place, that even the police did not enter it alone.

They called it the Devil's Acre, she said, populated by hucksters and costermongers and tramps and thieves and worse.

Eleanor walked ahead, holding her grey cotton skirts high above her ankles. He watched her, the way she was moving with determination, unflinching. Not a woman for hysteria or the vapours, he thought.

They arrived at an intact door, painted bright green, the colour glaring against the smoke-blackened brick.

Eleanor knocked loudly and called out, 'Mrs Johnson and Dr Borthwick.'

There was the sound of bolts being drawn back, then the door was opened by a middle-aged man dressed in a clean shirt and breeches.

'Good day to you, Mrs Johnson. And Dr Borthwick, thank you for visiting us here. I'm Arnold Wilson of the London City Mission.'

Dr Borthwick held out his hand which, after a moment's surprise, the other man shook.

'I am pleased to meet you, Mr Wilson. Mrs Johnson has spoken highly of the work done here,' the doctor said as they walked through the door.

It opened directly into a whitewashed room with a curtain across one end. Ten women sat crammed together on two benches, most of them visibly pregnant, all staring at him.

Eleanor looked at him, frowning slightly, then spoke to Mr Wilson.

'Mr Wilson, I am not sure Dr Borthwick will have time to see all these women. I asked him here to see our work, not necessarily to . . .'

Dr Borthwick shrugged. 'I am happy to set to the task, Mr Wilson, but I will need a bowl and hot water and soap. Could one of the older women act as chaperone?'

Afterwards he sat with Mr Wilson in another small white-washed room furnished with a well-scrubbed table and benches. He could hear Eleanor's voice through the ceiling above them. She was reading aloud from Mr Dickens's *Nicholas Nickleby*: a reward for the women who came to be taught their letters, she had told him.

Arnold Wilson poured them both a mug of strong black tea, made, he reassured Dr Borthwick, with sweet water which he brought in each day in a barrel from the pump at his home.

'Your first time here?' he said.

Dr Borthwick nodded.

'A shock then?'

'Indeed, yes. I've attended women in Southwark but this is, well, so much worse. And so close to the Abbey, the heart of Westminster, the carriages passing by.'

'The Devil's Acre. Every crime and vice is here. And disease and dirt aplenty.'

Dr Borthwick looked round the room. No wall was straight and the uncovered lathes in the low ceiling were buckled and patched.

'How old are the dwellings we walked through? Mrs Johnson said they are newer than the big houses on the lane. But surely not?'

'Most been put up in last thirty years. Stand on what were the gardens and yards of the old houses. Hence are called courts. This here would have been a stable, so better built. The new ones are just half-bricks and no foundations. Some built over the old ditches and cesspits.'

'How many live here?'

'Just in this court maybe two hundred and fifty people – men, women and children. Sleep ten in a room smaller than this.'

Dr Borthwick frowned. 'What do they do for water?'

'There's a pump in the next court but some take water from the drain.'

Both men were silent.

Dr Borthwick stood as Eleanor entered the room and pulled out a chair for her.

'I heard part of your lesson,' he said.

She glanced quickly at him.

'Some days are better than others. They like to be read to, but the writing is, well, a struggle. And sometimes they –' she paused and seemed to be choosing her words with care – 'sometimes some of the women are unwell.'

'With drink?'

'Yes. Or they have been beaten.'

He told them both about the women he had just seen. He, too, was careful with words, uncertain how much Eleanor knew about pregnancy and disease. Two of them were very young, children not women. All were undernourished. All were pregnant; two for the first time and one of those had severe rickets; one probably had consumption and two had other ailments. Eleanor looked up at him.

'I know about syphilis. I understand what these women do.' There was a faint splash of colour on her pale cheeks as she looked down again.

'It will probably affect their babies, if they live,' Dr Borthwick said.

'A lot of the children here carry the marks of their mother's sin,' Mr Wilson said but his voice was sad, not judgemental, not righteous.

Dr Borthwick said nothing, made no comment on the sins of the fathers and the pimps and bawds, suppressing his irritation.

'What about the girl with rickets? She's very young,' Eleanor asked.

Dr Borthwick looked directly at her. 'I doubt the baby can be born. Even if properly cared for the girl will likely die. The bones around the birth canal are deformed.'

Eleanor met his gaze and her voice was calm but the colour burned in her cheeks. 'Will you come back and help them, the women here?'

'As much as I can. I will come one day each week.'

They travelled back in his hot and stuffy coach, Hayward seeming as pleased to leave the area as they were. Dr Borthwick could not decide if the persistent noxious smell was his clothes, the air outside or just his nose remembering. Eleanor must have heard him sniffing and she smiled as she passed him a handkerchief heavily scented with lavender. He took it and inhaled deeply.

'Thank you. I am too sensitive to bad smells for a man in my profession.'

'It was my husband who told me always to carry a scented handkerchief when visiting the poor or the sick.'

'He was both good and sensible then. An admirable combination.'

'You are right; he was.' She hesitated for a moment. 'But I had never thought of it quite so. A very good man, a religious man, but always thinking of how to improve the lives of the people, their bodies as well as their souls. That is why he worked with the London Mission. The bishop does not approve of them, of course. They are not of the established Church.'

'No, but Mr Wilson struck me as a good man, even if he is an evangelical.'

Eleanor nodded but he could see the slight frown which he now knew presaged a difficult question. He was saved by the carriage turning into the wide road where the Swans lived.

He got out first and helped her down.

'You must change your clothes and wash with plenty of water and soap, before you do anything else.'

He saw the flicker of amusement.

'Thank you, doctor,' she said demurely, as she walked past him to the house.

As Hayward drove him home he thought about Eleanor. He realized that he admired her very much. Too much.

Mrs Bates was waiting in the hall. She was sitting straight-backed in the chair, radiating more disapproval than usual.

He gave her a warm smile. It was always the best defence.

'Good day, Mrs Bates. Am I needed?' he said, walking across towards her.

'No. But I need to speak to you. In private,' she said, glowering at Betty who had appeared in haste from the kitchen.

'Mrs Bates said as she must wait for you . . .' Betty's voice tailed off. Usually Mrs Bates was kind to her.

'Of course. Please, Mrs Bates, do come into the study.' He opened the door for her and turned back to Betty: 'Please tell Mrs Hayward we have a guest for dinner.' Then, turning again: 'You do have time to join me, I hope, Mrs Bates?'

The midwife looked at him in surprise and then gave him the briefest of smiles as she nodded.

'Good. Do sit down by the window. It is cooler there. Forgive me, but I must wash and change. I've been in Duck Lane. Filthy place. I will be only a few minutes.'

He ran upstairs to his room, locking the door behind him. He stripped off his neckcloth and shirt and trousers and washed thoroughly in the bowl of tepid water with expensive soap, a luxury he allowed himself. For a moment he felt almost cool. As he dressed in clean linen he eyed the clothes on the floor. The shirt could go to soak but he would keep the trousers separate, just for his visits to Duck Lane. He needed to speak to Mrs Hayward: the trousers would have to be brushed and aired in the sun. He paused for a moment as he tied the neckcloth. He needed to be sure Eleanor did the same, that her dresses could be washed.

Eleanor again.

Mrs Bates had never called at the house before. Her news

would not be good. He shook his head and made himself think about how best to help the women of Duck Lane. That was not easy either.

When he returned to the study, Mrs Bates wasted no time, starting to speak in her flat voice as soon as he was seated.

'I've just been with Mrs Fitzharris.'

He nodded. Mrs Fitzharris was another new patient following Mr Davies's recommendation to her husband. He now had a number of patients who were wives to the wealthy men of business.

'She said as Mr Fitzharris had heard at his club about Lady Florence. That she'd bled to death and you did nothing,' Mrs Bates said.

'From Sir Alfred? Mr Fitzharris heard that from Sir Alfred?'

'No.' Her tone was scathing. 'Dr Preston. He's been telling all his patients about the risks of young doctors with modern ideas, then telling about a lady who has died recently. Careful not to name her. Or you. But all know it's her. And you.'

'And what did Mrs Fitzharris think?'

'She wants to stay with you. She's heard nothing but good. But Mr Fitzharris will be there when you call next month.'

He nodded. 'It is, of course, true that Lady Florence bled to death and that I did nothing.'

She was surprised. 'No doctor could. Once they start to bleed like that.'

'Indeed. And even Dr Preston must be aware that there is nothing can be done if the placenta haemorrhages.'

She did not reply but remained tense, sitting on the edge of her seat. They sat silent for a while.

'What will you do?' she said.

'Nothing yet. We'll just try to weather the storm.'

'So you'll stay in London?'

'Yes. Most certainly. But I'm very grateful that you came to tell me about Dr Preston. Thank you. Now, dinner should be ready.'

As soon as Mrs Bates had gone, he went out and walked rapidly ten times round the square, which made him feel far too hot. Slowing to a gentle stroll, he tried to enjoy the sudden emergence of people from their houses as the temperature started to fall. There were families with children and dogs, maidservants pushing baby carriages, even one young couple strolling slowly by, the woman visibly pregnant. He doffed his hat to one of his neighbours who bowed politely back.

He was, after all, a man of some substance: he kept a carriage and three servants.

But the evening breeze, which should have been welcome, became increasingly foul with the smell from the river. Driven back inside, he sat in his study reading a paper on the treatment of syphilis with mercury vapour which seemed somehow an unreasonable idea. After reading the same paragraph three times he put the paper down and picked up *Nicholas Nickleby*. Eleanor's voice kept intruding in his head as he tried to concentrate. A complication that he would have to address.

Later, as he moved restlessly in bed in the humid darkness, he heard a heavy knocking at the front of the house. He was almost pleased when Betty rapped in turn on his door, which he unlocked and opened promptly, already in his dressing gown. She was barely awake, her nightcap half off the tight black curls, swaying sleepily as she handed him the note. He decided to be less than happy when he saw the name and address.

He sent Betty to waken Hayward and ask him to bring round the horse, firmly repeating 'the horse, not the carriage', and then dressed quickly. He collected his bag from the study and opened the front door just as Hayward appeared, leading the fully saddled mare from the mews. It was a never-acknowledged game they played, who would be ready first at night. 'Betty said as you just needed the horse,' Hayward said in his loud night-time whisper, making it clear any mistake was Betty's.

'Yes, Mrs Mallory has her own nurse. There'll be no need to take Mrs Bates home tonight.'

'Well, here she is, all ready to go,' the manservant said, patting the mare.

Giving him the bag, Dr Borthwick mounted from the step as Hayward fastened the bag to the saddle behind him.

'Thank you, Hayward. You go back to bed. I'll be a while, I think. Goodnight.'

'Goodnight, doctor.'

It would be Mrs Mallory on a hot and smelly night. The horse trotted along the quiet street as he thought about her. He made it a rule to be able to find at least one attribute he could like or even admire in each of his patients. Sometimes it was as little as that they were polite to their servants; often it was courage. He struggled with Mrs Mallory: she was pink and plump and wore over-trimmed silk dresses, and had an unprepossessing three-year-old daughter and a fat pug dog which seemed interchangeable in her affections. She was deeply concerned by every manifestation of pregnancy and he had been called to see her countless times.

A night-soil cart announced itself by a worsening of the feculent stench as it was pulled out of a mews entrance. He stopped and nodded politely to the two men as they pushed the cart out in front of him and then he pulled the horse to the other side of the road. The smell as he passed the cart was atrocious, but it was necessary work and apparently the money was good for those who could bear the odours. Good in relative terms, he thought, good enough to live in a hovel on the edge of the city rather than in Devil's Acre. Mrs Mallory, of course, would never even contemplate what happened to night-soil.

Dr Borthwick tried to discipline his thoughts, to be kind. He had never spoken properly to Mrs Mallory. She was always attended by the fussing nurse or her plumper, pinker, fussier mother. The nurse was another problem; he had no evidence of her competence. Not like Mrs Bates. That was something else he needed to do: to ask Mrs Bates to work with him at the refuge. He would need to give her a higher rate to work there, Mrs Bates having a very clear idea of her own status. Yet she still attended women local to her lodging house. Perhaps he was misjudging her too.

As he turned the mare into the very smart road where the Mallory family lived, the sky was already lightening. The morning breeze started to blow and for a moment the air seemed fresher. He smiled and patted the horse.

The Midwife

He arrived to a house in uproar. The footman who opened the door with visible enthusiasm was the first and last fully clothed person he saw. The butler, still in his nightcap, rushed across the hall, candle wobbling precariously.

'Ah, Dr Borthwick. So pleased you are here. Mrs Mallory is calling for you and the gas has gone off. All the mantles are out.' He gesticulated round the large hall with the candlestick.

'It is getting light and I can manage well enough with lamps and candles. Could someone stable my horse?'

'Yes, of course. Please go on up. Robert will light the way.'

Dr Borthwick turned to the stairs as the footman reappeared with a lamp.

Robert walked ahead along the landing to Mrs Mallory's room and hesitated.

'Do you wish me to wait here, doctor, in case you need me to fetch anything, more lamps or hot water perhaps?'

'Has the nurse not requested anything?'

'No, doctor. She seems a little –' he paused – 'unwell.'

'In that case, please do wait.'

Inside the hot bedroom, the nurse was moderately drunk and in her nightgown, and Mrs Mallory was sprawled across the bed, shrieking continuously. Dr Borthwick took a deep breath and went back to the door, opening it slightly to speak to Robert.

'Where is Mr Mallory?'

'At his club, I believe.'

'Ah. Could you bring as many bright lamps as you can and two large bowls of hot water and two of cold, freshly drawn. I need clean sheets – six to start with. Is there a maid who could help, not a young girl?'

'The parlourmaid is a sensible woman.'

'Her then. Thank you.'

He closed the door.

Martha, the parlourmaid, was quiet and composed, dressed in a clean striped frock with her night-time plait hanging down her back. She did all he asked with a willing efficiency, volunteering that she had seen her sister and brother born and was always the one to see to the pug when it whelped, but otherwise just nodding to each of his instructions. Between them they settled Mrs Mallory and, when all was calm, he examined her between her increasingly frequent contractions.

The baby's head was still not engaged. He knew that Mrs Mallory's daughter had been small and born early, but this was a big baby.

'Mrs Mallory, we need you up and walking around. Martha will help you.'

She walked through the dawn and into the morning, leaning on Martha and later on both of them, as she followed his instructions to breathe through the contractions. She showed a fortitude which surprised him, but as the early-morning hours passed he knew that she was not only exhausted but becoming afraid. He examined her again and then, as Martha was settling her, he went to the door and called for Robert.

'Is Mr Mallory home yet?'

'Yes, doctor, he's just taking his breakfast.'

'I need to speak to him. Now, if you please.'

*

Dr Borthwick waited impatiently outside the bedroom.

'Well, doctor, is my son born?' Mr Mallory said loudly as he reached the top of the stairs, red-faced and panting.

'No, I am afraid not. Until now good progress has been made but the baby is large and Mrs Mallory is tiring,' said Dr Borthwick.

'Is it alive?'

'Yes, the baby's heartbeat remains strong and Mrs Mallory has coped admirably but—'

'There were no problems last time. It was all over in a few hours,' Mr Mallory interrupted.

Dr Borthwick could see the beads of sweat forming on the bulbous nose. 'No, but I am told that your daughter was born early and was a small baby. Prolonged labour is dangerous for the mother and baby and I may need to intervene.'

'What do you mean?'

'If labour progresses it may be possible to use forceps to assist in delivering the baby. If not, we may not be able to save the baby.'

'It's a boy though, if it's big.'

'That can't be known.'

'I want a son. You must save it.'

'Mr Mallory, regretfully, sometimes we have to sacrifice the baby to try to save the mother. I hope it won't come to that, but it might.'

'I need a son.'

'I understand, but if I have to sacrifice the baby, boy or girl, to save the mother then that is what I must do.'

'Can't you just cut the baby out? I've heard say it can be done.'

'No, your wife would certainly die. Excuse me, I must return to Mrs Mallory.'

He turned away, but Mr Mallory grabbed his arm, shouting into his face. He reeked of bacon fat and whisky and an unpleasantly strong floral scent.

'I will seek another opinion.'

'Please do.'

The second opinion did not arrive in time. Two hours later Mrs Mallory's son was delivered alive with the help of forceps and laudanum. She had screamed only twice as he applied the forceps and she had pushed to order, even through the opiate confusion. He could admire that.

He washed the baby, a large boy with a tuft of black hair, with his back politely turned as Martha washed the mother. The almost forgotten nurse continued to snore quite loudly in the chair beside the window: she had been undisturbed by her patient's distress.

After he dried and swaddled the baby, he held him close for a moment. There was a faint smell of lavender from the cloth, mixed with the acrid tang of newborn skin. Here was contentment. Here was justification for how he lived.

Mrs Mallory took her baby in her arms.

'Thank you, Dr Borthwick.'

'You did all the work. You were very brave. Well done.' He smiled.

'Thank you all the same.'

'Well, a lot of the thanks go to Martha, who makes a good nurse.'

'Better than Nurse Simms.' Martha looked up and

nodded towards the sleeping woman, who gave an unfortunate grunting snort as she moved and settled again in her chair.

Mr Mallory was waiting in the hall as Dr Borthwick came down the stairs.

'Congratulations once more, Mr Mallory. Mrs Mallory is very well and you have a fine son. All is ready for you to greet him.' He moved to shake the man's proffered hand.

'My thanks to you, Dr Borthwick. I was over-hasty when we spoke earlier, very anxious and all that.'

Dr Borthwick nodded politely. He watched as the beads of sweat started to form again on the red face.

'I hear that there were problems in the house when you arrived – the gas lights and so on,' said Mr Mallory.

'The footman, Robert, provided me with lamps. He has been most helpful. But the nurse was in an unfit condition.'

'So I hear. She will be out of the house today, I can assure you. And with no pay.'

Dr Borthwick disliked him more and more.

'That is your decision,' he said and nodded again. 'But Mrs Mallory will need care. Martha, your parlourmaid, was very useful, a capable young woman. You may wish to promote her to being nurse. My own midwife, Mrs Bates, could provide some training.'

'Of course. Thank you, doctor. You'll be sending your bill?'

'Within the fortnight.' Dr Borthwick smiled, mentally adding extra guineas to the total for each time Mr Mallory had spoken.

Robert opened the door for him and escorted him to his

horse, which was being held by the stable boy; the horse was chewing contentedly from a borrowed nosebag.

'Thank you for feeding her,' Dr Borthwick said, giving the boy a penny.

'Thanks, mister. Gave 'er water an' all,' the boy grinned.

Dr Borthwick nodded and turned to Robert, giving him two silver crowns.

'One for you and one for Martha. And please tell the butler about the nursing. Martha should be paid extra for that.' With that, he got on his horse and rode away, tired but in a much better mood. There was even a slight breeze, although it was already very hot.

Then he saw Dr Preston, riding composedly along the far side of the road.

He rode slowly over and pulled in alongside him.

'Good morning, Dr Preston. Perhaps I could ride with you a while?' Dr Borthwick said with a polite smile and nod of the head.

'Good day, Dr Borthwick. What a pleasant surprise. But I am only going along the road to Lord Havers's house. His heart again. They will see no one but me, of course. Inconvenient. But one's duty.'

'Well, what I have to say will not take long.'

'Please, then do carry on.'

Dr Borthwick paused, taking time apparently to steady his horse, to think before speaking.

'I have been told by a friend that it is said, in his club, that you have been commenting on my care of one of my patients.'

'Indeed not. You are mistaken. I am after all a physician

so would not comment on the actions of an –' Dr Preston paused as if searching for the word – 'an *accoucheur*.' The tone he employed was that used in polite society to refer to unfortunate occupations; to dustmen, night-soil men and gravediggers.

Dr Borthwick replied in a level voice, 'Indeed, then you have been misreported. I am happy that is the case. I have no doubt that Lady Florence died of *placenta praevia* and I know of no physician nor *accoucheur* who could have saved her.'

Dr Preston smiled, his fleshy lips folding back over his large teeth. Doffing his hat, he pulled his horse to a stop and dismounted. Two footmen in full livery rushed down the impressive steps, one to take the horse, the other to escort the doctor through the gleaming double doors.

Dr Borthwick rode home in the rapidly increasing heat.

Betty was sweeping the front steps when he arrived and she ran down to take the horse as he dismounted, dropping the broom behind her.

'Good morning, Betty. I hope you were able to go back to sleep?'

'Yes, doctor.' She looked down.

'It was a hot night, though,' he said. Even after a year, he usually struggled to get a response from her.

She looked up, straight at him. 'I like it warm. It's the cold here is terrible.' She stopped, seeming surprised at saying so much.

'I think I prefer the cold but then I am better used to it, coming from the north.' He smiled at her and patted the horse. 'Is Mr Hayward up?'

She nodded.

'Take her round to the stable then. Make sure you tie her up, just as he has shown you.'

She nodded again with some enthusiasm.

He climbed the steps, picking up the fallen broom, and she called after him, 'Doctor, shall I say to Mrs Hayward as you want to take your luncheon early?'

He looked back, delighted that she had spoken unprompted. 'That will do very well. Thank you, Betty.'

Part Two

13

Northumberland, July 1838

S he stood in front of the long mirror and studied Mrs
Sharp: thin face framed by the white cap, grey-blue eyes,
straight nose and pale lips, long grey dress. She reached up
and pulled a few brown wisps forwards over her forehead, as
Alice had done, then tucked them back under the lace. Like
a nun, she thought, and saw women walking side by side, dark
dresses and white veils, across a sun-drenched square. Then
the picture in her head was gone. She watched the lips tighten
and the shoulders pull back, before Mrs Sharp turned away
and went downstairs.

She walked into the warm and fragrant kitchen, closing the
heavy door carefully behind her.

'Good morning, Mrs Godwin. As Mr Black has gone home,
I think it will be easier for you if I take breakfast in here,' she
said.

Jenny looked up from her porridge then hurriedly away
again but Peter put down his spoon and watched Mrs Godwin,
expressionless. After a long moment, the cook turned away
from her frying pan. 'Dr Soames takes breakfast in his study.'

'Well, I'm sure he'll not want to be disturbed. May I sit down?'

Mrs Godwin gave her attention back to the bacon, tipping it out neatly on to a plate and passing it to Peter, then said, 'Porridge then bacon is what we're having.'

'That sounds perfect, thank you,' said Mrs Sharp, sitting down on the bench next to Jenny.

Peter stood up and silently passed her a plate and cup and then slowly and methodically served her some porridge with a large blob of honey.

She smiled at him as he gave her the bowl and to her surprise he smiled back and spoke. 'Mrs Godwin gets the honey herself, keeps bees and all,' he said, nodding towards the garden.

It was the most he had said directly to her and she was grateful. 'I have such admiration for anyone who keeps bees. Perhaps, Mrs Godwin, when you have time you could tell me how it is done?' she said.

'Well, it's the bees as choose to stay, but if you're interested I'll show you the hives. Perhaps tomorrow,' Mrs Godwin said as she sat down heavily next to Peter.

The rest of breakfast was mainly silent, but Mrs Sharp was content to concentrate on the food: she was still hungry almost all the time. As she spooned up the porridge, thick and creamy, she thought of Mary and the half-cup of gruel she would already have finished; something else to discuss with Dr Soames.

Her two weeks were up today.

*

She walked along to Dr Soames's study, aware of the clicking of her boots on the tiled floor. They were Arthur Black's final gift to her. She had tried to refuse when he summoned the bootmaker, telling her she had to be 'shod decent to go with dress'. He had simply laughed and told her his life was surely worth more than a pair of boots.

The study door opened, and Dr Soames nodded to her. 'Good morning, Mrs Sharp. We start visits at a half past eight. Peter will take us to Denwick. I'll see you at the front door.'

'I'm to stay then?'

'Yes. We'll discuss your payment over dinner, which Mrs Godwin serves at two o'clock and is only held over for a birth or a death. Best otherwise never to be late. You'll take dinner each day with me so we can discuss our patients. Except for Sundays.' He smiled briefly and walked past her into the hall.

She only realized afterwards that it was another of Dr Soames's many acts of considered kindness to exhibit her first in his smart two-horse carriage, sitting beside him, with Peter driving in front, and so to establish her position as almost (but not quite) gentry.

She looked firmly ahead as they went slowly down the cobbled hill past the market square, aware of the occasional touch of Dr Soames's arm against hers as the carriage swayed. The passers-by almost all called out, 'Good morning, doctor,' and he responded by a nod of the head or occasionally by doffing his hat and replying. She knew they all stared at her. She moved only to pull the borrowed shawl, Mrs Godwin's again, across her chest as they picked up speed, leaving the cobbles for a long lane which curved away ahead.

The sun was bright in her eyes and then she was there in the other place, his hand warm on her back as the sand crunched under her toes. Walking towards the sun. Where? Who? She tried to hold the picture, the place. The carriage lurched and the light shattered into whirling fragments. Her stomach heaved.

'What is it?' A man's voice, Dr Soames, the smell of tobacco and tweed.

She had to be in control, had to assure him that she was strong and fit to work.

'I just felt dizzy for a moment. Not used to the movement of the carriage, I think. I am well now. Thank you.' She swallowed down the rising vomit, trying to slow her breathing, aware of her heart pounding.

He turned away for a moment and then back again.

'Our first patient is old Mr Jenkins who has a wasting illness. Later we'll see his daughter, Mrs Coultar, who lives on the farm at the end of the village.'

So they went on to see seven people. At each house Dr Soames introduced her as Mrs Sharp the new nurse and midwife, and watched her as she spoke to them, examined them or dressed their wounds and ulcers. He quizzed her gently as they left.

They were back promptly at a quarter to two; she went across the yard to the surgery and without pausing filled a bowl from the jug and started to wash her hands. He stood by the table, looking at her.

'I noticed you washed your hands a lot when nursing Arthur and again on our visits. Why?'

She paused and then the words came easily. 'It's what I was taught.'

'By whom?'

'I have no idea. I wish that I did.'

Dr Soames said nothing more until they were seated in the dining room. She was looking around at the highly polished sideboard and the heavy damask drapes, trying to stop her mouth from watering at the smells from the kitchen: food was such a priority, even an obsession, and she was embarrassed by her greed.

'I was impressed by the way in which you examined Mrs Coultar. I agree it must be twins,' he said.

'She looks anaemic,' said Mrs Sharp.

'What would you recommend?

'Same as for Arthur, liver or blood pudding with fresh greens.'

'We agree on the first two but why the greens?'

'Because I know it's correct. But I can't remember how I know.' She looked directly at him, almost defiantly, feeling the beginning of irritation and knowing she must suppress it.

He looked back, brown eyes under bushy grey brows, a big, slightly hooked nose and thick, greying hair. She lowered her gaze first, trying to find something to distract him, to distract them both.

There was a portrait over the fireplace of a young woman in a pale muslin gown, dark hair loosely bound by a wide blue ribbon. She was sitting with a book open but the painter had captured her in a moment of raising her eyes, with a half-smile. Mrs Sharp found herself almost smiling back.

'My wife, Clara, before we married,' Dr Soames said. 'Her

father gave me the portrait as a wedding present. But she was too modest to have it on show in a public room. I hung it here after she died.' His voice was calm, face expressionless.

She already knew that Dr Soames was a widower and that his daughter Charlotte was married: Alice had told her.

She thought, fleetingly, about what to say, but the words came easily, measured and quiet. 'When did she die?'

'A long time ago now. Twenty-four years.'

She looked straight at him then, at the tightening of the lines around his eyes and mouth.

'I am sorry.' She paused. 'Alice Black said you have a married daughter.'

'Yes. Charlotte is Mrs Robert Thorpe, and lives some distance away, near Newcastle. That is her portrait by the window, painted a few years ago now.'

She turned around to look. Two portraits: in one, a pretty young woman with her fair hair arranged in curls and her face arranged in a simper; and, in the other, a child with her mother's dark hair looking solemnly out at the world. Alice had said nothing about another daughter.

'The younger girl is much like your wife.' She spoke without turning back to him.

'Yes. They were alike. Our first child, named Elizabeth for her grandmother. She died of the measles the year after the portrait was done. Eight years of age. Charlotte is our second child, a year younger. Her mother . . .' He paused and then continued, his voice roughened. 'My wife died in childbirth, her third child with her, the following winter.'

Such pain unsaid. She knew then she had done this before, talked with those who were grieving and bereaved. She knew not to say she understood, not to offer empty sympathy. She turned back to face him.

'It must have taken great courage to carry on living,' she said.

He inclined his head slightly and started to speak but was interrupted by Mrs Godwin bringing in a pie, golden pastry standing tall on a big platter. It was placed with some ceremony on the sideboard.

'Mrs Godwin's pies are renowned,' he said, instead.

As Mrs Godwin cut into the crust the steam escaped and a smell of hot meat and vegetables filled the room. Mrs Sharp felt the rush of saliva in her mouth and swallowed hard. The first thick wedge was carried over and placed in front of Dr Soames and then a large wedge brought to her.

'Thank you, Mrs Godwin. It looks and smells very good indeed,' she said.

Dr Soames nodded and then waited until Mrs Godwin had left the room. He started to eat.

She ate with concentration, wiping the last drop of gravy from her plate with a piece of pastry. She could feel him watching her.

'I can still feel what the hunger pains were like,' she said as she placed her knife and fork neatly on the plate. She looked past him at the sideboard and the blue platter. 'That piece of pie I've just eaten would be three days' worth of meat on the farm and there'd have been nothing else. No pastry.'

Dr Soames nodded. 'John Elliott said he found you on the high moor very ill and that he fed and clothed you.'

'He did find me. He saved my life. But it was Mary who

nursed me, who shared her food and her clothes. Rags, as you saw. They have very little.'

'He said you owe him money.'

He was looking directly at her and she held his gaze, kept her voice slow and level.

'He earned money from me. Once I was able, I worked on the farm and then afterwards he was paid for me acting as midwife and nurse. But he didn't spend the money on food for Mary or me. I've paid my debts to him.' She could feel the anger and the shame rising. She looked down.

'I agree. You owe him nothing. John Elliott is not a good man.'

'No, but I did hold money back from him. I got a shilling from Blacksmith Weddell and a few other pennies. I know I should give it to you now, that you must have paid him off. But I need the money. I have to buy some meat and oatmeal and send it out to Mary.'

She looked up then and was horrified by his pity.

Hot rage consumed her and the words started to spew out, unstoppable. 'This is all wrong. The farm was wrong, that poor starving girl and her baby and the smells and the filth and John . . . It's all wrong, bent, bad. This is not where I should be. This is not me. This is not me!'

She heard the echo of her shouting as she rushed out of the room.

She lay on the bed, listening to the sounds of the house: heard Dr Soames go out again; heard footsteps and then a knock, and Jenny's voice saying there was a tray with tea by the door;

heard the footsteps go away again. She lay on the bed, waiting for the dark.

There were no tears left. She was so tired, so very tired of knowing nothing of herself except that this place was not hers. No pictures, no words, just the greyness stretching ahead. Anyway, there could be no life here for her now, not after that outburst, and in a way she was glad. She knew how to get to the sea: just walk along the lane to Denwick and keep going until she was there. Then keep walking into the water, then swim for a little while. Her dress would soon get wet and heavy.

She woke into full night, surprised she had slept. Lit only by the moon, she stood up, careful to be quiet, and removed her crumpled cap and white cuffs, smoothing them out before folding them. She patted down her dress, momentarily saddened at the thought of Alice and Arthur Black – but it was Mrs Sharp they had befriended, not her. Not whoever she really was.

She turned the doorknob slowly and opened the door. There was a small pool of light on the landing; Dr Soames was sitting at his bedroom door, reading. He looked up. 'Mrs Godwin has left out some cocoa in the kitchen, if you would like a drink? I might join you if that is acceptable.'

'Thank you, but I think I should leave. I have somewhere to go.' She was pleased that her voice was calm.

'There is a life for you here as Mrs Sharp. If nothing else you can help others as you did Arthur, at least for now. I have written to a colleague in Edinburgh who has some knowledge of memory problems. He might be able to help. But it is your choice. The kitchen door is unlocked,' he said.

He walked downstairs with her. Mrs Godwin was there, swathed in a paisley robe with her hair in a nightcap, sitting at the table and writing something by candlelight.

'Oh, I'm sorry, Dr Soames, I couldn't sleep so I'm just doing the grocery list. I'll go,' she said, pushing back her chair.

'Well, as you are here, Mrs Godwin, perhaps you could pour us some cocoa and maybe Mrs Sharp could manage some of your excellent gooseberry pie,' said Dr Soames.

Mrs Godwin left them, declaring she would be making pancakes for breakfast, and Mrs Sharp sat down and drank cocoa and ate gooseberry pie whilst despair lapped at her feet.

Dr Soames moved to sit beside her. 'I think, Mrs Sharp, that you are a little older than my daughter Charlotte. She will be arriving in the next few days as no doubt her spies will be telling her I have taken a strange woman into my house. I must admit to looking forward to you meeting her,' he said.

When she started to weep he held her arm gently, as a father would, and then she went back to the bedroom which she now knew was hers.

14

London, August 1841

This time the request to call had been written in Lady Gasgoine's own elegant handwriting on rose-scented notepaper. Dr Borthwick was intrigued.

The front door to the house in Belgrave Square was opened by the butler, Mr Burrows, a singular acknowledgement of Dr Borthwick's increased status with the family. Once inside the cool, quiet entrance hall, Dr Borthwick inhaled with pleasure: the scent of lilies filled the air, towering vases of white flowers standing on each of the side tables.

'Well, Mr Burrows, it is a good deal pleasanter in here. It is already hot and the breeze is carrying up the stench from the river again,' Dr Borthwick said, handing his hat to the butler with a smile.

'Her ladyship is receiving visitors in the conservatory for that very reason, doctor. Her ladyship has asked for coffee to be served there. She is accompanied by her sister, Lady Burnside,' the butler said.

So much information conveyed with so few words. Dr Borthwick felt he was becoming almost fluent in the code used by upper servants: Sir Jeremy had not been mentioned so was not at home; the conservatory was a very informal place to receive visitors; the serving of coffee suggested a meeting of those with equal status. Dr Borthwick raised his eyebrows slightly.

The butler, with whom Dr Borthwick had shared half a bottle of good port after he had safely delivered Lady Gasgoine's twins, nodded fractionally in response.

A footman, resplendent in a summer uniform of white breeches, shirt and stockings and a pale blue waistcoat, escorted Dr Borthwick out of the hall and along a wide corridor. The doctor surreptitiously touched the pale green wall. It was not covered with one of the new papers, which were expensive enough, but with stretched silk. He wondered fleetingly how much it had cost as the footman opened the double doors on to a scene that must have cost very much more.

There were orange trees in terracotta pots and the warm air was scented with their blossom. The two women were sitting in padded bamboo chairs beneath a hanging vine, framed by two pineapples growing in blue-and-yellow glazed pots. High above them arched white ironwork, supporting curved glass panels.

Lady Gasgoine smiled, gesturing to the chair beside her as he bowed, and then she introduced him to her sister. Lady Burnside also smiled but her eyes were red-rimmed and her fingers were plucking at her elegant skirts.

He made polite enquiries about the twins and Lady Gasgoine spoke of them with affection but not passion. She was, he knew, highly intelligent and had been remarkably brave during her long labour but he usually found her to be quite detached, almost passive. According to Mrs Bates, Lady Gasgoine had married her own choice of husband and had her own considerable fortune.

He sipped his coffee, poured with offhand grace by Lady Gasgoine, and thought how lovely and how alike they were: both in brightly patterned chintz day-dresses; both with pale blue eyes; both with uncovered fair hair, smoothly looped over their ears. Alike but not identical, he decided. Their faces were slightly different, and Lady Gasgoine was always spoken of as being a famous beauty and her twin sister less so. Lady Burnside perhaps had the more fashionable looks, the smaller heart-shaped face, but her sister was the one who stopped conversation when she entered a room. He thought that must be hard for Lady Burnside, to be always second best.

He saw that she was struggling to remain composed, so turned slightly to address Lady Gasgoine.

'Thank you for the excellent coffee and respite from the heat, and also, I'm afraid, the smell by the river. It is particularly objectionable today, alas.' He paused. 'Is there a problem on which you require my advice? You are looking, I am pleased to say, very well.'

'I am very well, and grateful for your care,' said Lady Gasgoine.

He smiled his acknowledgement and waited.

'It is my sister who is in need of advice and we did not know who best to ask,' she said.

An interesting phrase. Dr Borthwick felt the first stirrings of anxiety.

'As you are aware, Lady Gasgoine, I do not practise as a physician in London but only as an *accoucheur*.'

'Yes, and it is for that reason I – we – felt you could advise.'

He looked at Lady Burnside, but her head was down. He knew now what might be coming next and his response was prepared.

'Lady Burnside, what is the problem?' he said, his voice professional, quiet.

She shook her head and he saw a tear drop down on to her dress.

Lady Gasgoine leaned forward and patted her hand then turned back to face him.

'It is best if I explain. My sister is in great distress.'

He waited again.

'My sister is with child. Only a few weeks.'

'Are you – is she – certain?'

'Yes.'

'But why is this causing her and you such concern? Surely this is welcome news?'

He watched as Lady Gasgoine took a deep breath and then looked directly at him again. Her voice was steady. 'The child is not her husband's. The father is not Lord Burnside.'

'Forgive me, but I need to understand. Is your sister certain that her husband is not the father?'

'Yes. There have been no . . .' She paused, and the colour flared in her cheeks. 'No relations for over a year. Lord Burnside is very much older than my sister and is often ill.'

'Forgive me again. Sometimes a much older husband will accept a child . . . ?'

'No. That is not possible.' Lady Gasgoine looked across at her sister who was now sobbing quietly.

'Then arrangements need to be made for Lady Burnside to

go away, abroad perhaps? It can be said that she has signs of a weakness in the lungs. I have details of a sanatorium in Switzerland which will make arrangements including for care of the child afterwards.' His voice was gentle.

Lady Gasgoine nodded and looked at her sister.

He waited again.

'I can't have it, not anywhere.' Lady Burnside's voice was slurred with tears but the words were almost shouted.

Lady Gasgoine looked at him. And here was the passion he had not seen before, both a deep love for her twin sister and real fear. There were tears filling her eyes now but her voice was still steady.

'The father is my brother-in-law's secretary, Jacob. He is the son of a slave whom Lord Burnside freed in Jamaica and who became his trusted manservant. Jacob was brought up and educated as part of the family. Lord Burnside treats him almost as his own son.'

Lady Burnside wept and her sister went and knelt beside her, holding her close. Dr Borthwick stood up and walked over to the citrus trees. Each of them was standing on a circular wooden platform with a handle, presumably to rotate the heavy pots. Leaning over, he tried to concentrate on the mechanism.

Lady Burnside was right. The story would get out. Even the discreet Swiss clinic would not be able to keep this secret. She would be ruined and Jacob would quite possibly be hanged. It would be called a rape, of course. He sniffed the orange blossom and went back to his chair.

He had to refuse the request he knew would be made.

Lady Burnside was quiet, just now and then a shuddering sob. Lady Gasgoine sat opposite him again and he saw the effort it took her to regain her usual composure.

'Dr Borthwick, I love my sister most dearly. Please understand that I ask this only because I am certain that there is no other way.' She paused but the blue eyes held his. 'I know that unwanted babies can be got rid of. Will you help us?'

'It is unlawful and considered gravely sinful by many. It is also very risky for the woman,' he said.

'I thought it would be safe for her if you would—'

'No, it is never safe. The drugs and potions are useless. The only sure way involves a form of surgery. It is often not successful. There is serious risk of putrefaction, of bleeding, of death. It is, as I said before, against the law,' he said.

He turned to Lady Burnside. 'I am sorry. Please do not think me unsympathetic to your distress. I think travel abroad is the best option.' He stood up, bowing to them both.

Lady Burnside leapt up and took his arm, her fingers gripping tight. She looked at him, fierce and unwavering. He saw the courage her sister had shown in labour, delivering her twins. 'If you will not help me then I must kill myself. If I have this baby then Jacob's life as well as mine is over. They will hang him. So I will save him. I will pay with my life. For him.'

He believed her.

Mr Burrows, the butler, opened the door for Dr Borthwick again the next day and a footman was sent out to bring in his bags.

The Midwife

'Lady Gasgoine is with her sister. They are in Lady Gasgoine's room. Everything has been made ready as you requested,' the butler said.

'Thank you. Lady Burnside is most embarrassed about the abscess, because of its position. It is essential that there is no talk of it by her maid.' Dr Borthwick's voice was clear, louder than necessary.

'I have spoken to Marie-Claire myself. She is a sensible girl, though French, of course. Do you think, doctor, that the ladies do too much riding?'

'Well, in this case, perhaps. Lady Burnside tells me that she had ridden out every day for several weeks before she came to London.'

'And, I gather, in the rain. The possibility of chafing of the . . .' Mr Burrows coughed, and continued in a hoarse but loud whisper. 'Of the lower regions.'

'Indeed.'

Confident that the conversation had been heard by the footman and the under maid, Dr Borthwick went slowly upstairs.

He had no choice but to care for her as best he could: she was desperate.

A different woman from the elegant society beauty now, Lady Gasgoine was dressed in a plain cotton gown, her hair scraped back beneath a white cap. The passivity was gone; she was concentrating hard as he explained again what she must do. They were sitting by the large window, waiting for the opium he had given her sister to take effect.

125

He went over again to check Lady Burnside, who was now barely conscious.

Lady Gasgoine did exactly as he asked. She held apart her sister's flopping legs as Dr Borthwick washed Lady Burnside, then examined her and inserted the metal tube and then poured in the soapy, now cool, boiled water. Lady Burnside screamed just once and then sobbed, sinking back into a half-sleep. Her sister sat on the bed and held her as she moved fitfully with the cramps that followed.

Two hours later Dr Borthwick carried the bloody cloths downstairs himself and put them in the hot fire beneath the huge boiler. When he came back into the room, Lady Gasgoine was washing her sister's face, speaking to her in a loving whisper. He paused, unwilling to interrupt such tenderness.

'Is it done?' Lady Burnside's voice was weak.

'Yes,' he said, coming to the bedside and gently taking her pulse. It was steady. 'Yes, it is done but the danger is in the next few days. You must rest and drink and eat as your sister tells you. She is an excellent nurse.'

Lady Gasgoine looked at him and to his surprise she raised her eyebrows and smiled a little.

He spoke directly to her. 'I will call tomorrow morning but sooner if she becomes feverish or there is heavy bleeding.'

Lady Gasgoine nodded.

'You recall what I said to tell your maid?'

She nodded again. 'That there was a large quantity of foul green matter came from the abscess. It had such a terrible smell that I retched.'

'What is the worst smell you can ever remember?'

She thought, concentrating.

'When we were children we found a dead deer in the lake. Our brother tried to pull it on to the shore and it burst open. All its guts spilled out. I can still smell it.' Her face portrayed real disgust.

'So, remember that smell when you tell your maid. It is very important.'

As Hayward drove him in the carriage to the Devil's Acre, Dr Borthwick thought how expert he had become at lying. Always have some truth in what you say: try to reflect a memory of something similar, something real, if you can. Even better, something which had caused a physical response, actual revulsion or anger. He had his set-piece lies and his rules and his reputation for being polite and reserved. It was usually easy now.

The stench of the river worsened as they plodded south. All the traffic was slow, the horses' heads drooping in the heat. There were few people on foot; even the boys who jostled to hold horses for a ha'penny had gone. Dr Borthwick felt the sweat trickling down his temples.

Hayward left him at the entrance to the alley on Duck Lane, taking the horse and carriage to find some shelter from the sun. As Dr Borthwick walked towards the refuge he could hardly breathe; there was no movement in the air trapped between the blackened walls, and the feculent smell was strong enough to taste. He reached the green doors with relief. Inside, the room was packed, every bench filled with women. For a brief moment, the smell of soap overlaid the smells of human sweat and excrement. He shook his head, annoyed with his weakness.

Eleanor came down the ladder stair, neat as always in her movements. As she came closer he could see a sweat-damp curl escaping from her cap on to her cheek. He ignored the urge to push it back, to touch her face.

'Dr Borthwick, you are late,' she announced.

'I regret to tell you, Mrs Johnson, that I have been in a drinking and gambling club all night and never been home,' he said, smiling.

'And now you are in this low place. Shame on you,' she smiled back. 'Mrs Bates is already hard at work and wants you to see Mrs Smith,' she said, waving him away towards the curtain.

When at last the room was empty, he offered to take Mrs Bates back to her lodgings in his carriage, along with Eleanor. She refused at first, but he insisted: it was a dirty and dangerous walk and tempers were fraying in the heat.

It had taken him some time to persuade Mrs Bates to come to the Duck Lane refuge. He had assured her she would not be expected to come there alone to attend women in labour, that he wanted her instead to train the local women to help each other. The lying-in hospital was massively overcrowded and those from the Devil's Acre were very often turned away.

Her reluctance had been overcome by him offering her double her usual day rate of pay. But on her first visit she had been shaken, even with all her experience.

The child was heavily pregnant, bruised and scarred, every rib visible, with a suppurating syphilitic chancre in her groin. Mrs Bates had swept out through the curtain, shouting at the women on the benches. He followed her, surprised.

'How could you let this be done to a child so young? How could you let her . . . let her . . .' She stumbled for the word and spat out, 'Work.'

The women on the benches stared at her, some lost in apathy but others always near to anger. One laughed and turned to Dr Borthwick.

'Her ma died and her . . . gentleman –' the word was said with scorn – 'he said as he would have the child for his use instead. One of your people, he was. Not one of us.'

Mrs Bates turned back and looked at Dr Borthwick and for just a moment he saw the rage that she felt against all men: the impregnators, the rapists.

He went behind the curtain to talk to the child, his voice gentle.

On the way back to her lodgings that evening Mrs Bates had sat silent opposite him in the coach. Eventually she spoke in her usual flat voice.

'I should not have shouted.'

'Sometimes we see something so bad, so awful, that perhaps we need to shout,' Dr Borthwick said.

'Not at those women, some almost children themselves.'

'No.'

'It's a terrible place. The worst I've seen even here in this filthy city.'

'You were not always in London?'

'No. A village. My mother was a midwife and taught me.'

It was the first thing she had ever told him about her past. He thought and then spoke carefully.

'Would you go back?'

She laughed harshly, an unused sound.

'I ran off with a sailor, burned my boats all ways, you could say. Not worth it but seemed so at the time. Young and foolish.'

'We all make mistakes. But it is to the benefit of women that you are working here now. You must see how important your work is.' He smiled at her and she nodded and looked away.

They had finished the journey in their usual silence.

Now, Mrs Bates sat rigid beside Eleanor in the carriage, defying even Eleanor's good humour. She did agree, somewhat grudgingly, to Eleanor's comments on the excessive heat and need for rain. Dr Borthwick leaned back and watched them, knowing he should help Eleanor, but admitting to himself that he was enjoying the tussle.

At her lodgings, he got out to help Mrs Bates down and then discreetly handed her the day's pay. She nodded and turned away, then hesitated.

'Dr Preston's been saying things again. Things he oughtn't. Lies,' she said, voice low.

'About Lady Florence?'

'Yes, but no one bothers with that now. No, he says that you're –' she hesitated – 'well, over close with some of your patients.'

'For heaven's sake! I'm sorry, please excuse my language. Who does this relate to? Which lady?'

'No names. Yet, anyways.'

The Midwife

'Well, how ridiculous.' He smiled at her then. 'Your reputation as a midwife and chaperone protects me.'

'Aye. Most think the same. But there are still men who don't want a doctor to touch their wives. It's them he aims at.' She turned to go but he reached out and patted her arm very briefly.

'Thank you, Mrs Bates. Thank you for your frankness and your loyalty. Indeed, for your friendship. It is highly valued.'

She nodded once and walked briskly into her lodging house.

As they travelled back to the Swans' house, Eleanor made no secret of the fact that she had been listening.

'Is it a serious problem?' she said.

'Did you hear it all?'

'Yes.'

'More nonsense.' He shrugged.

She frowned and was about to speak but stopped and then leaned forward. 'Do you pay Mrs Bates when she comes to the refuge?'

'Of course. I pay her for all the work she does for me. She only has what she earns.'

'But you're not paid for what you do there.'

He shook his head, surprised at her sudden intensity.

She spoke firmly then, very much the woman he admired. 'I'll make sure Mr Swan tells of your good work at the Mission, of your charity to the poor women. He is well respected. Men will listen to him.'

They sat in companionable silence for the rest of the journey.

*

Late that evening, he was sitting in a pleasantly tepid bath mulling over the day when he heard Betty's knock, tentative as always, on the door.

'What is it, Betty?' he called, climbing over the high bath side and starting to dry himself.

'A note from Lady Gasgoine. The footman says is urgent. There's a coach waiting,' she shouted through the door.

'Go down and tell him I will be five minutes,' he shouted back.

This soon, it was more likely to be bleeding. If it was infection now she would have no chance. Damn, he thought.

As he walked briskly down the stairs, he saw Betty struggling out of his study with both bags. He went to the footman who bowed and gave him the note.

Lady Gasgoine's hand, but the paper was plain, and the ink smudged:

Lady Burnside appears unwell. Please come at once. Anne Gasgoine.

They moved through London at considerable speed. As soon as the coach started to slow, he heard the footman call to the coachman and start to climb down. The door was jerked open and the step pulled out the instant the coach stopped. The footman rushed ahead of him to bow him through the already-opened front door.

Sir Jeremy himself was in the hall and the doctor felt his pulse start to pound.

'Dr Borthwick, I am not sure we should have disturbed you but Lady Burnside is in some discomfort and my wife is concerned for her. Would you go straight up?' The footman led him at a run up the sweeping stairs and he rehearsed what he might find; what he could do.

The footman knocked on the door then stood back, clearly following instructions. Lady Gasgoine, still in her plain dress and cap, opened the door just enough to let Dr Borthwick in and then closed it behind him. He went straight over to Lady Burnside who was sitting propped up in bed. He exhaled slowly as she opened her eyes, fully conscious.

'I am feeling much better. I think my sister panicked a little.' She smiled and then took her sister's hand. Lady Gasgoine stood, tensed, on the far side of the bed.

He nodded as he felt Lady Burnside's forehead and then her pulse. It was steady and she was not febrile.

'What happened?' he said.

Lady Gasgoine replied, her voice trembling slightly. 'My sister started to have bad cramps again. I looked at the rags as you had told me and there was a small amount of blood. But then a great clot of blood came out. I have it here.'

She passed him a covered basin and looked directly at him. She was struggling to hold back the tears she had never shed when in labour with her twins. He realized that she was near the end of her courage.

'But, Dr Borthwick, since then I have had no more pain. Indeed, I am comfortable,' Lady Burnside said, glancing at her sister and taking her hand again.

He walked over to the table lamp and examined the contents of the basin. A simple blood clot.

He washed his hands and then examined Lady Burnside's abdomen and checked the rags. He straightened up and smiled at her as her sister covered her with the sheet.

'I think everything is as it should be. The bleeding is no more than expected and there is no sign of infection. Some more boiled water and honey to drink and a little light food if you wish. And then a good sleep. I will call back tomorrow.'

He washed his hands again and turned to find Lady Gasgoine holding out the towel, which he took with a small bow. Then, at the door, she paused and, defying convention, took his hand for a moment in both of hers. She looked directly at him; the blue eyes almost bruised by fatigue.

'Thank you. You have been more than a good doctor and more than kind. I know how much my sister and I have asked of you.' She stopped and opened the door and then closed it softly behind him.

The waiting footman escorted him downstairs, telling him that Sir Jeremy had asked if Dr Borthwick would be good enough to attend him in his study. Dr Borthwick, feeling considerably relieved that his patient was doing well, so far, agreed promptly.

Sir Jeremy was polite but slightly distant, reflecting his status. He offered the doctor refreshments, which he declined, and then they discussed the weather. After propriety had been satisfied, Sir Jeremy leaned slightly forward in his chair.

'My wife is devoted to her sister and I consider Lady Burnside to be my own very dear sister also,' he said, then paused, frowning, seeming uncertain.

'Yes, indeed. I have been most impressed by the care with which Lady Gasgoine is attending to Lady Burnside,' Dr Borthwick said, filling the silence which was too long.

'Will she recover?' Sir Jeremy said, looking at him, intent now.

Dr Borthwick was expecting a different question. He chose his words with even more than his usual care.

'You will understand, I know, that I cannot speak in any detail of my patient. What I can say is that the problem has been dealt with and I am hopeful Lady Burnside will make a full recovery.'

Sir Jeremy paused before nodding briskly. 'I understand. Thank you,' he said.

Later, Dr Borthwick was escorted with ceremony to the door by the footman and Mr Burrows, the butler, and then driven back to his house in a four-horse carriage. The pace was stately, so he had time to admire the silk wall linings and herb-filled cushions on the silk-upholstered seats.

As the carriage turned into his road there was a flash of lightning and then rolling thunder. The rain started.

15

Northumberland, August 1838

To Mrs Sharp's relief, storms and heavy rain delayed the much-anticipated visit of Mrs Robert Thorpe, Charlotte, Dr Soames's only living child. According to Mrs Godwin, Mrs Thorpe now resided in great style in Corbridge following her marriage three years ago to a very rich colliery owner. Mrs Godwin had been there twice, called upon to help cater for large house parties when, she said, the Thorpes' cook was unable to cope. She described the kitchen, the modern iron stove and the new boiler in the scullery with considerable enthusiasm. She was even more enthusiastic about Mrs Thorpe, describing her as a mighty fine lady now, moving in the best company. Mrs Sharp, listening carefully to the unsaid, restricted her responses to comments on the importance of a good boiler and how useful one would be in the surgery.

On the morning of Mrs Thorpe's now expected arrival, Mrs Sharp woke early to bright sunshine coming through the wide-open shutters. She lay feeling the warmth from the patch of sunlight across her legs and then grimaced: no last-minute reprieve by more rain then. She sat up, stretched, and looked around at what she now felt was hers: a white-painted room with a large east-facing window looking over the walled garden; a washstand and chair; a wardrobe; a fireplace with a bowl of roses in the grate. Worth fighting for, she decided.

She washed and put on her newest dress, a lighter cotton in pale grey but the same style, her uniform. This one she had made herself, cutting it out on the big table in Alice's kitchen and then sitting in the light evenings in the garden, both of them stitching. She was almost as quick on the straight seams now, but the draper's daughter was very much better at the tiny buttonholes. Smiling at the memory, she checked herself in the mirror. She pulled her cap back from her forehead just enough to show the line of smoothly swept-back brown hair, re-pinned it and then nodded. No shadows or ghosts, just Mrs Sharp.

She arrived downstairs to find the kitchen in overheated chaos. Mrs Godwin was already applying pastry to three copper pie tins; Peter was piling coal into the stove; and Jenny was weeping over the porridge pot.

'Jenny, go and fetch the bowls whilst I finish the porridge,' Mrs Sharp said, tying on an apron and taking the spoon from the girl's hand.

'Feckless girl's burned one lot already. And Dr Soames'll be ringing soon,' Mrs Godwin said, picking up her rolling pin.

'Well, this lot looks fine. How do you want me to do Dr Soames's eggs?'

When the bell rang from the study, Mrs Sharp carried through the large serving tray, leaving Peter to cope with an ever-redder Mrs Godwin and a still snivelling Jenny.

'Good morning, Dr Soames,' she said.

He turned from his newspaper and raised his eyebrows.

'Mrs Godwin is busy,' she said, putting the tray down. 'She is making several pies.' Her voice was calm.

'Mrs Godwin's best pies are always saved for my daughter,' he said with a small smile.

'Will the visits to patients be at the usual time today?'

He looked at her for a moment.

'The weather is fine, and the road should be dry enough now. Jane Weddell is needing a visit and you could call in on Old Mr Weddell too, lives with his daughter, the miller's wife. Peter will take you. If you want to, you could go to see Mary Elliott.' He paused. 'Mrs Godwin would give you a pie to take to Mary but better not ask today.' He turned back to his reading.

'How late should we get back?'

He looked up and caught the smile she was trying to suppress.

'Oh, Charlotte will most certainly wish to meet you. Perhaps you would be kind enough to join us for a bite of light supper this evening?' he said.

'Of course. It will be a great pleasure to meet Mrs Thorpe at last.'

It was a lovely day. The sun was already warm as they set off in the trap, turning from the cobbles, heading westwards out of the town. The long straight road ahead divided the still mist-shrouded valley from the dark green moorside. The ruts in the road were softened by the heavy rains of previous weeks but the huge pools of water were gone, so they made good time.

138

Peter pointed out the cottages and the farms as they passed, naming those inhabitants who were Dr Soames's patients and occasionally giving some more information, but his comments were, as always, brief and non-judgemental. She was content, listening to his soft voice, watching the view as the mist lifted over the woodland, feeling the warmth on her back increase as the sun rose higher. She had not expected to feel contentment, had forgotten for a while what it meant, but here it was, flowing slowly over her, and she let herself be.

They stopped at the forge first and she stepped down quickly as Peter pulled up. Blacksmith Weddell came out in response to Peter's shouted greeting and stopped, looking at Mrs Sharp, silent and frowning. She felt her smile tighten: she had expected a kinder welcome.

'Good morning to you, Mr Weddell,' she said, chin high.

'This is Mrs Sharp,' said Peter, looking from one to the other.

The blacksmith kept looking and then grinned hugely at her. 'Good day to you, Mrs Sharp. I didn't recognize you. You look very well.'

She looked down at her crisp skirts and shining boots. 'Indeed, thank you. I am very well indeed. Dr Soames asked me to call on Mrs Weddell.'

'Aye, and Jane will be right pleased to see you. Go on over to the house.'

Jane Weddell was in her kitchen lifting biscuits from a tray and setting them to cool. She looked up as Mrs Sharp walked in and paused, eyebrows raised. '*You* are Mrs Sharp! Oh, it

139

suits you to be so smart and well looking! Come in, sit down, be welcome.'

Sitting on the settle, drinking milk and eating a warm biscuit, Mrs Sharp smiled at Jane's delight in seeing her in the new grey frock and starched cap, at Jane's genuine pleasure in knowing her settled in Dr Soames's household. But as she watched Jane, she could see only too well the bright flushed cheeks, the extreme thinness of the pale wrists: the disease was progressing.

After a while, she asked gently, 'How is the coughing?'

'It was better for a few weeks. I had some hope of . . . Perhaps . . . But it started again last week. I try to keep it from him,' Jane said.

'Is there blood?'

'Specks, sometimes a little more. Sometimes quite a lot.' The younger woman looked directly at her, voice level, face composed. 'I know what it means.'

Mrs Sharp took her hand. 'Dr Soames has sent some medicine to reduce the cough at night. It will help you sleep.'

'If it is God's will to take me then I go to Him willingly. I am ready at His command. But is it wrong for me to want to have a little more time here with my husband? I fear to leave him.'

Jane wanted to come with her to see Old Mr Weddell, her father-in-law, and Rose, his daughter. They walked slowly down through the small village to the mill. Mrs Sharp carried her own bag and Jane's basket filled with biscuits and Jane carried a small bunch of roses, freshly picked from her garden. Even so, she was soon short of breath and they stopped for her to sit for a while on the wall by the flood-filled stream,

140

running deep and fast to the wheel. When they set off again Mrs Sharp offered Jane her arm, which she took with a quiet thank-you.

The noise of the wheel clanking on each ratchet and the rush of the spilling water were loud enough to hear inside the cottage, though it was separate from the mill. It competed with the combined efforts of three young children, a baby, two dogs and a loud welcome from Rose, the miller's wife. A great fuss was made of Jane by Rose and the oldest child, and a seat was found for her by displacing a dog. Jane then sat serene amidst the chaos, rapidly acquiring a small child on her knee, and starting to tell a story.

Mrs Sharp introduced herself to Old Mr Weddell who was sitting very upright in a chair padded with cushions. He was almost completely blind now, his eyes milky white, but the hands holding the chair arms were still big, blackened and scarred like his son's. He had remained strong even after his vision failed and his son became the eighth Blacksmith Weddell. A continuous line since the forge was first built, Jane had told her, sharing the family pride.

He showed Mrs Sharp his swollen knees and admitted to some pain in his back. When she helped him up he moved with difficulty and could not straighten, the tall body bent over almost double. She and Rose helped him sit back down and Rose passed him his pipe.

'We give him the medicine at night and if the pain's bad he has a tot of rum. That's right, Father?' Rose said, patting the old man's hand.

He took her hand in his huge one. 'My Rose looks after me

141

well and Miller's a good man. I like to sit here and listen to the childer,' he said.

'You're a lucky man,' Mrs Sharp said.

They were interrupted by the miller coming loudly through the door, bringing the musty smell of drying grain and flour. The dogs went wild and the children shrieked. He cuffed the dogs, lifted up two children, bellowed a general greeting and then sat down beside Jane.

Rose took Mrs Sharp's arm. 'Come outside a bit and I'll show you my pigs.'

Mrs Sharp escaped with gratitude.

The three pigs were Rose's own, bought each year and fattened on scraps from the village which she boiled up on a stove her brother had made for her in the outhouse.

'I pays people back for the scraps in fresh meat when we kill a one and sell on rest, though family eat most of it now.' She leaned over the wall and scratched the largest pig around its ears. 'This one's near ready,' she said with no sentimentality.

Mrs Sharp nodded and waited.

A long moment passed, just the sound of snuffling and rooting and the clack-clacking of the wheel.

'Jane's fading faster now,' Rose said. 'Each day I sees it.'

'Yes. Her breathing is worse than when I last saw her.'

'Thomas said as she'll not last next winter through.'

Mrs Sharp looked at the young woman, so strong and healthy. 'I don't think so.'

'Naught to be done, then?'

'No. But we can look after her. Try to make it easier.'

'I had no sister afore her. Just me and Thomas. We all love her very dear. Thomas's heart will be broke.'

'Dr Soames has sent more medicine for her and I'll come up every month, sooner if she needs,' Mrs Sharp said.

Peter arrived with the trap then. Mrs Sharp thought he was keeping them to time but then realized, as he lifted Jane up on to the seat, that he had thought about Jane and the uphill walk to the forge. There was a sack half-full of coal behind them.

'Blacksmith sent it for Mary Elliott,' Peter said with a smile at Jane beside him.

'How very kind of him,' Mrs Sharp said.

'If you can wait a minute at the cottage I'll get some biscuits for Mary too,' Jane said.

It was a basket filled with potatoes and carrots and a package of meat, as well as biscuits, which Jane gave her for Mary.

'Not Rose's pork?' said Mrs Sharp, laughing.

'No. Beef in payment of Farmer Turnbull's new hung gates.' Jane paused. 'I think it's from being brought up in town but I can't see how Rose can be so fond with those pigs and still be counting the sausages to come.' She shook her head. 'Thomas says I'm too soft-hearted.'

She stood laughing and waving as they left.

Further up the valley they passed the Turnbulls' farm and then turned up the narrow path. She told Peter the story of her first ride down the hill on Farmer Turnbull's big horse, laughing, and realized she was talking too much, overfilling the time. She could feel her heart thudding. Peter stopped the trap at the final gate and helped her down. He picked up the basket and her bag and walked with her up the steep mud path to the door.

He knocked firmly and then opened it for her, calling out, 'Mrs Sharp to see Mary Elliott.'

She walked in and was overwhelmed – but not with fear, not with what she had expected. The room smelled of despair: of unwashed bodies and urine, of stale food layered with smoke and dampness, of never being clean and warm and dry. A small mewling cry came from the cradle and she went and picked up baby James, a sodden filthy bundle. Peter walked out into the yard, calling for John and Mary.

Mary came in first, carrying a milk pail, putting it down and looking at Mrs Sharp. 'He needs his milk. Give'm here. Mine.' Her voice cracked with fear. Not anger, only fear.

'Hello, Mary,' Mrs Sharp said.

Mary stared at her and then slowly nodded. 'Joanna? Is it ee?'

'They call me Mrs Sharp now,' she said in her nurse's voice. 'Where's John?'

'Up in top field.' Mary was still staring at her, mouth slightly open.

'I'm going to change baby James and then I'll make some stew while you feed him.'

'Ee look well,' Mary said, looking at Mrs Sharp's dress.

'Thank you. Now let us sort out James. Why don't you sit down?'

Mrs Sharp turned as Peter came back in. 'Peter, could you heat up some water?'

Mary remained motionless. Mrs Sharp transferred the

baby to one arm and helped the girl to sit down, feeling her thin shoulders, smelling the acrid tang of stale vomit. James was crying more loudly now.

'Do you want to feed him first?' Mrs Sharp said.

Mary shook her head. 'Can't. No milk since Sabbath day. Nothing. I've been trying with yow's milk but . . .' She dropped her head and sobbed.

Mrs Sharp was counting the weeks, but she already knew. 'Mary,' she said, her voice almost a whisper, 'are you being sick?'

The girl nodded.

The monster, the evil foul monster, Mrs Sharp thought, the words slamming into her head.

'Is the milk in the pail fresh?' she said.

'Yes, I just took it but there's not much. Yow's near dry.'

'How are you giving it to baby James?'

'From cup,' Mary said. 'But it just runs away over his mouth.'

'Well, let's try another way.'

Peter made up the fire and heated a pan of water and then started to cook the meat and potatoes from Jane's basket. Mrs Sharp fed baby James from a piece of cloth torn from her underskirt and washed in hot water, then soaked in the milk which was still warm. He fed ravenously, screaming each time she took the cloth away to soak it. Once he was replete, she washed him, and wrapped him in more of the cloth.

John Elliott arrived back then, throwing open the door and slamming it closed behind him. She looked up briefly, before turning back to the baby, settling him down into the cot. The noises in the cottage seemed louder: Mary making little mewling noises as she slept on the bed, Peter slowly scrubbing the table, the fire hissing. John remained silent but she knew he was watching her.

She stood up slowly and looked first at Peter, seeing his anger, and shook her head slightly. Then she smoothed her skirt with steady hands and turned to face John. She walked over to him and stopped, standing tall.

'Baby James was near dead of starvation when we arrived.' She wanted to scream but kept her voice low. 'You need to bring down two ewes in milk and make sure the baby is fed. Mary is pregnant again, her milk's gone. I'll send more food for her and a pap cup and clothes for the baby.'

He looked her up and down and then leered slowly, showing his blackened teeth. 'You'm looking mighty fine. Filled out nice.' He paused. 'Be a better poke now.'

She heard Peter move behind her, but she needed to do this, to face him alone. Her back rigid and her voice steady, she said, 'You're beneath my contempt. But if baby James dies, I will see you hang.'

She was shaking with anger as Peter helped her up on to the trap. After a while she managed to speak. 'Thank you. For the cooking and cleaning. Well, and . . .' She shrugged.

Peter nodded and said nothing for a while.

The sun was behind them now and the shadow of the trap was lengthening in front. Her mind was almost empty again, lulled by the swaying of the trap and the warm breeze. Then she sat bolt upright, realizing what the shadows meant.

'Will we be home in time to see Mrs Thorpe? I'll need to change. I reek of urine and milk.'

'Yes. We'll go in from the yard. She never comes to the back of the house.' He paused then and looked at her, frowning a little. 'Good you've had time to calm down. She's a mighty irritating woman is Mrs Thorpe.'

Mrs Sharp realized that a barrier was being breached and waited.

'Dr Soames took me in too. I'd been in the gutter. Drink, after I left the Navy,' Peter said.

And the barrier had fallen.

'How long ago?'

'Near twenty years. Don't even remember how I got to Alnwick. But I do remember the Navy. Not a place for a man like me but better than the streets. I learned my letters, saw some of the world. Ended up surgeon's mate so knew a bit and Dr Soames, he recognized something. Mind, I reckon I was even filthier than you when he took me back to the house.' He stopped, seeming almost as surprised as she was by so much speech.

'Thank you,' she said. 'For helping me.'

'Aye. Like you help others. Best we can do.'

They sat in easy silence until they reached the edge of the town. He turned suddenly to her. 'Mrs Thorpe's a hard one, none of her father in her. And jealous. You'll need be careful.'

'Jealous of what?'

'Of a woman in her father's house. She'll be looking to keep her inheritance safe.'

Mrs Sharp began to laugh. 'How ridiculous. I knew she

wasn't a kind person – Jenny's terrified of her. But jealous? Of me?'

They arrived at the house and Peter drove through the archway to the yard. As he handed her down he said, 'Just remember, be careful.'

She went in quietly through the scullery door.

Mrs Sharp arrived in the dining room in her Sunday dress, clean and smelling of lavender. The room was already fragrant with vases of flowers on the sideboard and the table shone, polished mahogany and silver cutlery. Dr Soames stood as she entered but Mrs Thorpe did not move other than to nod graciously as he introduced them to each other. She then continued her conversation with her father, earnestly asking him to tell her all about dear Mr Sealy, the lawyer.

Mrs Thorpe was a beauty and fortunate enough to have the looks of the moment. Her face was small, pale and oval, framed by shining blonde hair smoothly parted and fastened in a large chignon. The first woman to be seen in Alnwick last spring with hair done in the style of the young Queen, as Mrs Godwin had told Mrs Sharp at length earlier in the week. Mrs Sharp tried to listen to the high-pitched girlish voice, but found her mind drifting to how much Mrs Thorpe's blue silk dress must have cost and how many dresses she must have.

At the first opportunity, Dr Soames turned to Mrs Sharp. 'Charlotte and Jane Weddell were friends when young girls. She knows Jane is ill. How was she today?'

'I am very sorry to say that your friend is troubled with being more short of breath and a recurrence of coughing and fever,' Mrs Sharp said to Mrs Thorpe.

'Poor Jane. We lost touch, I'm afraid, once I had my governess. And now we move in such different circles.'

Mrs Sharp could feel Dr Soames's disquiet. His daughter must realize that Jane's death sentence had just been given.

'It will be a consolation for you that your friend is the centre of her husband and his family's attention, and her own family in Alnwick make every effort to visit. She is loved deeply for her charity and piety,' she said. She felt a passing moment of guilt in using Jane's goodness as a weapon.

Mrs Thorpe paused a moment, looking intently at Mrs Sharp, her head tilted prettily to one side. 'Are you also a pious woman, Mrs Sharp?'

'I make no claim to being deeply religious, but I hope I practise charity in my work and to my friends,' Mrs Sharp said, and looked down demurely at her hands. And was suddenly afraid she had gone too far, had presumed too much on Dr Soames's good nature.

Mrs Godwin protected her from Mrs Thorpe's riposte by bringing in a large pie, beautifully glazed and decorated with a pattern of leaves. Mrs Sharp ate a small amount in polite silence as Mrs Thorpe pointedly reminisced with her father about past family meals. For once she did not enjoy her food.

She was saved again by Peter entering and coming over to Dr Soames to say quietly that Jack Coultar had sent a message; his Elsie was having pains and his mother had said to tell the doctor.

'We have not even finished supper. Can she not go?' Mrs Thorpe said to her father, gesturing vaguely in Mrs Sharp's direction.

149

'I am happy to go. If Peter can take me I can send for you when needed?' Mrs Sharp said to Dr Soames. She was already standing, needing him to say the right thing.

'Thank you, Mrs Sharp. That seems an excellent way to proceed. I'll ride over as soon as it is light in the morning, unless you send for me first. Peter, take my instrument bag with you and whatever else Mrs Sharp requires.'

'Thank you, Dr Soames.' She turned to Mrs Thorpe and nodded politely. 'It has been a pleasure to meet you.'

She walked out of the room, realizing she had unwisely, but perhaps unavoidably, reinforced Mrs Thorpe's resentment, but feeling quite pleased.

After first seeing Mrs Coultar last month, she had read the chapter about twins in Dr Soames's book and discussed it with him, and had rehearsed carefully in her head what to do during the woman's labour. She sat next to Peter, barely noticing the swaying and jolting as the trap wheels caught in the ruts, and thought it through again.

The moon was full and bright. And then she was in the other place, walking in bright light, talking, planning. His hand was holding hers but as she turned to him he was gone again.

'Mrs Sharp.' She heard Peter's voice and felt his hand on her arm, the trap stopping.

'Sorry. I must have been dreaming.' She took her bag and climbed down quickly.

The farmhouse was much bigger than those up the valley but it contained the whole Coultar family: Farmer Coultar and his wife, their two grown sons and their wives, their oldest daughter and her husband, and three other children down to a seven-year-old. Mrs Sharp had been introduced to some of them on her first visit but had found it difficult to tell apart the dark and wiry men who were all heavily bearded. The farmer's wife and their daughters were also dark-haired but Elsie, their son Jack's wife, had shining copper curls. The curls were sweat-darkened now as she walked round the kitchen leaning on her mother-in-law.

'When did it start?' Mrs Sharp said as she put down her bag.

'Just afore sunset. We was setting up for the morning when Elsie put down the pan and gave a groan. Knew that sound straight away. Done plenty of it.' The older Mrs Coultar laughed as she helped her daughter-in-law to sit down.

Mrs Sharp knelt in front of the chair and looked directly at Elsie, holding her gaze. 'Elsie, I need to feel your belly, see where the babies are. Which room are we using?'

'Mother and Father Coultar's room. Over there. Mother Coultar said easier than going upstairs,' said Elsie.

'Aye, and it's a good bed for birthing. I've had my last six on it,' said Mrs Coultar.

'So, after the next pain we'll go through to the bedroom.' She turned to Mrs Coultar. 'Peter needs to boil some water.'

'Aye, the copper's full and there's a big pan aside it. Clean linen is on the chair by fire, just like you asked.'

Mrs Sharp smiled. 'Where is everyone?'

'Jack and Mr Coultar are just finishing off outside. Others are with my sister. Thought Elsie would want a bit of quiet.'

*

Elsie's waters broke just before dawn as she and Mrs Sharp were walking round and round the kitchen. Mrs Coultar was snoring quietly in the bedroom chair and Peter was sleeping on the kitchen settle. Jack and his father had gone upstairs, leaving the women to their work.

'Well, best not in Mother Coultar's bed,' Elsie said, watching the liquid run across the stone floor, and then she groaned.

'That's good, the pains will get stronger now. It means one of the babies is coming. Lean on me until it passes, and we'll get you back to the bedroom,' Mrs Sharp said.

When Dr Soames arrived an hour later Elsie was sitting on the edge of the bed supported by Mrs Coultar and groaning loudly. Mrs Sharp was kneeling on the floor, sleeves rolled up and swathed in a white apron. 'She's just started pushing but there's a lot of pressure on the fourchette. I'm going to get her to squat.'

'Head down?' he said.

'Yes.'

'Carry on. I'll just take off my jacket.'

'And wash your hands. Over there, basin and soap.'

The first baby, a boy, arrived half an hour later, pink and squalling, and Dr Soames held him as Mrs Sharp tied and cut the cord. He quickly wrapped the baby and put him into his mother's arms and Elsie smiled as the sweat and tears ran down her face.

Dr Soames went to get Jack, already working out in the yard, as Mrs Sharp and Mrs Coultar cleared away the soiled linen and covered Elsie with a clean sheet. Mrs Sharp gently washed Elsie's face and smoothed back the wet curls. When

Jack came in, she left them alone for a moment and stood outside the bedroom door. Mrs Coultar came over with a cup of gruel for her. They stood together, waiting.

'Her mam died with the second baby still in her,' Mrs Coultar said.

'I know. Elsie's a sensible, healthy woman. She has a good chance. I'm going back in now to check for the second baby. Where's Dr Soames?'

'He's gone outside again. Peter's riding back to town, leaving trap for you and Doctor.'

Mrs Sharp nodded. She opened the door and then stopped, realizing she had done this many times before, had set the confident smile in place, had stormed the castle. She went in.

Jack was leaning over Elsie, one hand on hers as she held the baby. He turned and smiled and then the smile faltered. He knew the risk.

'Any pains, Elsie?'

Elsie shook her head.

'Well, we need to get on with this. Mrs Coultar, can you help Elsie get that lovely baby boy on the breast. It should get things going again. Jack, are you staying?'

He shook his head, kissed his wife and child and left.

Dr Soames came in as she was pulling the sheet back over Elsie's swollen belly.

'Longitudinal definitely and head down, I think. No bleeding. No lengthening of the cord,' she said.

He looked at her for a long moment, seeming surprised. She realized that the certainty in her head had sounded in her voice. He turned to Elsie.

'Well, Elsie, I'm going to go sit with Jack and leave you and Mrs Sharp to do all the work.' He nodded to Mrs Sharp and put his pocket watch next to her. She smiled her thanks.

She watched as Mrs Coultar unconcernedly handled Elsie's breast, trying to get the baby to suck, and saw Elsie's calm acceptance of what needed to be done. But the young woman's eyes were almost closing. Mrs Sharp looked at the watch and a minute dragged by and then she looked again, and five minutes had gone and she realized she too must have slept. She took a deep breath and stood up. Time was the enemy now.

She roused Elsie whilst Mrs Coultar put the baby boy in the basket by the bed and between them they helped Elsie to stand. She was very tired now, almost sleeping as they walked her. Dr Soames came in and Mrs Sharp just shook her head. He went over and got the instrument bag and went out again. Another ten minutes and then the waters broke, the girl becoming fully awake as the warm liquid ran over her foot.

'Oh, very good,' Mrs Sharp said. 'Elsie, I need you back on the bed so I can check what's happening.'

Elsie managed to push and to breathe and to deliver her baby girl who was small and blue but gave a little mewling cry as Dr Soames took hold of her and Mrs Sharp tied the cord. Mrs Sharp carefully pulled away the dirty linen and pushed a clean sheet under Elsie's buttocks, always watching the two cords, watching for bleeding. Nothing yet.

She covered Elsie with another clean sheet and watched, her professional smile firmly in place, as Mrs Coultar helped the now pink baby start to suckle. Elsie was smiling but she was very nearly asleep. Jack came in then and held his wife and daughter.

Mrs Sharp and Dr Soames waited by the bed. Jack looked up.

'We just need to wait now for the afterbirth,' Mrs Sharp said, voice low.

Fifteen minutes later it was all done. Mrs Sharp carried out the bowl with the afterbirth and the dirty linen feeling quietly triumphant: mother alive and apparently undamaged and two living babies.

A little later she sat at the big scrubbed table eating a huge bowl of porridge with stewed plums, tired and contented.

Jack came over and sat down opposite her. 'Dr Soames says as you'll call back each day to check Elsie and the babbies.'

'Yes, of course.'

'We're glad on that. Priest's coming to see babbies this afternoon. Seen as they're twins. Get them baptized. In case.' His voice was matter-of-fact, but his face was drawn.

She nodded.

'Boy's to be called John, as we do in the family. But Elsie, and me, we would like to call our girl for you.'

'Thank you. That is very kind. I would be honoured.'

There was a pause.

'I don't think as we can call her Mrs Sharp,' Jack said.

She looked down, trying to think. Not Joanna. Not a name tarnished and shamed. Then she looked up.

'I've always preferred my middle name, Elizabeth. If that is a name which you like. It was Dr Soames's daughter's name too.'

'Aye, and she was a good girl. Remember her from school. Allus kind. Elizabeth Grace, then.'

He paused and looked towards the bedroom, where his young wife was sleeping. 'Grace, after Elsie's mam.'

16

London, October 1841

They were too exotic, too bright and shining for the small room: Lady Gasgoine in peacock blue and her sister in vibrant green. Dr Borthwick watched as they settled, their full silk skirts spilling over the narrow chairs, lace falling over their wrists beneath wide brocade sleeves. They brought with them the scent of lilies.

Mrs Hayward served the coffee with unusual ceremony, Betty holding open the door with a look near to terror. Mrs Hayward, rustling in her best black, went to the side table and poured out the coffee and then carried the first cup to Lady Gasgoine, held steady on a small silver tray which Dr Borthwick thought he had not seen before; preparations for their ladyships' visit had been under way in the kitchen since the note arrived three days ago. Betty followed with the sugar on another small tray, clasped firmly in both her hands, frowning with concentration. Lady Gasgoine served herself with sugar and gave Betty a polite nod and a hint of her smile. However, when Lady Burnside was served, she defied convention by first thanking Mrs Hayward and then by speaking directly to Betty.

'Thank you, child. Have you worked here for a long time?'
Betty turned and looked at Dr Borthwick, eyes wide.

He could see the row of hairpins pulling back her curls beneath the freshly starched cap; it looked painful. 'Do you want me to answer for you?'

She nodded, biting her lip, eyes now fixed on the floor.

'Betty has been here with us for almost a year now. Mrs Bates found her for us.' He paused and then added with a polite nod to the cook, 'Mrs Hayward is training Betty as a parlourmaid and she will no doubt be a credit to her. That will be all for now, thank you, Mrs Hayward.' That, he thought, should prevent any unfounded recriminations in the kitchen.

Lady Burnside smiled, turning her head to encompass Mrs Hayward in her largesse as the servants left the room.

Lady Gasgoine spoke then in her low, rather slow, voice. 'I assume Mrs Bates found the child in some distress?' The voice was that of the society beauty, but the look was serious, the look of the woman who had surprised him in her plain cotton dress, nursing her sister.

'Mrs Bates was called to her mother who died in child-birth. The mother's circumstances were very poor indeed and there were no other relatives. Mrs Bates feared for the child, so she brought her here,' he said.

He looked across at the two women, each dressed in a skilled workman's wages for a year. Lady Burnside was frowning slightly at him.

'Was her mother a freed slave, a servant?' she said.

'I don't know. The owner of the . . .' He paused, unsure how much to say.

'Bawdy house, I assume,' Lady Gasgoine said, as if commenting on the weather.

'Yes. The owner of the house told Mrs Bates that she had taken in the woman and her young child a few years ago. Out of kindness, of course.' He could not keep the contempt from his voice.

The sisters exchanged a look, and Lady Gasgoine shook her head at her sister. She turned to him and spoke again, still with her usual detachment.

'In a way the issues are linked, I think. We came to ask you to engage yourself with our cause. We are determined to establish a proper hospital for women. Would you speak at our next meeting, indeed join our committee?'

'Another lying-in hospital?' he said.

'No. Or perhaps I should say not just that. Certainly a hospital for the care of women's particular conditions but also for other ailments,' Lady Gasgoine said.

'Many women's conditions arise from poor care in childbirth.'

'Yes, of course. But is it not safer for women in childbirth to be cared for at home?'

'Yes. For a woman with a clean home able to pay a good midwife. Not for most women in London.' He paused and looked at his guests in turn. How much did they understand? Or want to hear? 'May I speak frankly?'

'We expect nothing else,' Lady Burnside said with a sudden smile.

He acknowledged it with a brief nod. 'I see women at the London Mission in the Devil's Acre. They live two and three families to a room smaller than this with no glass at the windows, no source of water and filth flowing in the lanes. All the fevers rage there. The lying-in hospitals usually refuse them.'

Lady Burnside looked away but Lady Gasgoine met his gaze and she was still calm and measured. 'I have heard of these things and they must be changed but I cannot do that. What I can do is raise money for a decent hospital for women. And training for nurses. Surely you support that?'

'Of course. And training for midwives too?' he said.

'Indeed. So, you will assist us then.' It was more of a statement than a question.

'It will be my pleasure.'

Lady Gasgoine rewarded him with her smile, which even now he found extraordinary.

'Do you know the works of Mrs Wollstonecraft?' she then said, surprising him again.

'I do indeed—'

'You think she should still be read, in spite of her unusual life?' Lady Burnside interrupted quickly.

'Perhaps the more because of it,' he said.

He saw the swift glance between the two women.

'Well then, Dr Borthwick, we will tell you our secret mission. We aim that one or other of us will live long enough to see a woman qualified as a doctor, though we may need to be very old. We will do all we can to support this,' Lady Gasgoine said.

'Bravo.'

As they were leaving, Lady Burnside gave him her hand. 'If ever the child needs another position, I will take her into my own household.'

'Thank you,' he said as he bowed over the pale, slender fingers and the huge emerald which exactly matched her dress.

It had been nearly a year ago, the early morning of a dark and cold November day, rain clattering down the window. Dr Borthwick was already up and in his study, waiting for breakfast, when Mrs Hayward came to tell him that Mrs Bates had arrived with 'a personage'. Her disdain was evident. It was clear from her manner that she was not about to bring the 'personage' into the room.

He stood up and followed her into the hall, his curiosity piqued. Surely Mrs Bates had not brought a patient here?

The child was standing slightly apart from Mrs Bates, a dripping blanket round her shoulders, just her thin legs and bare feet visible. Her eyes were wide and staring but she looked down as soon as she saw him.

'I ought not to have brought her here, but I couldn't leave her and she'd have got no welcome at my lodgings,' Mrs Bates said, the words rushed. She sounded, for her, uncertain.

'You look cold,' he said to the child. 'Would you like some milk and porridge?'

She looked up at him very quickly and nodded just once.

He called for Mrs Hayward who would certainly be listening through the kitchen door. 'My apologies, Mrs Hayward, but could you sit the child by the fire in the kitchen and give her milk and my porridge and the eggs if she wants them. Mrs Bates and I will take some tea in the study.'

He heard Mrs Hayward's intake of breath and turned and

smiled directly at her. 'Thank you,' he said and turned away again as he opened the study door.

Sitting there with Mrs Bates he had been unsurprised by the story she told in her flat voice, her distaste made clear when she described where the child's mother had lived. A bawdy house. The bawd had sent for Mrs Bates out of concern for her source of income, but the baby was stillborn and the mother bled to death shortly afterwards. The bawd told her that the child, sitting silent in the passageway, was twelve but Mrs Bates thought she was younger. It was very clear that she would replace her mother.

If the story hadn't surprised him, Mrs Bates's account of her next actions did.

'I told her as I'd do the laying-out. Save her paying someone else. But only if she went out and brought me some gin to drink. When she'd gone I wrapped a blanket, a filthy lousy thing, round the child and we ran. A dustman carried us on his cart.' She stopped and looked up at him. 'I couldn't leave her to that.'

'No, indeed not.'

'I'll enquire at the workhouse but they might not take her with the colour. Well, a family would have to say she was theirs, and all.'

'We can think about that later. Mrs Hayward looked somewhat unhappy. It would help if you would stay and bathe the girl?'

'Yes, I'll do that gladly.'

'No doubt Mrs Hayward can be persuaded to find her some clothes. Perhaps you could make it clear that you have told me I should pay her extra to care for the child. Quite a lot extra.'

Mrs Bates nodded, almost smiling.

He laughed. 'I doubt I'll get any breakfast, though.'

So Betty had stayed and was being trained as a maid. He knew that her life was not easy, that Mrs Hayward was not always a kind woman. But Betty had good food and a safe place to sleep, her own tiny room in the attic, and he was teaching her to read. That was something.

Betty handed him the note from Eleanor as soon as he arrived home from his afternoon visits. The writing was neat, but the message was hasty:

Can you come to the Mission today? Many children have a severe illness of the throat. Eleanor Johnson.

He decided to ride: Eleanor would have travelled to Duck Lane in Mr Swan's coach, so he could send her home in that.

As he turned down Duck Lane it was already becoming dark and he could taste the fog as it rolled up from the river. There were plenty of boys waiting, ready to hold the reins as he dismounted. Picking out the one who looked to be the leader, he gave him a penny. 'There'll be a thrupenny piece for you if the horse is here when I get back. And the police if she's not,' he said firmly.

The alley was strangely quiet as he followed the flickering lamp. The house walls were barely visible, though he could reach out and touch them on both sides. There were none of the usual shouts and catcalls, only muted coughs and groans

163

through the gaping holes of the windows. There was no glass in the windows in the courts of Devil's Acre.

He did not usually worry about his own safety: he carried little money and had always felt his profession offered some protection, but it was a relief to see the green door. Giving the lamp boy an extra ha'penny, he went in.

There was a new and different smell in the whitewashed room, the sweet-foul tang of putrefaction. The benches were crammed with women and even men holding young children, but no sounds except laboured breathing, occasional harsh coughing and sometimes a sob.

Behind the curtain he found Eleanor wiping the face of a small boy. His neck was massively swollen, and the stench was so strong he could taste it. Each breath was a terrible effort, but the boy was barely conscious. On the next table was the flaccid body of a baby, unmoving, skin grey.

'Do they all have the same?'

Eleanor nodded.

'I need to look at the baby's throat. Can you hold the lamp?' he said.

She stood calm beside him as he opened the small and for ever silent mouth. Easy to examine in death, he could see the swollen, ulcerated throat, the thick leather-like membrane lying completely across both tonsils, no gap between, no space for the air to pass.

'Mr Wilson thought it was scarlet fever at first, but they have no rash,' Eleanor said in a whisper.

'Where is he?'

'He has gone to seek a carrier to take away the dead—' Her voice cracked slightly but she carried on. 'At least five have died here since yesterday. There are many sick in this court and also, we think, in the next.'

'All children?'

'I think so. That's all who have been brought here today and yesterday.'

'You were here yesterday too?'

'Yes. But Mr Wilson said there were cases the day before as well. What is it?'

'Diphtheritis, it is called now. I've seen it before, in the north when I worked there. It is not scarlet fever or the mumps. You've not been aware of it before? No one had it when you were a child?'

'No. I don't remember it being spoken of. Scarlet fever and the measles and croup, but not this.'

He looked at her and tried to speak slowly but he was afraid. 'Then you must leave. Go back to the Swans' house. You must go straight upstairs there and take a hot bath. All your outer clothes must be boiled or burned. Keep to your room and above all keep away from the baby.'

She looked at him in horror. 'But surely this is a disease of the foul humours here?'

'It will be worst here, where people live without food and fresh air, but I have seen the sickness in a man of business's family, the richest almost in the town.'

'But then surely you should leave too?'

'No, I did not become ill last time. Some do not. I'll do what I can here, but it will be little enough. Where is the carriage?'

'At the corner on Duck Lane.'

'Go now. The boy will light the way.'

She nodded and turned away to wash her hands, as he had taught her, before she put on her coat and bonnet. Her voice was calm as she pulled on her gloves. 'Will you call on me at Mr Swan's house, later tonight?'

'No, it will be too late an hour. But I'll call on you tomorrow.'

Tired beyond sleep, he watched Arnold Wilson pour out the tea. The green door was locked and the children had been taken home to the cold rooms in the broken houses, sleeping five or more to a bed, if there was one. Some, a few, of them would live but not, he knew, because of the tinctures he had given them. They would survive and the others would not. The disease would run its course through the courts of Duck Lane and Old Pye Street and then would disappear for a few years. That is what happened.

Thoughts were jumping in his head: children red and gasping, choking; Eleanor leaning over the dead baby holding the lamp still; a woman sobbing as Arnold took her dead child from her arms. Grief was the same for a lost child; the same here, where life seemed cheap, as in the rich squares, only here the pain was hidden under the daily effort of living. But his anger couldn't help them.

Arnold passed him the cup and he drank quickly, even though it was too hot.

'The carter said there was bull throat here about fifteen years ago,' Arnold said.

'Bull throat. Boulogne throat. It's what it was called then, blaming the French. Diphtheritis now. Still kills,' Dr Borthwick said.

'It is hard, but it is God's will.'

Dr Borthwick bit back his reply and just shook his head.

'You are a good man, and knowing the Lord is a comfort to us all,' Arnold said.

'I only see the pain and the horror of poverty here.'

'And it is the work of the Mission to help. To do God's work. To bring Jesus to these sad people.'

'I'm sorry, Mr Wilson, but I can't help but think that a loving God might have done a better job to start with.'

He expected Arnold to shy away from this blasphemy but instead he smiled. 'You do His work anyway. But it is a lonely path you must walk without His hand.'

Dr Borthwick shook his head. 'I'll not argue with you, Mr Wilson. But you are right about the lonely path. Some days more than others.'

Arnold poured him some more tea and they drank it in an easy silence. After a while Dr Borthwick stood up, stretched a little and put on his coat.

'I hope someone has been watching over my horse,' he said.

'I'll walk you to the lane,' Arnold said.

'Thank you.'

Late that night he sat in his study, the dull red of the dying fire reflected in the one small glass of port he allowed himself. He had read and re-read all that was in his textbooks on malignant croup, and the other diseases that might be diphtheritis, but it was incomplete, useless. There were no cures. Just althaea and liquorice root, thyme, sage and honey to ease the throat and perhaps, in those that must die, laudanum to ease the passing.

He put down the glass and closed his eyes, unwilling to break one of the rules by which he had survived in London, the rule about living day by day, looking forward and never back. Opening his eyes again, he stared at the darkening coals and made himself remember. It was undoubtedly the same disease, and it had taken a young child and sometimes more than one from almost every household in some parts of the small town. They had been able to do so very little.

After a while he wiped the tears from his eyes and went upstairs, silent as a ghost.

When he arrived at the Swans' house early the next morning, he was taken straight into the morning room where Mrs Swan was already dressed and waiting for him with, for her, an unusual degree of agitation.

'Dr Borthwick, I know you are here to see Eleanor, but I must ask you if there is any risk to baby James. Eleanor was most clear that she must keep apart from us and particularly from him. But she had dined with us the night before last, after she got back from the Mission. Though she always follows your instructions to change her clothes.' She stopped to take a breath.

'I think the risk to James is very small indeed because Eleanor herself was well,' he said, voice firm and confident.

'Was. But then you fear for Eleanor?'

'I hope not. But it is best for her to keep apart from the family for a few days.'

'She has left her room only to take a turn in the garden but insisted on being alone.'

'I will come to check her each day. Try not to be too concerned.' Meaningless words, he knew, but expected words held a certain power.

He waited for Eleanor in Mr Swan's study. Called his room but used, Dr Borthwick knew, by both of the Swans. Mrs Swan had a table under the window where she drew pen-and-ink sketches, illustrations for a reading primer for children. He had thought at first that it was Mr Swan's business connections which had secured her a publisher but later learned that she had worked from her father's house as an illustrator before she married. He felt that the Swans lived a secret life, a life of shared intelligence, camouflaged by the rules of polite society. He was admiring a sketch of a dog, of how Mrs Swan had conveyed that it was running fast, when the door opened.

Eleanor let herself in and walked over to the fire. She was wearing a full-skirted dress of deep amber and a brightly patterned shawl. Perhaps it was the colour of her dress, or the firelight, but he could see strands of amber in her brown hair.

'Good morning, Dr Borthwick,' she said as she sat down with her usual neatness and composure.

He bowed and crossed the room to sit opposite her.

'You are well, Mrs Johnson?'

'Thank you, yes.' She smiled. 'Abigail sent up several bowls full of broth and then hot milk and fruit posset, so I slept soundly.'

It was the first time she had referred to her friend as other than Mrs Swan when speaking to him. Another sign of intimacy.

'Have you had breakfast?' he said.

'Yes, and I ate well. I ate in my room, of course, and then I took a turn round the garden.'

'May I examine your neck?'

She nodded and dropped the shawl down from her shoulders. He knelt on one knee beside her chair and gently examined her neck. Her pulse quickened beneath his fingers.

'Could you turn to the window and open your mouth?'

She complied, opening wide at his request and then giving a small embarrassed smile, her face flushing, as he stood up.

He went back to his chair. He shouldn't be her doctor any more, couldn't be. But how to tell her?

'I am pleased to agree with you, Mrs Johnson. You do indeed seem well and there are no signs of any condition of the throat.'

'But I may still become ill, may be a risk to baby James?'

He thought then that he admired her composure – no, her courage more than anything.

'I think that is unlikely but to be safe it would be better for you to stay mainly in your room and take your meals there for a few more days.'

'Of course. I will do anything needed to keep the house free of contagion.'

She asked him more then, about the disease. Her questions were sensible: what could be done to protect the household; what could be done at the Mission; how long would the contagion run? He answered as best he could and then told her about Boulogne throat and found himself admiring her smile at the blaming of the French for the condition.

He knew that he must distance himself from her, that it

must be done now. He started to make his farewells and was almost ready to stand up and bow and leave before he could make himself say the words. He looked directly at her.

'I have a colleague whom I trust considerably, Dr Atkins. I am going to ask him to call on you each day for the next three days. If you are well, then he will be able to advise you as to when you should rejoin the normal family meals and activities. But he will agree, I am sure, that you should not attend the Mission until the illness there has abated.'

As she listened, she started to frown but did not interrupt. When he had finished she took a breath and spoke, calm but firm, looking directly back at him. 'You are my doctor. I know you would not recommend Dr Atkins unless he were most skilled, but I have no need of a further opinion.'

He held her gaze. 'Mrs Johnson, I am honoured now to think of you as my friend. We have shared sad events at the Mission. Another doctor should visit you.' As he spoke, he knew these were the wrong words: he was inviting intimacy and he must destroy it.

She leaned forward and touched his hand. 'Then you should address me as Eleanor, surely.'

He stood up and riddled the fire, desperate now to say the kindest words he could and also to say what he must.

He turned to look at her. She looked back and he could not ignore the smile she gave him, what it meant.

'Eleanor,' he said, but he did not return her smile. 'Eleanor, I cannot offer you anything more than friendship, no matter how I might wish to. I must take my leave and put you in the care of Dr Atkins.'

He bowed and moved to the door.

'No. You may not leave.'

He turned, surprised by her tone, and, seeing her anger, he admired her even more. He waited, keeping his breathing steady, looking at his hands, feeling where she had touched him.

'I am as independent as a woman can be. You know that I have my own house in Winchester. I also have a good income. You know my reputation and my friends. I loved and respected my late husband and was his good wife. It was his wish when we knew of his illness that after his death I should marry again. Of my own choice.'

It was as if she had removed her clothes and was naked before him, and they both knew it.

'Please, my dear Eleanor, please stop. It cannot be. My past is unhappy, and I do not consider myself free to marry. If only it were not so. But nothing can be done. We must not speak of this again.'

He watched the colour flooding into her cheeks and the tears starting, and he hated himself. She ran past him and the door slammed closed behind her.

After a few minutes he walked out into the hall. Mrs Swan was waiting.

'Will you come into the morning room and take coffee?' she said.

'Thank you but I must go. I have patients I need to visit.'

'Eleanor told me that she is not ill. But she was very distressed. Have you and she had a misunderstanding?'

Another woman he admired whom he must disappoint.

Another friendship lost. 'She will need to tell you herself. I cannot,' he said.

'I know she has become attached to you and we all thought you must reciprocate this. We hoped it so. Indeed, that is how you have behaved, as if with a proper attachment.'

'And I should not have sought her friendship when I can offer nothing more. I realize that and I am sorry. Deeply sorry. Good day to you, Mrs Swan.' He was struggling for composure as he watched her face, the change from concern to disappointment and then the flush of anger.

'Good day then, Dr Borthwick.' She turned away. The footman appeared, opened the front door and then closed it behind him.

He didn't look back.

17

Northumberland, October 1838

Mrs Sharp brushed her hair with some vigour and parted it along the centre, pulling a wing of brown hair down each cheek. She folded up each side in turn, pinning the still-too-short hair behind her ears with a greater than usual degree of irritation. The new linen cap with its starched lace frill covered the pins as Alice had said it would, and the overall effect was similar to the much-admired picture displayed in the draper's shop: hair was now to be worn smoothly curved in front of the ears, in the new style adopted by the Queen. She smiled then, a little at Alice's earnest advice and slightly more at herself for following it.

For a moment the grey-blue eyes and level brows looked back and she saw the face she thought she should have. There were no voices, no one else there in the mirror, just a tall, respectable-looking woman in a grey dress. Mrs Sharp watched as the eyebrows frowned and then she laughed at whoever she was and turned away.

She thought about Alice as she walked downstairs, deter-mined to keep from thinking about the anticipated unpleas-antness of the day. How she had insisted on a new hairstyle now her hair was almost long enough to tie back. Alice was also trying to persuade her to have another dress for the winter not only in a warmer cloth but with a pattern, although, she had reassured her, nothing gaudy or unseemly. It would be a pleasure to sit in the Blacks' warm kitchen, stitching side by side with Alice under the lamp, whilst old Mrs Black knitted or darned. Something to look forward to after today, she thought, as she went into the kitchen.

Mrs Godwin turned from her egg pan just enough to address Mrs Sharp.

'Blacksmith Weddell's been already to leave you a parcel. I told him as you were still abed.'

As always now, Mrs Godwin seemed to imply that Mrs Sharp was indulging in gross self-indulgence, if not depravity, by sleeping.

'I'm sorry to have missed him. Will he call back?' she said.

'I told him as you would be too busy with Dr Soames and his guest.'

Mrs Sharp was spared the need for reply by Peter handing her a bowl of porridge.

'I've put the parcel in the surgery. Blacksmith said if them isn't right, send a message any time this week. He's over at Howick Hall. Doing new gates for the earl,' Peter said.

Mrs Sharp smiled back, acknowledging both the length of the communication and the fact that he hadn't said what was in the parcel, which would, they both knew, irritate Mrs Godwin.

'Thank you. I'll look at it after breakfast,' she said.

*

She was standing outside Dr Soames's study, putting off knocking. She had made a detour via the surgery to collect her parcel and had brought it with her but could find no other excuse to delay. She swallowed, took one long slow breath, then knocked and walked in.

Dr Soames stood up. 'Good morning, Mrs Sharp. Come and sit with us. May I have the pleasure of introducing my old friend and colleague, Dr Mackay.' He turned formally. 'Dr Mackay, this is Mrs Sharp, about whom we have corresponded.'

Dr Mackay stood to greet her, a small thin man with red hair whitening at the temples and a pinched and lined face. Dr Soames was attentive to her, making sure she was comfortable, and by pouring her coffee declaring her status in the household as more than a servant. Once they were settled Dr Mackay spoke first.

'Dr Soames wrote to me, as you know, about your unusual –' he hesitated and resettled himself in the chair – 'your very unusual problem. He has just been telling me a little more. I should say first that I have an interest in memory and its afflictions. It is not a well-understood area.' He stopped again and shrugged. 'My patients have mainly been those who have suffered an apoplexy or an injury to the head.'

Mrs Sharp nodded. Her heart was thudding.

'It would be most helpful if you could answer some questions?' His voice was quiet, with an accent similar to Reverend MacPherson, but he moved restlessly as he spoke.

'Yes,' she said and looked across at Dr Soames.

'I'll stay for a little while,' he said.

She answered Dr Mackay as fully as she could, aware

initially of Dr Soames sitting to the side but then becoming lost in the telling of her story, from waking in the dark room to Butcher Black's injury in the market square to becoming Mrs Sharp, nurse and midwife. Almost all her story.

Dr Mackay listened, very still now, looking sometimes at her and sometimes at his fingers, steepled together. He interrupted only occasionally: she could recognize his skill.

'Mrs Sharp,' he said when she had finished, 'if you are in agreement I would like to talk with you for a while longer but in private.'

'Yes, that is acceptable to me,' she said and turned to Dr Soames, questioning.

'Then I will go,' he said. 'Dinner will be at the usual time of two o'clock. I will see you both then.'

Dr Mackay stood as his friend left and then sat again, fidgeting as he settled in the chair. Mrs Sharp felt her heart rate rise again. What now?

'Dr Soames said that you were very low after Arthur Black recovered. That at one point he thought you considered taking your own life.'

'I was still not fully well. I had been starved and ill with fever.'

He said nothing but continued to watch her, motionless again.

'It was too hard, not knowing who I was, what I was. I was tired, so very tired.'

'Do you feel like that now?'

She looked down at her clean, trimmed nails, her long fingers resting motionless on the grey skirt.

'No.'

'And why might that be?'

'Because I'm Mrs Sharp now. I have a home. I have work to do. I am useful.'

'And?'

'Dr Soames lets me use his study and read his books. I have friends. I am content.' She stopped and knew that it was true, there was contentment.

'You are good at counting your blessings, Mrs Sharp.'

She smiled. 'I was starving and filthy and Dr Soames took me in. He saved me.'

Dr Mackay smiled fully for the first time, relaxed back in the chair and lifted his arms, shrugging again.

'I was concerned when Dr Soames first wrote that you must be some sort of trickster but he seemed sure you were not. He is a very charitable man but also a rational one. He says you have considerable knowledge of medical matters.' He paused, waiting for her to respond.

How to begin? She looked up at the shelves, at the books and papers. 'I don't know how I know.' She wanted to make him understand but how could she? 'When I was on the farm, when Mary had her baby, I did things without any understanding. As the weeks went by what I needed to do as a midwife became something I knew in my own head. It didn't just drift in.'

'Drift in?' As he spoke he leaned slightly forward; she could feel his concentration.

'Words just appeared. Sometimes I could get hold of them but sometimes they disappeared. Not just words, pictures.' She struggled, trying to find an example. 'So when Arthur Black was injured I knew it was the femoral artery and I knew how quickly he would bleed to death and how I had to press on the wound.'

'Ah yes, the femoral artery. Dr Soames wrote about it and he and I discussed it again when I arrived last night. Not arteria femoralis. He says you do not know Latin?'

'No. I recognize some of the words in his medical books, but I don't know the language.'

'Parlez-vous français? Il fait froid aujourd'hui.'

'Oui, je le parle. Et oui, il fait plus froid aujourd'hui. Je pense que cela annonce l'hiver,' she replied, his meaning clear in her head though she had to think of the French word for 'winter'. And then it was there.

'Avez-vous étudié pour être médecin en France?'

'Je ne sais pas.'

'Où avez-vous appris la langue?'

'Je n'en ai aucune idée. J'aurais aimé savoir.'

'Mrs Sharp, you present a most interesting case.'

As the long morning passed, Mrs Sharp found it easier and easier to talk to him. She realized she was saying things that she hadn't intended to, that she hadn't even known before. Perhaps it was because she knew that Dr Mackay was interested in her now as a patient, not as a trickster, or worse, a fallen woman out to seduce his friend.

She talked about the face in the mirror which had seemed not to be hers and the image of her hand next to a man's hand on a ship's rail; the feeling of the ship moving and some memory of the sound of crashing waves; and then another storm but on land, with rain on her face and neck and a brilliant white flash of lightning. And then a different memory of her skin, sun-warmed, and then the burning heat and a sky bleached white in the glare. And her hands again, sometimes shining in a different light.

He listened intently, sometimes repeating back to her what she had said and asking her to explain. 'Can we talk a little more about your other place?'

'It's the name I give to where all this comes from.'

'So, it's not an actual place. You have spoken of being in a hot country and on a ship.'

'No, it's more than that.' She stopped, uncertain of what more to say.

He waited for her.

'Sometimes things here seem wrong. At the farm it was everything but here it's less, less obvious but still some things are wrong.' She stopped, struggling again to explain.

He waited once more, his eyes on hers.

'Sometimes I read something in one of Dr Soames's books and it just seems wrong. But then I don't know why. It's maddening.' Unexpectedly, she felt a lump start to rise in her throat and her heart was beating faster, blood rushing in her ears.

She felt Dr Mackay's hand on her shoulder. 'I think we should stop for now. Here, take this,' he said, putting a glass gently into her hand.

She nodded and sipped the water, forcing herself to breathe slowly.

'Perhaps you would like a brief rest in your room before dinner? It is a half past one already.'

'Thank you,' she said and stood up, catching sight as she did of the parcel she had brought in with her and put on the side table.

'Oh, I should show you this.'

She undid the parcel and passed the contents to Dr Mackay.

'Ah, a test for me now. Forceps, I believe, but I must confess I have not delivered a baby since I was a student. Though these seem different from the forceps I remember,' he said.

'Yes. They have been made for me by Blacksmith Weddell to my design. Dr Soames's forceps were not right. This shape is better. But don't ask me how I know.'

Mrs Godwin provided them with an excellent dinner: brown soup, a magnificent game pie with buttered turnip 'especially for Dr Mackay', and apple pudding. Dr Mackay ate with such single-minded attention that Mrs Sharp started to feel concerned about his domestic arrangements and his thinness.

'Guid God, man, but that woman makes a tasty pie,' he said to Dr Soames, his accent much more pronounced than in his professional conversations.

'Indeed, we are fortunate in Mrs Godwin's excellent cooking, would you not agree, Mrs Sharp?' Dr Soames said.

'Yes, indeed. I am torn between my admiration for her pies and my delight in her cakes,' she said with a smile to both men.

Dr Mackay turned to her. 'Forgive my poor manners, Mrs Sharp. Not only am I used to inferior food, but I do not often have the pleasure of dining in mixed company.' He smiled with warmth and then tacitly acknowledged the status which Dr Soames accorded her. 'My dear wife, Margaret, may she rest in peace, died very young of consumption. I have adopted the habits of an old bachelor.'

181

'I am deeply sorry to hear of such a great sadness,' said Mrs Sharp, understanding better the friendship between these two very different men.

'Thank you. But I am comfortable enough with my profession and other interests. I spend a great deal of time studying the new subject of geology, which my good friend Dr Soames considers very boring.'

The conversation became general and both men deferred to her from time to time for comments. The room was warm and the autumn sun was shining in through the window and she felt that she belonged.

Perhaps this was enough.

Mrs Sharp stamped the filth from her boots with considerable irritation when she came back from her visits late that afternoon.

She had a number of regular patients now but was busiest with expectant mothers. Her first call had been to a woman who seemed wanly vague about how many children she had borne but certain enough that she was near her time with another. Mrs Sharp had examined her in a bed alcove alongside a young child who was sleeping and watched by three others. All were in ragged clothes and their faces had the grey pinched look of too little food, even though their father was in work as a labourer at the masons' yard at the castle.

It was wrong that women here were constantly pregnant; she knew it was wrong. She needed to discuss it with Dr Soames or perhaps even with Reverend MacPherson, though that would be unkind. He was too easily embarrassed. She would tell the reverend about the family: he was the parish officer for the Alnwick Poor Law Union and decided who should be admitted to the workhouse. More importantly, he had organized the wives of the Freemen and other gentry into the Alnwick Relief Committee which doled out food and clothing, even to those judged either not poor enough or too feckless for the workhouse.

Her next visits were to families living in the grim alleys and courts behind Market Street. A reeking place with the tanners' yards at one end and the new gas-making factory at the other. A place of ramshackle huts built against the walls of the older buildings; of itinerant labourers taking turns to sleep, four to a bed; of families crammed together with no access to a privy, slop buckets still being emptied into a sewage pit each morning.

Finally, in the fading light she had slipped on the wet cobbles and one foot had ended up in a liquid manure-filled hole. She had only just managed to keep upright and, after a quick glance up and down the road, had hitched her skirts and walked briskly on.

As Mrs Sharp was assessing the sad state of her clothes, Jenny appeared from the kitchen, slightly breathless and pink-cheeked. Mrs Godwin was agitated by visitors and Jenny, as always, suffered most.

'Oh, Mrs Sharp, Dr Soames said as could you go and see him when you get in.'

'I need to change first. My skirts are filthy and wet.'

'Well . . .' Jenny hesitated, almost in tears.

Mrs Sharp took a breath and raised her eyebrows. 'What is it, Jenny?'

'Well, Dr Soames has asked for supper in the dining room, not his study.'

'Dr Soames has a visitor. I'm sure Mrs Godwin expected supper to be set in the dining room.'

Jenny twitched at her apron, the equivalent, Mrs Sharp felt, of the wringing of hands. 'Dr Soames has asked it to be set for three,' Jenny said.

That was the cause of Mrs Godwin's upset, thought Mrs Sharp. Mrs Godwin had accepted her taking dinner with Dr Soames as a time for discussion of medical matters, except of course on Sundays. Mrs Sharp taking dinner with the visiting doctor was therefore acceptable, but an informal evening supper with both doctors would be challenging Mrs Godwin's firmly held views on the social order. No doubt it would also require Mrs Godwin to write to Mrs Thorpe, even result in a further visit from Mrs Thorpe.

Mrs Sharp decided to be amused rather than cross. She walked into the kitchen. 'Good evening, Mrs Godwin,' she said. 'Jenny has said I must take supper with Dr Soames and Dr Mackay. Is that so?'

'Yes, and not convenient at all. I was planning omelette for the doctors and I can't be expected to do that for three.' Mrs Godwin was beating a lump of dough into submission.

'No, of course not. I must say I would have preferred a quiet supper with you in the kitchen. I'm soaked in filthy mud and I'll have to change. Now it will have to be my best black. What a nuisance.'

Mrs Godwin looked slightly mollified and nodded.

Mrs Sharp continued, 'I was going to say how impressed Dr Mackay was with that magnificent pie. Perhaps some hard-boiled egg and a small slice of cold pie might please him for supper? And your pickled plums? That would delight him. He is clearly not used to well prepared and wholesome food.'

Mrs Sharp had found the best common ground with Mrs Godwin was fulsome, even excessive, praise of her cooking. This had the benefit not only of ameliorating the cook's sensitivities about Mrs Sharp's station but led to her being served larger portions.

There was quite a lot she would still do for good food.

Conversation over supper was initially general, with Dr Soames relating some of his many stories about the townsfolk and their enthusiasm for the latest quackery. The current fad was for a 'blue pill' enthusiastically promoted by Dr Selby, the apothecary, who now called himself a doctor. A person about whom Dr Soames, an Edinburgh medical school graduate, made uncharacteristically caustic comments. The blue pill cured all diseases and had the added advantage of turning the patient's urine a marvellously intense deep turquoise colour. Mrs Sharp, having heard all this before, simply nodded at the appropriate moments, suppressing a smile.

Dr Mackay meanwhile ate again with enthusiasm and only spoke at any length when his plate was finally empty.

'Well, I can understand your view on the blue pill and indeed on Dr Selby. Though he is of course legally licensed, I suppose?'

Dr Soames nodded and speared a final piece of pie with unnecessary force.

'But here is an interesting question – what do you think of mesmerism?' Dr Mackay said, becoming more animated.

'Another remarkable foolishness,' said Dr Soames.

'My apologies, Mrs Sharp, are you aware of the practice of mesmerism?' Dr Mackay said, looking across at her.

'Only what Dr Soames has told me. He showed me an article in the *Lancet* which described it as gravely mistaken and unscientific.'

'That is so. The editor of the *Lancet* is now vehemently opposed. And I can only agree. I saw a demonstration by Dr Elliotson two years ago which was frankly alarming. He was claiming strange forces, animal magnetism and such. And all with young women patients who were behaving, alas, with some abandonment,' said Dr Soames.

'But I have a colleague in Edinburgh who has done some sober and sensible work using mesmerism which does seem to help those with memory problems.' Dr Mackay was moving in his chair, arms adrift again.

'So, you think there is something of science to it?' Dr Soames said, frowning.

'Not in the animal magnetism, certainly not. You are correct, I am sure, in calling it a foolishness. But in using certain techniques to calm patients, yes, I think so. I have used these now on some of my patients, to help them find their memories.'

Dr Mackay turned to her again. 'Indeed, Mrs Sharp, I had thought to ask you if you might consider a further discussion but under mesmerism. You would be sitting quietly, and I would ask you questions about your past, about before you awakened on the farm.'

*

186

Later, in the study, he placed an armchair by the fire and asked her to sit comfortably. Standing a little way in front and to the side of her, he unfastened his watch from his waistcoat pocket and held it out. All the nervous movements were suppressed and he stood very still. The watch hung steady on its chain, its shiny gold back towards her. He spoke slowly and quietly, his accent soft.

'Now, Mrs Sharp, please keep your eyes on the watch and breathe slowly. Think only of looking at the watch as your breath moves slowly in . . . and then out.'

She concentrated on the watch, which was moving very slightly now, catching the light from the fire, sparkling. She could feel the breath moving slowly across her lips. Dr Mackay's voice faded then became louder again.

'Hello, Mrs Sharp, hello. We are finished.'

A fleeting moment of dizziness and a smell of lavender and then . . . something, then gone, and she was aware of stiffness in her neck and back. Dr Mackay was leaning forward, handing her a glass of water.

'Thank you,' she said. 'Is it over?'

'Yes. We were talking for almost a half-hour.'

She looked over at the clock. The time had passed.

'Was there anything? Before I arrived on the moor?'

'No. Nothing. Nothing at all. Extraordinary.'

'So, what did I say?'

'You told me the same as this morning, about waking at the farm and your life here in Alnwick.'

He sat down opposite her and leaned forwards, his fingers laced together. She looked at them, realizing that was how he

187

composed himself, concentrated his attention. She did not want to look at his face.

'You did say something more . . . about John Elliott,' he said, and waited.

A long moment passed.

'John Elliott raped me,' she said, and swallowed as bitter liquid rose in her throat.

She looked up and Dr Mackay was watching her, expressionless.

'I don't want Dr Soames to know,' she said.

'I understand. I will not speak of it,' he said.

He stood up and went to the door, holding it open for her. As she walked past him he bowed.

Dr Soames rejoined them and sent for hot chocolate which Mrs Godwin brought in herself, with rather pointed cere-mony. Mrs Sharp listened as Dr Mackay told Dr Soames almost all she had said. He described her as a unique case and offered to seek advice from other Edinburgh colleagues, to which she agreed. The doctors were still discussing the merits of mesmerism when she said goodnight and went to bed.

She lay awake, listening as they came upstairs, listening as Peter pulled the bolts across the front door, listening as the house settled into silence.

And then there were just Dr Mackay's words, over and over. 'Nothing. Nothing at all.'

18

London, January 1842

He awakened, knowing he was being watched, and sat back suddenly, frowning as his neck cricked. He was sitting at his desk in the study.

'Oh sorry, doctor. Dursn't mean to startle you. There's a note,' Betty said.

'I shouldn't have been asleep over my books,' he smiled at her.

'You was back home awful late. Mr Hayward is still abed, not even taken his tea yet.' She stopped, seeming as amazed as he was by her spontaneous comments.

She had become more talkative with him over the last few months and was no longer almost mute with terror in her reading lessons. She held out the small tray. 'Mr Swan's footman is waiting on reply.'

The note was from Mrs Swan, asking him to call that afternoon if convenient. He wrote his reply, *'Yes, honoured to attend at 4 o'clock'*, and watched Betty walk quite briskly into the hall.

*

He hadn't been to the Swans' house since October and the painful interview with Eleanor. He knew, though, from Mrs Bates that both Mr and Mrs Swan continued to advocate his skills as an *accoucheur*. They were kind. He had even received a politely worded invitation to a Christmas Eve soirée but he had declined, knowing that was what was expected, but grateful that he was not being publicly excluded from their set.

He had anticipated spending Christmas alone, but was instead invited to Dr John Atkins's house and enjoyed goose followed by plum pudding in the company of Mrs Atkins, their two young children and old Mr Atkins, a retired surveyor of roads. Dr Borthwick managed to keep the conversation focused on the construction of the Great North Road and the drawing skills of the children, and enjoyed the day. He still considered John Atkins a respected colleague rather than a friend, but recognized the man's good humour and the warmth of his family.

Which brought his thoughts back to Eleanor. He knew she was still staying with the Swans: they had met twice by accident at the Mission, despite Eleanor avoiding his usual Tuesdays. They were formal and polite, uncomfortable in the same space, and she left directly after her reading classes. But while she was there, he was distracted by her voice in the next room, seeming to hear it over the noise of the women; her quiet voice. Mrs Bates in turn had seemed unusually talkative and kept asking for his opinion when he knew she didn't need it. So was Eleanor now leaving London, returning to her Winchester house? Or was this a medical matter: Mrs Swan or the child?

He stood up, impatient with himself, and called for Betty.

The Midwife

It was time to make a morning call on Lady Gasgoine; a planned visit at her request; an elegant, scented note hinting at a happy event.

The welcome at Belgrave Square was warm, Mr Burrows the butler again taking his hat and coat and escorting him to the morning room, the footman rushing ahead to open the door. Dr Borthwick smiled his thanks to Mr Burrows as he was announced. Sir Jeremy came over to shake his hand as they exchanged polite greetings and then offered him a seat by the fire. Very different from the formality of a year ago.

Dr Borthwick felt well established now as part of the outer circle of what he realized was one of the most powerful couples in London: prominent Whigs attended their soirées, Sir Jeremy being certain to be returned as MP in the next elections, and his wife was applauded for her wealth and beauty. There was less unanimity about her campaigns for women's education and the hospital for women. Dr Borthwick had observed Lady Gasgoine in the many roles she played: he thought she was the most intelligent person he had met in London.

They both stood again as Lady Gasgoine swept into the room in a rustle of claret-coloured silk, bringing a scent this time of jasmine with her. She was immaculate, from the sweep of blonde hair coiled and dressed with long lace ribbons to the just-visible silk shoes. She was, he thought, a work of art. Then added, wryly, to this perhaps not completely professional appraisal, that she was not as tightly corseted as usual.

She settled herself and turned to Dr Borthwick.

'Well, it seems I am about to do my duty to the Gasgoine name again,' she said in her languid society tones.

'Which is another great blessing,' her husband said.

'Indeed. But, dear Dr Borthwick, I hope you will tell me not twins. Not again,' she said.

He shrugged very slightly. 'Alas, that is not something that can be ascertained until nearer to the time of your confinement. May I ask, are you certain that you are with child?'

'You may be open, indeed scientific, if you wish. My husband has a strong constitution,' she said, with a vague gesture in Sir Jeremy's direction.

She was looking at Dr Borthwick directly, a challenge he thought.

'When was the last bleeding?' he said.

'I have missed twice now.'

'So about eight or nine weeks ago?'

'Nine.'

He looked briefly at Sir Jeremy who was sitting back in his chair, but watching the exchange, and then back to Lady Gasgoine.

'Are you well?'

'Better than last time, certainly. But I am of course following your rules: stays are well loosened and I am taking fresh air and milk and plenty of greens,' she almost chanted, perhaps slightly mocking.

He smiled then, full into the level stare from the blue eyes, and was bathed in her lovely smile in return.

'And fresh cow's liver, cooked, once a week?' he said.

'Even that, though it still disgusts me.'

'Then you do not need my advice.'

'I am very certain that I do. I will see no other doctor this time. Just you and Mrs Bates.'

She was serious now and he could see the memory of last time, of the hours and hours she had laboured. The fear that all women shared.

He leaned towards her and his voice was gentle. 'I meant only that you do not need Mrs Bates's and my attention as yet. I will need to see you with Mrs Bates in a month's time. We will look after you.'

She nodded.

He asked then after the health of the twins and they were brought down from the nursery to be viewed. Both regarded him solemnly at first but condescended to be placed in turn on his knee. A pigeon pair: the girl brown-eyed like her father but still blonde; the boy with his mother's blue eyes; both well fed and lively. It was Sir Jeremy who took the girl from him and held her on his own knee and she played contentedly with his watch chain. Lady Gasgoine watched, unperturbed. The children were removed when tea was served.

Afterwards, Sir Jeremy escorted him to the door, the footmen discreetly vanishing at a nod from him. 'My wife has great faith in you. We all do. But she is afraid. And in truth so am I. I did not know that such an ordeal could be survived,' Sir Jeremy said.

'Lady Gasgoine is a healthy and intelligent woman. And it is very unlikely to be twins again. But you understand there can be no guarantees,' Dr Borthwick replied.

Later that day, riding to the Swans' house, he wondered if Sir Jeremy knew about his sister-in-law, about Lady Burnside. He thought that he probably did. Then he worried about the very long list of women due to deliver their babies in the next few weeks. He had had no choice but to engage a second midwife, a sober widow who came with Mrs Bates's recommendation. His reputation as an *accoucheur* continued to rise: Dr Preston's campaign against him had faltered, due in no small part to Eleanor's efforts in the autumn. Eleanor. Why had Mrs Swan sent for him?

Mrs Swan was waiting for him in the warm and well-lit morning room with its pale green walls and botanical prints. She stood as he was announced and so did the tall man sitting near her. Not Mr Swan, though. It was Charles Darrow, which was a surprise. He had seen both Charles and Mr Swan at meetings of the Anti-Slavery Society, of which Mr Swan was a founder member, but had only made polite, public conversation.

Why was Charles here?

The exchange of greetings gave him time to slow his breathing. He took the offered seat opposite Mrs Swan and Charles.

'I trust you and the family are all well?' he said, looking at Mrs Swan.

'Thank you. Yes, we are all well. James does very well and Mr Swan, of course. Very well. Indeed,' she said, flustered and dropping her eyes.

He felt an actual pain in his gut.

'And Mrs Johnson?'

Mrs Swan looked up in sudden comprehension.

'Of course. Yes, Eleanor, Mrs Johnson, is well. She plans to leave us soon, in the spring. Her tenants in Winchester will move out next month. We will miss her . . .' She was speaking very quickly and she paused and then looked at him, her gaze level. 'It is not about Eleanor. Not directly. I did not mean to alarm you. But it is a serious matter. I'm going to leave Charles to explain. Then I will rejoin you.'

She smiled, a small, tense smile, and they stood as she left the room.

Charles raised his eyebrows and grimaced slightly as they sat once more.

'It's Dr Preston again. He has been spreading very specific rumours that you are – well – a sodomite, and that he has proof. It's going around all the clubs, the high and the low. A few of my – well – very close friends have even asked me if I'm the lucky man. I have told them alas, no, that you were indifferent to my charms.' Charles stopped and shrugged.

'There have been rumours before, mostly that I was too interested in my patients as women. So, sodomy now,' Dr Borthwick said. He felt unsure, even confused, by Charles's level of concern. The Swans had known about the earlier rumours.

'This is different. People believe it. Because of the source,' said Charles.

'The source?' He felt the pain in his gut again.

'Yes. The source is thought to be reliable.'

'What? Who?'

'Eleanor's maid.'

Charles told him all they knew. Since Christmas, Dr Preston's valet had been approaching the maidservants of Dr Borthwick's friends, looking for scandal, even offering money. Eleanor's maid had told the valet the story of Eleanor's distress in October and conversations she said she had overheard between Eleanor and Dr Borthwick, and Eleanor and Mrs Swan. It was a good story, based on truth, as good stories are.

Dr Preston had then embellished it well: he told the story that Mrs Johnson, a most respectable and wealthy widow, had welcomed her friendship with Dr Borthwick and had rightly expected that the growing intimacy would lead to a proposal of marriage. The Swans had been certain of it as had others in their circle. But Dr Borthwick had spurned her, though with some distress, admitting that he was unable to marry. Telling her he was unable to marry due to his 'tendencies and ungovernable weaknesses'.

Dr Borthwick could hear Dr Preston's voice, see the fleshy lips forming the words, lingering over 'ungovernable weaknesses'. Charles was right: this was serious. Why would any doctor turn down the opportunity of marrying a young and wealthy widow, a woman of excellent reputation and personal elegance? It made no sense, otherwise. That would be the solemn conclusion of the men in their smart clubs and probably in the brothels too.

He was vaguely aware of Charles leaving the room and then returning with Mrs Swan.

'Tea will be brought in shortly,' she said.

'Thank you.'

The tea came and he drank it as Charles talked about the plans for the expedition to South America: the ship he was to travel on to the Azores and then on to Rio de Janeiro; the supplies that he had to take with him; the new specimen boxes with walls of glass. Dr Borthwick tried to listen, but the words drifted by.

He nodded at intervals until Mrs Swan took the empty cup from him.

It was time to leave, to go home and decide what to do next. He started to stand up and make his farewells, but Mrs Swan interrupted him. 'Dr Borthwick, Eleanor is distraught to have caused you this trouble.'

'No, she must not be. The fault is not hers at all. Please tell her so.'

'She is in the study. She asks if you would speak with her.'

He couldn't refuse.

Eleanor was standing by the hearth as he entered. She looked quickly towards him and then back to the fire. He didn't know what to say but knew he must speak first.

Moving slowly across the room, he stopped and stood some distance from her, but close enough to see that she was struggling for composure. He could think of nothing that would not make it worse for her, for them both. The silence stretched.

'Mrs Johnson, I fear that I am causing you more distress—' he said, his throat aching.

He stopped as she turned and spoke rapidly, interrupting him, saying words that were thickened with tears.

'No, Dr Borthwick, I must speak first. Through my fault, this terrible scandal is being made of you. If I had exhibited more control, there would have been nothing for my maid to tell.' She stopped, swallowing down a sob.

He looked at her, at her pale, thin cheeks and the tears escaping, at the hand wiping them away.

'Mrs Johnson, Eleanor, there is no fault here except my own. I have caused you pain and I am so deeply sorry.'

He felt her agony as she tried to speak but couldn't and then she dropped her head and moved blindly towards the door. He couldn't let her go, though he should, though he must. 'Eleanor,' he said and he reached out and held her gently, his hands on her shoulders, and she turned towards him. He held her tight against him as she wept.

A moment passed. He kissed her hair just once and then, with his arm around her, walked back to the fireside and sat her down in the chair, pulling the other across so he faced her. She still had not looked at him.

'Eleanor. My dear Eleanor. I owe you an explanation, but I cannot be as open as you deserve, and as I want to be. I am not free to marry, for reasons I cannot give you. But the friendship, the affection between us has been very real. If I were a free man then there could be no other woman for me, none to surpass your courage, your intelligence, your compassion.' He stopped as she looked up at him and then he added, his voice very gentle, 'Your loveliness.'

'Why then? Why are you not free?' she said.

He loved her, of course, he knew that. But he could not compromise her. Could not expect her to understand.

'It is a matter of protecting someone else. I cannot say more. You deserve a man who can marry you free of any constraints.'

She dropped her face into her hands, and as he waited he watched her, and knew he had said goodbye.

After a while she took a deep breath and straightened her shoulders. When she spoke her voice was steady but she didn't look at him. 'Charles says it is definitely not true that you are –' she stopped and then said the word – 'a sodomite. I know the word, what it means. Abigail told me.'

'No, I am not. But I know men who are. Good men. I do not judge them.'

'But God does,' she said, looking directly at him now.

'So men say.'

She frowned and dropped her gaze.

He was unsure if she knew about Charles. In many ways she was not as aware of the world as the Swans, even though she spent time in Duck Lane and saw the effects of drunkenness and violence and prostitution. But her husband had been a religious man and much older, and she was still quietly but deeply devout. He had listened to some of her intense conversations with Andrew Wilson at the Mission: she a moderate Anglican, he a nonconformist evangelist.

She was looking at him again.

'What will you do?'

'About the slander?'

She nodded.

'See what happens. I have had no patients change doctor yet. Indeed, I am almost too busy.' He shrugged and managed to smile. 'Perhaps Dr Preston is helping me.'

'We will all speak for you, and you have powerful support from Sir Jeremy and Lady Gasgoine.'

'Thank you. Your continued good words are what matter most.'

'But not enough. Mr Swan has already told his circle that my maid took money for telling lies and has been dismissed.

But there needs to be a reason why . . . why we are not to be married. That Mr Swan can tell.'

'No, I do not want any more discussion of your private life. Any fault is mine and that is how the world must see it. That I have wronged you.'

And then to his surprise she smiled, the first smile she had given him today, the first since October.

'Abigail and I have already made up an explanation for Mr Swan to spread, if you will agree?'

She told him his new story.

When he stood to leave she gave him her hand, and he could barely see her tears through his own. He kissed her fingers lightly then turned away. But at the door he turned back.

'My story is not the same as the one you make for me, but it is the true reason why I cannot marry. There is a woman I must protect.'

He closed the door behind him.

He heard the story back from Mrs Bates the following week. It was already much embellished. He had, so it went, gone to Edinburgh to study medicine and then found a good position in a small northern town, working with a friend of his deceased father, a well-respected country doctor. He had rapidly developed an attachment to the oldest daughter which was very acceptable to both families, indeed, may have been the hope of both. Not long after the engagement, the young woman had become unwell and then increasingly deranged, a recurrence of a former condition. She was still alive, cared for at home by her devoted parents but often needing to be locked in her room with her nurse. Her father had released Dr Borthwick from the engagement and sent him away to London. But Dr Borthwick did not consider himself to be free.

By the time he heard the story from Sir Jeremy, another week later, his erstwhile fiancée had spent time in the past in an asylum and her family had concealed this from him. Sir Jeremy asked him if it was true and he replied that there was some truth but that most of the re-telling owed a great deal to the novels of Sir Walter Scott, or even Mrs Radcliffe. Sir Jeremy smiled and said that Dr Preston seemed to have lost his appreciation for literature and then added in a quiet aside, 'Dr Preston is a difficult man and his malice has made him look foolish. He will keep on trying to discredit you. Be careful.'

19

Northumberland, January 1839

Mrs Sharp walked behind Dr Soames as he strode up Fenkle Street. He was greeted by Mr Sealy in his lawyer's black, and a tweed-cloaked man who she thought was the duke's new agent but did not have a chance for a proper look. She kept her gaze modestly on the cobbles, aware of the pleasing clicking of the heels of her newly shod boots and the swish of her dutiful, dark-checked winter skirt.

They had a comfortable routine: she would accompany Dr Soames on his morning visits to the gentry if the patients were new to her; then pay her own calls, first to expectant mothers and later to apply poultices, replace bandages and give what comfort she could to the dying. Tradespeople were visited by the doctor in the afternoons if needed and the poor were seen at four o'clock at the dispensary. She helped wherever he wanted and secretly, though he certainly knew, visited those who could not pay.

Over the half-year since she had been Mrs Sharp she had put on weight, so was slender rather than gaunt. Her hair had grown enough to be neatly fastened in a chignon beneath her cap and alongside Dr Soames's tall, solid figure she no longer felt quite so different. The general view, the doctor said, was that she was useful to him and therefore to the citizenry. She even had her own advocates now in terms of her skills as a nurse and midwife, though her advice on diet continued to be considered outlandish.

Her assumed identity as the daughter of a doctor and widow of a silk trader, who had lived for many years in Calcutta, was firmly established and had indeed been embellished for her through local gossip. That she had fallen on hard times and been rescued by Dr Soames was, she knew, still discussed but the extent of her fall and the enthusiasm for detail varied, with Dr Soames quashing any particularly lurid stories when they got back to him. Links to John Elliott were now rarely made: the cloak of respectability created for her by Dr Soames was encompassing and warm.

Dr Soames left her at the top of Fenkle Street with a small bow and she crossed the road to the butcher's shop where Arthur Black's smile was warm as always.

'Good morning to you, Mrs Sharp. Here, Mother made up a package for the Elliotts.'

'And good morning to you, Mr Black. And thank you. Will you take payment?' she said.

'You know I'll not dare to,' he replied, laughing loudly at the shared joke.

His mother, old Mrs Black, was formidable; no one defaulted for long on their butcher's bill without it becoming public knowledge. It was an accepted fact that Arthur was his mother's darling, her only living child; she had ruled her lugubrious husband with an acid tongue but had only honey for her handsome son, even more after his father died. Dr Soames's household had had all their meat free since the butcher's injury and the full fury of old Mrs Black descended on anyone who dared to criticize Mrs Sharp in her hearing.

Arthur pulled on his coat and, limping only a little, helped her up on to the bench seat of his cart. They were going together up the valley, she for her regular visits to Jane Weddell and Mary Elliott, and he to see some bullocks who might come to slaughter before the first market.

'Bit o' warmth in the sun today,' he said as they turned up the hill out of town.

'At last. And no more snow this week.'

'Aye. Bad winter. And those many bairns lost. People about were right pleased Dr Soames had help through that. And grateful for all you did and do for them.'

'Thank you. I'm very grateful to be here.'

'Aye. Better than living up valley. You look a sight better than when I first met you and all,' he added with easy familiarity.

'I do hope so,' she said, pulling her thick woollen cloak tighter round her shoulders.

All through November the disease had raged through the town, blighting most families but passing some others by. Diphtheritis, Dr Soames had called it. No respecter of rank or income, it had taken children from the workhouse and the smart streets, but most of those who died were from the alleys and courts behind Market Street.

The worst affected was the Kirkup family: four adults and eight children living in one room. Mrs Sharp had held one child and then another upright in her arms as they struggled for breath, dosing them with althaea and liquorice root for the breathing and thyme, sage and honey to ease the throat; knowing it was useless. When they could no longer swallow and the desperate choking started, she did what Dr Soames gravely suggested, and slowly trickled laudanum into the gasping mouths, to try to ease the final terrible hours. All the children except the youngest baby were desperately ill. Three died the choking death; the four oldest survived the swollen throat but two of them died in the weeks that followed. Five children dead from that one family, from that one cold, dark room.

Then came the snow, a three-day blizzard and after that a bitter cold, the snow hard frozen for two weeks and no water from the pumps. And more deaths each day: some expected in the old and the consumptive; some in children who seemed to have survived the diphtheritis but then sickened and died with their lungs flooded with clear fluid; some, but not so many, in the well fed and previously healthy, but most in the poor.

The days and nights blurred as she trudged across the white roads, feet sliding even though Peter had put short nails into the soles of her boots. She slept for just odd hours at a time and some days saw Dr Soames only as they passed each other in the hall, or sat together in the kitchen to eat a bowl of broth, speaking only of their patients, rushing to set out again. There were no dinners, no pies, no cakes. Mrs Godwin spent her days making bread and pan after pan of broth to be carried by Peter to the soup kitchen in the market square, or delivered to those too sick to go out. Jenny's hands bled from keens and chilblains on every finger as she chopped piles of half-frozen cabbages and turnips. They never complained: they were all bound by Dr Soames's compassion.

It was perhaps an apple pie which caused Mrs Sharp to shout at Dr Selby, the apothecary. The smell of warm pastry and soft apple, so fragrantly intense after weeks of broth, after the sickly smell of laudanum, after the terrible stench of the dying children's mouths. Or perhaps it was just being so tired. Alice said later that it was righteous anger but Arthur said it was still foolish, though he laughed.

She called into the apothecary's shop to collect an order of powdered herbs. The assistant, a pale, thin young man who rarely spoke, was apologetic: he was behind with his work and he was just now making up the powders. The jars were on his bench and he was weighing and mixing as they spoke.

'I can't wait,' she said, thinking that she must go now to the Turnbulls' child who had a high fever and then trek back up the hill to collect the powders, then back to old Mr Mason. An extra ten minutes' walk on the frozen snow.

'I'm sorry. Dr Selby told as I must make up the blue pills first. But I can do half of the powders straight away,' the assistant said.

She turned as Dr Selby walked in from his rooms behind the shop. He was chewing and swallowing, a napkin tucked at his neck. Through the open door came a wave of warmth and then the smell of hot apple pie.

Her first slow thought was surprise that it was dinner time and then a physical wave of anger that he was sitting eating apple pie; that he wasn't out visiting the sick and dying; that he wasn't ruining his own health as she was certain Dr Soames was doing.

'Now, Mrs Sharp, there is no need to be rushing the boy. He has plenty to do.' He ran his tongue over his lips, removing the crumbs.

'The powders are needed. They were promised to be ready this morning,' she said, her voice quiet.

'Well then, Mrs Sharp, you should have collected them on time.'

'But they wouldn't have been ready then. They are not ready even now.' She was struggling to keep her voice level.

Making no reply, he smiled and stared at her.

'I don't think Dr Soames slept at all last night and he is away up at Edlingham now. How can you be sitting eating apple pie when—?' She stopped. This would not help. She breathed out slowly.

'But Mrs Sharp, forgive me, would you like to take a piece of pie with you?' He smiled again.

'It is not about the pie. It's about you getting off your fat arse and doing your job.'

The silence stretched.

'Well, so you really are from the gutter. I've always said as much.' He smirked and walked back into his rooms, closing the door firmly behind him.

She turned to the assistant, feeling the heat in her face and neck.

'I'll bring the rest of the powders to Dr Soames's house if that is satisfactory, Mrs Sharp,' he said, eyes lowered.

'Thank you, yes.'

'He deserves worse,' he whispered as he handed her the parcel.

*

Dr Soames said nothing until after Mrs Godwin brought in the first apple pie at the end of the first proper dinner they had taken together for weeks. He waited until the door closed again.

'I hear you had an altercation with Dr Selby in relation to apple pie, the fortnight gone?'

'I was unconscionably rude. I wrote a note to apologize,' she said.

'So he says. He is an irritating man but best not, I think, to comment on physical attributes, however well evidenced, unless in a medical discussion.'

'Of course.'

Nothing more was said, but she had eaten her slice of pie with less enjoyment than usual.

Butcher Black left her at the forge, waving and smiling to the blacksmith, then setting off to see Farmer Turnbull's bullocks.

'Good day to you, Mrs Sharp,' Blacksmith Weddell said with his usual shy formality as they walked over to the cottage.

'Good day. A better journey than a fortnight past,' she said.

'Jane was worried for you then, going back through snow.'

'How is she?'

'Worse. Bad fever at nights. Always coughing. Rose is with her.'

She looked up at him and patted his huge arm as he opened the door.

'Mrs Sharp's come,' he called and then went back to his forge, giant's shoulders hunched forwards over his pain.

The Midwife

Rose came into the kitchen and took Mrs Sharp's cloak and bonnet, hanging them by the fire, and started putting on her own.

'I'll be going home whilst you're with Jane. Father Weddell is with bairns but he tires quick,' Rose said, not looking at her, her voice choked.

Mrs Sharp reached out and helped Rose to put on her cloak, and then the two women held hands for a moment as tears for her sister-in-law ran down Rose's healthy red cheeks.

Mrs Sharp pushed open the bedroom door and stopped, silent as she saw her friend. Jane's greeting was barely audible, but she lifted her hand in welcome, a memory of a smile stretching the pale lips against the paler skin.

Later, after she had so gently washed Jane and brushed the remnants of the blonde curls and settled her back against fresh pillows, they gossiped for a while as usual. But Jane could barely listen now, drifting away and then back. Mrs Sharp continued to talk, soft-voiced; to tell Jane about Dr Selby's latest coloured pills, Alice's desire for side ringlets, anything and everything. Then she watched and waited.

'Will it be long?' said Jane.

'No, not long,' said Mrs Sharp, taking Jane's thin hand in hers, squeezing the cold fingers gently.

'I'm afraid of the coughing and the blood. There's so much.'

'Dr Soames has made up a stronger medicine. It will help to stop the coughing.'

'Will you stay? For Thomas, so he's not alone when I go.'

'Yes.'

'Well then, it's best I see Reverend MacPherson soon.'

'I'll ask Butcher Black to take a message. He'll be here in a little while.'

Butcher Black came and took the package of meat and the coins she had saved and delivered them to Mary Elliott for her and then returned to Alnwick.

Reverend MacPherson arrived in the evening darkness, his old horse well used to the half-frozen road. He came straight in to Jane. Mrs Sharp took his coat and left them together. She went into the kitchen and served up the blacksmith's supper and watched him try to eat. Neither of them spoke. She let Jane's whispered voice and the reverend's prayers play background to her thoughts.

She knew Jane's story: Jane had told it to her piece by piece over the winter months, wanting to share the joy of her life. She was born in Alnwick, youngest of the four daughters of the undertaker; she had kept house for him after her mother died and then come to live in the village with her father's sister after her father's death. She had married the young blacksmith within six months and filled her life with teaching at the village school, keeping his accounts, tending her small garden, making jams and pickles, busy every day. Mrs Sharp had heard much more from others of Jane's quiet religious devotion, of her care of the old and sick, of her and the blacksmith's charity. But there was more to Jane, to her friend, than piety and charity – there was laughter too.

Mrs Sharp looked across at the blacksmith, who was sitting with his eyes closed, his lips moving slightly as he prayed.

She closed her own eyes and let herself remember the warmth and the sunshine and the red ribbons, that day at Alnwick Fair.

It had been the first letter she could remember receiving. It was the end of August last year, two weeks after Mrs Sharp in her grey dress and white cap had first visited Jane in Edlingham village. Peter carried the letter into the kitchen on the silver letter tray from Dr Soames's study, and presented it to her with some formality.

'A letter for you, Mrs Sharp. Dr Soames told me to bring it straight through.'

Mrs Godwin's back visibly tensed as she listened, leaning over the stove, tending Dr Soames's poached eggs. Mrs Sharp studied the letter carefully. It was addressed to her, *Mrs Sharp, Dr Soames's House, Alnwick,* in neat and confident script on good thick paper. She turned it over slowly, broke the seal and unfolded the page. Then she read it, folded it again and put it in her pocket.

She caught Peter's eye as they both watched Mrs Godwin serve out Dr Soames's eggs and put the plate on his tray. Peter smiled.

'So, what are you waiting for?' Mrs Godwin said to Jenny. 'Get this through to the doctor before his eggs are cold.'

She served Mrs Sharp next with an unsurprisingly hard egg which Mrs Sharp felt she probably deserved. She decided to make peace.

'Well, how nice of Jane Weddell to write to me,' she said.

'She could have sent a message, blacksmith's in and out of town. Waste of money, a letter,' Mrs Godwin said.

211

'It's an invitation to go with them to the fair on Saturday.'

There was really nothing to which Mrs Godwin could object: Dr Soames had already given them all permission to go to the fair, had said he would need no meals after breakfast.

'What if you're needed?' Mrs Godwin said.

'People will know where I am. Dr Soames said he was happy with that.'

So Mrs Sharp had gone to the fair. The blacksmith drove them down to the Pleasance, the crowds giving way good-naturedly enough when they saw it was him. Though most of the shouted greetings were for Jane, who smiled and replied, always knowing their names. Jane was in a pale blue dress and straw bonnet with sprigs of pink dog roses tucked into the blue ribbons. Her eyes were clear and as sky-coloured as the dress. She should have looked beautiful, but the light emphasized the pallor of her skin and sharp angles of her face and the sleeves hung loose on her bone-thin arms. Mrs Sharp, looking at her, felt a moment of despair. There must be more to treat consumption than potions to ease the cough. For a fleeting instant she felt sure that there was.

Jane touched her hand. 'We are so blessed to have such a beautiful day for the fair. I am most looking forward to it. Did you know that my dear Thomas is to wrestle?'

'Wrestle? But how?'

Jane laughed. 'It's new here in the last few years. Called Cumbrian wrestling. The men do it in their winter combinations.'

'In public?'

'Indeed, yes. We women watch at a discreet distance. We're not meant to be there.'

Mrs Sharp looked at Jane, thinking she must be teasing. But Blacksmith Weddell, Thomas, was nodding.

They spent the day at the fair, watching the mummers and the dancers and the children singing. Jane bought another straw bonnet and some deep red ribbons and Blacksmith Weddell won the competition for strongest man, seeing off the challenger from Amble to the delight of the highly partisan crowd. When Jane was tired, Mrs Sharp took her to sit on the cart. The blacksmith arrived with three pies and some lardy cakes and a jug of small beer. Jane swallowed a mouthful of pie and nibbled at one of the cakes and then slept on the bench seat, her head in Mrs Sharp's lap.

'She eats an egg for breakfast most days and Rose brings her good stew and green stuff like you said, but she takes very little. She eats to please us now,' he said and then paused and shook his head. 'Is there any more to be done?'

'No,' she said. 'But the food will help to keep up her strength.'

'You said afore that she would likely not live another winter,' he whispered, looking down at his sleeping wife. 'I pray to God every day that you'll be wrong.'

'I hope so too.'

But she knew she was not.

The blacksmith took the cart to the edge of the field, up the slope so Jane could have a good though distant view of the wrestling. The crowd was huge, everyone at the fair drifting over as the bell was rung. The men and boys formed a big circle and the women ended up round the cart, lifting the children up to stand in the back. The contestants appeared from a huddle of men dressed, as Jane had said, in their long winter combinations, varying shades of cream and grey and some more than a little stained, but all decently covered from neck to ankle. Jane told her the rules with enthusiasm and provided a detailed commentary: three weight categories; bouts for boys and light men first; best of three throws goes on to the next round.

Alice arrived breathless at the cart just in time to see the start of the middleweight men's bouts. She announced she was pleased with the day, all fifty pies sold; she had been up baking since dawn.

'Surely you could have had the day off. Arthur's been here all day,' Mrs Sharp said, surprised.

'But the pie money is mine,' Alice said.

'As it should be,' agreed Jane, eyes still on the wrestling. 'That lad from Alwinton is good.'

'Aye. I think Arthur was pleased to have an excuse not to fight him this year. Said as all his teeth rattled on that second throw last year. Reckon it was more his pride, though,' Alice said.

Jane nodded, smiling, but eyes still on the two men who were circling round, bent double with arms locked across each other's backs. They tussled together until the Alwinton lad hooked his leg across and toppled his opponent hard down on to the field. Jane clapped, frowning slightly.

'What is he? Shepherd?' she asked Alice.

Alice shrugged. 'Don't rightly know but not much else goes on up there.'

'So you have your own money?' Mrs Sharp asked Alice.

'Aye, I have a little put by.'

'Is that usual?'

Jane and Alice both looked at her.

'No. I don't know many else as do it. But I've always kept my pin money,' Alice said.

'I don't have any,' said Jane.

'You don't live with Mother Black,' said Alice.

There was a silence then as Blacksmith Weddell appeared, huge and magnificent in startlingly clean combinations. Mrs Sharp felt the colour rising in her cheeks and looked hurriedly down as Alice poked her arm. Alice leaned over and whispered, 'We all feel same. Menfolk are right jealous. Does them good.'

He won all his bouts on two throws to massive cheers from the crowd.

The blacksmith brought his winner's rosette back for Jane and Mrs Sharp pinned it on to Jane's hat. The cart was surrounded by well-wishers and Jane sat smiling beside her husband, who was now fully clothed, her cheeks flushed pink and eyes sparkling. Mrs Sharp watched her, watched them both, and unexpectedly felt her eyes fill with tears.

A fiddler came over to the crowd and shouted up, 'Will you call for a tune, Mrs Weddell?'

'You know my favourite,' Jane said.

He laughed and started to play and the music filled her head, louder and louder.

The day fractured. She was in the other place spinning in his arms, laughing, but when she looked up the light was blinding white and he was gone. And she hadn't seen his face again.

It was Alice's voice: 'What is it? Mrs Sharp . . . Mrs Sharp . . .' Alice's arm was tight on hers.

'Sorry. Just felt a little faint for a moment. I am well now.'

She looked around. No one else seemed to have noticed. 'What's the tune called?'

'"Apprentice Lads of Alnwick". Do you recognize it?' said Alice.

'I don't know. It's . . . I don't know.'

Jane turned round, frowning with concern at her. 'My dear Mrs Sharp, are you ill?'

'No. Just the tune seemed familiar.'

She saw the glance between her friends.

'Anyhow,' Alice said to Jane, 'I need to find Arthur and get him home before he has any more ale. And you and Thomas can take Mrs Sharp home.' Alice climbed over the rail and off the cart. 'I'll see you tomorrow evening, Mrs Sharp. We've sewing to do.'

The blacksmith pulled up at Dr Soames's house and got down and took her hand as she stepped off the cart. Jane leaned from her seat and handed her the bonnet and red ribbons.

'Take that to Alice's tomorrow and she'll help you trim it.'

'But I have a bonnet.'

'It's too plain. Alice and I want you to have this. The colour will suit you.'

Red ribbons. She looked up as Reverend MacPherson came through the bedroom door and realized that tears were running down her cheeks. She wiped them away as she stood up.

'She is coughing again,' he said.

She nodded and turned to the blacksmith. 'I'll give her more medicine and then come for you.'

She went in to Jane and held her as she struggled for breath and coughed and choked. She talked quietly to her about that day last year at the fair, the sun shining, the men wrestling; about the red ribbons on the straw bonnet. When the opium had taken effect, she sponged Jane's face and cleared away the bloody cloths and pulled the bedcover carefully over her.

'Thank you,' Jane said, the blue lips barely moving.

'Thank you, my dear friend. I'll get Thomas.' She kissed Jane's forehead.

She brought him in, her arm on his.

And then she left them, the blacksmith lying beside his beloved wife, her thin hand hidden in his scarred and blackened one.

Reverend MacPherson stayed the night on the settle by the kitchen fire, sometimes reading his Bible, sometimes talking to her. They were easy now, had sat together so many times before, preparing for the ending.

It was the way here to be matter-of-fact about dying. She had learned this from Dr Soames. Even before the winter, she had realized that death was part of his daily work and it became hers: babies and mothers lost in childbirth; infants and children lost to the various fevers; men killed in accidents, trapped or trampled; all ages lost to sicknesses of the lungs; and some lucky old ones living out their years to pass quietly in the night. But the dead were mourned and the pain of loss was real; grief could be profound.

She sat by the fire and watched the flames, knowing she had watched and waited for death in the other place and it had been both different and the same. Shaking her head, she stood up and went to the bedroom door to check again. She could hear the blacksmith's deep voice speaking quietly to his Jane and she turned away.

'Will you take a drink of tea?' she asked Reverend MacPherson.

He smiled and nodded and they sat at the table for a while.

'We have never spoken of your past,' he said. His voice was kind; the question was not a challenge.

'No. There is very little to tell.'

'Do you want to tell me?'

She looked at him. Honesty was necessary in the dark waiting hours and made easy in the dim light from the fire.

'I don't know who I was, before. Before John Elliott found me on the moor.'

'How do you mean?'

'I have no real memory of it. I know some things, I can remember how to do things but . . . It is so hard to explain. Dr Soames had his friend from Edinburgh come to see me but he said—' She stopped and shrugged.

'So you do not remember your childhood, your parents?'

'No.'

'But how terrible. A terrible loss.'

'You are kind but I cannot mourn the loss of what I do not know.'

She could see his frown of concern in the firelight.

'I do mourn, though. But not so much now. The loss of myself, of who I was,' she said.

He nodded, saying nothing.

The Midwife

'When I was ill, at the farm, I used to have dreams and sometimes pictures would float into my head.'

'Pictures?'

'If I think of Alice Black, I can see a picture of her in my head. I can see her sewing by the fire in her kitchen.'

'Of course. Yes, we all do that.' He sounded relieved.

'I have none, almost nothing from before. So sometimes I see, I used to see, just a fragment of a picture but not what it meant.'

He looked at her, anxious now.

Perhaps too much honesty, she thought.

'But I am better now. I am very content in my work,' she said, using her brisk nurse's voice.

'And you have given great service to the people. You are well thought of, indeed, highly thought of.'

She could hear his relief.

'Thank you,' she said.

'I will pray for you.'

She thought, pray for me, whoever I am. But did not say it.

At the darkest hour she woke and walked past the sleeping minister to the bedroom. There was no sound, so she opened the door and walked into the quiet room. The blacksmith was kneeling beside the bed, still holding the cold hand. She held his shoulder for a few moments and then moved round the bed and touched the white and pulseless neck.

Reverend MacPherson went to tell Rose and old Mr Weddell, and Rose came back with him. Together she and Mrs Sharp washed Jane's so thin body, clothed her with the sky blue summer dress and put blue ribbons in her hair.

In the grey morning light, Mrs Sharp rode into Alnwick with Reverend MacPherson. There was only one comfort. In the end Jane's passing was gentle and quiet, as she had been.

20

London, February 1842

S now was falling heavily again, and Dr Borthwick decided to ride rather than risk the carriage. Hayward's relief at not having to drive was evident in his unusually quick saddling of the horse and willingness to advise about the best route to Gower Street on the slippery roads. Such information was usually withheld unless specifically requested. Dr Borthwick assumed it must be considered part of the accepted secrets of the trade, not for outsiders.

He still could not feel any real warmth for Hayward or his acerbic wife. They kept the household comfortable and well fed and Hayward never complained about the long waits when Dr Borthwick and Mrs Bates were busy with a patient. Both were always deferential and polite with his infrequent guests. But he was still not sure that they were always kind to Betty.

He was determined to get to the lecture at University College Hospital whatever the weather. The recent flurry of women needing his attention during birth had kept him so busy that he had hardly read the recent *Lancet*, let alone any of Mr Dickens's latest work. Added to which, the roads had been hard frozen for weeks and doubly treacherous after each new snowfall, making travel to his patients slow and difficult.

After one night-time delivery, a young woman with a breech baby, they had been forced to abandon the carriage as they got to the narrow streets near Mrs Bates's lodgings. He had sent Hayward back to stable the horses whilst he walked Mrs Bates to her home and then spent a most uncomfortable night there on a makeshift bed in the kitchen. At least it had been warm.

He frowned as he remembered the following morning. He had been woken by the kitchen skivvy, a thin girl in a shabby grey dress, as she came in to stoke the fire under the oven. She seemed unsurprised at finding a man in the kitchen, barely looking at him as she knelt down in front of the grate with the riddle. As he went out to the privy he said a quiet good morning and put a thrupenny bit beside her. She looked up quickly then, showing her deformed nose and notched teeth. Congenital syphilis, he thought, saddened.

He had been escorted by the landlady into the draughty dining room which was warmed only by a small fire in a large ornate grate. After a cold quarter-hour he had been joined by the ladies who had rooms in the house. There were six of them, all introduced to him as 'Mrs . . .' and all plainly dressed: the youngest was barely more than a girl and Mrs Bates was probably the oldest. Thin porridge was served with a flourish by the landlady from an ornate porcelain tureen. It was followed by surprisingly good bread of which each of the ladies got one thin slice but he, to his embarrassment, got two. He passed the butter to the landlady and watched the tiny sliver she took and how she watched that each of her tenants took the same. He caught Mrs Bates's glance as she, in turn, watched him. He smiled at her and she, unusually, did the same. A private exchange.

He had learned a little bit more about the women from Mrs Bates over the next few weeks: two milliners and two dressmakers, Mrs Bates, and a day-companion to an old, long-retired lawyer whose manservant looked after him at night. He was surprised only by the day-companion and then touched by the story Mrs Bates told him. The woman's husband had been the lawyer's clerk but had died, crushed by a fallen horse. The clerk and his wife had been kind, though always deferential, to the lawyer, a widower with no children. He in turn now provided for the clerk's widow. Mrs Bates was horrified at Dr Borthwick's suggestion that the widow would surely be better off living at the lawyer's house; she would certainly be better fed. It would, of course, not be proper; Mrs Bates had told him very firmly. He had said nothing more: her views on propriety were not to be challenged lightly.

The snowfall was lighter now, individual flakes drifting down. The horse slipped slightly from time to time but easily recovered her balance and plodded on. Beauty was large, a carriage horse, but very placid, and she suited Dr Borthwick who was the first to admit that he was an indifferent rider. They were well used to each other and she was always happier ridden than pulling the carriage. He patted her fondly and was ignored.

Turning on to Gower Street, the gas lights were very bright and the fresh snow sparkled. Beauty took herself into the line of horses and stood solidly as Dr Borthwick managed, he felt, a credibly smart dismount. A stable boy, with a sack draped over his head and shoulders, took the horse. Dr Borthwick thanked him and gave him a penny and then climbed the steps to the entrance of University College Hospital, brushing the snow from his waxed cape.

As he entered the large lecture theatre he saw his colleague Dr Atkins waving and went over and sat beside him. The audience were all medical men, soberly seated, prepared to listen with some cynicism to the latest defence of mesmerism by a Dr Braid from Manchester. Since Dr Elliotson's fall from grace three years ago, mesmerism had gone out of fashion. The public exhibitions, with galleries crammed to overflowing with curious spectators, were nowadays left to the surgeons wielding their dirty saws and scalpels.

'So, Borthwick, what do you think of it?' Dr Atkins asked.

'Mesmerism? I'm not sure.'

'I saw Dr Elliotson's last show here in '38.'

'Show?' Dr Borthwick raised his eyebrows slightly.

'Yes. It was a show. A spectacle. An embarrassment. It wasn't science.' Dr Atkins paused and then continued rather sadly. 'I studied under him, you know. He was a sound physician. But the animal magnetism idea. Well, it's discredited now. He appeared foolish.'

Dr Borthwick nodded, thinking for a while before he spoke.

'I have some knowledge of mesmerism. The doctor who demonstrated it was an Edinburgh man interested in memory. Very sound. It seemed to work. But it was very different, I think, from Dr Elliotson's theories. I gather Dr Braid's approach will also prove more scientific.'

'Well, in that case I will endeavour to listen with an open mind,' Dr Atkins said, smiling.

Dr Braid gave a quiet description of what he called 'hypnotism' which he said was 'attributable to a peculiar physiological state of the brain and the spinal cord'. He politely rejected any component of magnetism or unknown forces.

Dr Borthwick listened intently. The process of hypnotism which Dr Braid described was very familiar to him. He was thinking back, remembering, when he suddenly became aware of being watched. He looked across the lecture theatre.

To his horror, the very person in his memory was there, looking straight at him.

Dr Mackay of Edinburgh.

Too late, Dr Borthwick realized his jeopardy. He looked down quickly. He was in the middle of a bench and could not leave without drawing more attention to himself. He put his hands to his chin, covering as much of his face as possible, and stared fixedly at the lecturer.

Time passed unbearably slowly and he sat immobile, sweat starting to collect on his forehead. He realized the lecture was over when the clapping started. Looking down, he clapped vigorously and then turned to respond to Dr Atkins's comments. As the audience stood, he apologized, saying that he had to rush away – a patient to check on his way home – and tried to push through the crowd as he walked down the steps.

Dr Mackay was waiting for him in the hall.

'Dr Mackay, what a pleasure to see you in London,' he said, putting out his hand. 'We met in the north, some time ago.'

'Indeed, I remember it well,' Dr Mackay replied, equally calm.

They shook hands and then there was a pause. Before Dr Borthwick could decide what to do – and his options seemed severely limited – he heard Dr Preston's voice.

'Dr Borthwick, I did not realize you were interested in mesmerism. Perhaps you plan to mesmerize your patients? Another of your innovations?' His tone was smooth, but the sarcastic emphasis was explicit.

Dr Borthwick nodded and turned to Dr Mackay.

'Dr Mackay. May I introduce you to Dr Preston, a physician here in London. Dr Preston, this is Dr Mackay, an Edinburgh physician with an interest in mesmerism.'

They both bowed politely.

'You are a long way from home, Dr Mackay,' Dr Preston said.

'Indeed, yes. I have been staying the winter with my sister who lives here with her family. My nephew is alas gravely ill, and she wanted me near.' Dr Mackay's Edinburgh accent was muted.

'I am sorry to hear it. Will you be practising here in London?'

'No. I plan to return to Edinburgh as soon as the snow clears.'

Dr Preston smiled politely, his turf protected, and started to turn away but then turned back to Dr Borthwick.

'So, you worked with Dr Mackay in Edinburgh, Dr Borthwick.'

There was a pause, too long a pause. Was this to be the end?

'I did not have that honour,' Dr Borthwick said. 'I met Dr Mackay as a friend of my mentor when I worked in the north.'

And then, too quickly this time, Dr Mackay added, 'Yes, Dr Borthwick worked for my esteemed friend Dr Soames in Alnwick.'

Dr Preston made a little grunting noise and then bowed again as he turned away and left. He went briskly and, to Dr Borthwick, the rapid steps sounded to be filled with satisfaction.

'I said too much. I'm sorry,' Dr Mackay said.

Dr Borthwick smiled, a small, sad smile, and he saw the recognition again in the other man's face. 'If you have the time, Dr Mackay, perhaps you would do me the honour of joining me in some late supper?'

They rode through the new snow; it was quiet, the air still. As they turned into the narrower streets the gas lamps became infrequent. Dr Borthwick turned his head to speak over his shoulder. 'Careful here, there are deep ruts in the ice under the snow.' His voice seemed almost shockingly loud, echoing between the dark buildings.

'Indeed. But this nag's steady enough, though she'd not get up if she fell. Poor old lady,' Dr Mackay said, riding close in behind him. Then added, 'Good man that my brother-in-law is, he keeps a sorry stable.'

As Dr Borthwick had expected, Betty was thrown into confusion by his arrival home with a visitor and having to relight the fire in the study and, worst of all, having to convey his request to Mrs Hayward for some soup and toasted cheese. After nine o'clock at night!

Once they were settled in the study, Dr Mackay leaned forward and looked at him, staring intently at his face.

'I didn't realize straight away. I saw you entering the lecture hall and was trying to remember who you were, a young doctor trained in Edinburgh, perhaps? But when you looked directly at me . . .' He shrugged.

'I saw the recognition. I suppose I'm always looking for it. Waiting to be unmasked. Always,' Dr Borthwick said.

There was a silence. He picked up the poker and moved the coals. The flames flared for a moment.

'How long have you been . . . ?' Dr Mackay raised his hands, gesturing towards him.

'Dr Borthwick?'

Dr Mackay nodded, steepling his fingers together now, deeply intent.

'Since I left Alnwick. The day I wrote to you.'

'I was grateful for your letter. Grateful but deeply saddened to know of Dr Soames's passing. Albert was a good man. A good friend.'

Dr Borthwick turned to the fire again. He was determined to be in control. He blinked hard, stopping the tears, and his voice was calm. 'He was the best of men. I try to be like him. To be a good doctor and a good man.'

'So, you live always as a man now?'

'Yes. I am Dr Borthwick, *accoucheur*.'

There was a knock on the door and Mrs Hayward herself brought in the supper tray, trailed by Betty. Dr Borthwick helped put down the tray.

'Mrs Hayward, I am sorry to give you so much trouble so late in the evening. This is Dr Mackay, a friend from Edinburgh whom I had not realized to be in London. I have invited him to stay.' He turned to Dr Mackay. 'Mrs Hayward is very good to me, preparing excellent meals at all hours when my duties disturb the household.'

Dr Mackay stood up and gave Mrs Hayward a small bow which she acknowledged graciously.

'Come along, Betty, we have a bed to make up and a fire to lay,' she said, pushing the girl to the door.

They ate supper almost in silence, Dr Mackay showing the same concentration on his food as he had done in Alnwick. Dr Borthwick remembered it as if he, not Mrs Sharp, had been there. Usually now he thought of Mrs Sharp's life as a story that she had told him, that she was someone he knew well. Not himself, not any more. He started to eat, sure he would feel sick, but then realized he was hungry.

Dr Mackay cleared away the last piece of cheese, then pushed back his chair.

'You eat like a man, admittedly one with much better manners than mine, and your voice is convincing. How long did it take?'

'About three months after I got here. I'd practised the walking and voice before, at night in Alnwick. Modelled on Reverend MacPherson, though not his accent. Did you meet him?'

'Yes. Goodness. A man of the cloth. And a good Scot.' Dr Mackay shook his head, smiling, and continued. 'When Albert asked me to see Mrs Sharp, I wasn't convinced about the amnesia. I arrived in Alnwick intending to show she was a fraud, but she wasn't. But then where had she . . . ? You. Where had you learned midwifery and medicine?'

'I almost don't think of that now. I live as I am. Dr Borthwick, Edinburgh graduate.'

'But you're not Dr Borthwick. He died.'

Dr Borthwick shook his head and said nothing.

'Albert and I corresponded after I had seen you. He was more and more certain, Mrs Sharp, that you must have studied medicine. There was a medical student at Edinburgh, after Albert's and my time there, thought by some to be a woman in disguise. He graduated in 1812, I think. Dr James Barry. He is now an Army surgeon of some repute. But there is still talk. Albert thought you must have done the same, before you were ill, before you were Mrs Sharp.'

Dr Borthwick shook his head again. 'Perhaps. I don't know. That is the honest truth.'

They were interrupted by Betty coming in for the tray. He thanked her and told her they would need nothing more and that she should go to bed. Restless, he stood up and put more coals on the fire and stayed watching until the flames leapt up again. He sat back down and faced Dr Mackay.

Dr Mackay leaned forward again. 'And your memories of before, I think you called it your other place?'

'I've given that up. I never think of it. Whoever I once was found knowledge somewhere. I accept what I know. I try to do what I am certain of.' Dr Borthwick paused. 'I think that I would have gone mad, else.' His voice was level and he looked directly at Dr Mackay.

'And are you good at what you do? Are you a good *accoucheur*?'

'In truth?'

'Yes.'

'In truth, I am better than the rest. It is not good enough, I know that. But I am the best of what there is.'

Dr Mackay looked at his fingers for a while. Dr Borthwick waited.

'Are you content?' Dr Mackay said.

'I am useful. I have friends.'

'But what about marriage. Even children?'

'I have made the best choice I can. What would you do? Given a free choice, which would you rather be, a woman or a man?'

Dr Mackay sighed. 'I see how my sister lives. When we were children she was as quick as me with her letters, a lively mind but . . . Well, she married and has seemed happy enough. But she has nothing to distract her, nothing to turn to when her son dies. She would have benefited from more involvement in the world, more opportunity to use her talents. I can see that now.'

Dr Borthwick managed a smile. 'You should meet a friend of mine, Mrs Johnson. She has very strong views on the education of girls. And Lady Gasgoine, a woman with some power, is plotting medical education for women when her hospital is built.'

'They are right. There is also talk in Edinburgh of training women doctors to attend to women. But it is still too soon, I think.' He frowned. 'It is often my younger colleagues who are most opposed to even a discussion of it.'

Both men sat quiet for a while. Dr Borthwick knew he had to ask the question. They had both avoided it for long enough.

'I know you are in a difficult position. But I have made my case. Will you keep my secret?' He stopped and took a breath then smiled, without difficulty now. 'Will you let me have my life?'

'I have been trying to think what Albert would do. I know how much he cared for Mrs Sharp. And I keep hearing his voice, what he said about her, about you. That he couldn't understand how you were there but what you were doing was right. I suppose that's as true now. I'll protect you as he did.'

'Thank you.'

They shook hands and, to carry them over the moment, Dr Borthwick said, 'I have brandy in the cupboard. I think we should toast our absent friend.'

'And the education of women. And that I might live to see a woman graduate from Edinburgh University!' Dr Mackay said, making it easy for them both.

Dr Borthwick lay awake, regretting the number of other things that they had found to toast between them, half a bottle of brandy's worth. Each time he closed his eyes he would see Dr Preston's smug smile. How much had he heard? Dr Preston must have seen the initial constraint between Dr Mackay and himself. He had almost run out of the hall, eager to do what? Round and round chased the thoughts until he finally fell asleep; he woke still feeling the touch of a warm hand on his and hearing the waves, smelling the sea. He had not knowingly dreamed of the other place for over a year.

He turned on to his side and squeezed his eyes to clear the tears, then opened them again. It was almost completely dark in his bedroom, just the outline of the window in pale moonlight. There were few sounds in London in the deep night: the night-soil cart always at three o'clock of the morning, the occasional dog, less often a human shout. The house creaked sometimes but he knew those sounds well. What he feared were the memories he thought he had vanquished coming back.

He rolled over again and concentrated on his current patients in Duck Lane. He was due there tomorrow. More women arrived at the makeshift clinic every week and not just those that were pregnant. And then Eleanor, perhaps she might be there. Not Eleanor, he must not think of Eleanor. He sighed and turned to the moonlit window and closed his eyes but the image of Dr Preston was back, the fleshy lips curving in a satisfied smile.

The following morning Dr Mackay managed porridge followed by ham and eggs with an enthusiasm which Dr Borthwick felt unable to share. They parted with a firm handshake and Dr Mackay's solemn commitment to protect Dr Borthwick's identity; Dr Borthwick in turn agreed to become a regular correspondent on medical matters.

Two lonely men making the best of it.

21

Northumberland, February 1939

Mrs Sharp returned from dressing ulcers and examining the undertaker's wife, who was cheerfully pregnant for the fourth time, to the welcome smell of Mrs Godwin's mutton pie. She washed her hands carefully with the lavender soap, giving yet another mental thanks to Dr Soames, this time for her soft skin, no longer chapped and broken even during the long winter. Passing through the kitchen, she exchanged pleasantries with Mrs Godwin and noted with pleasure that there was a tray of jam tarts ready to go in the oven.

She walked briskly into the dining room and stopped, appalled.

He was sitting bolt upright in his chair, gasping through blue lips, unable to call for help. She rushed to him, calling out for Jenny, and started loosening his cravat.

'Oh, Dr Soames, my dear, I'm here now. We'll get Dr Selby to come and see you again. Jenny, go for Dr Soames's medicine. It's by his bed, bring it to me. Then get Peter to run for Dr Selby. Go now, quickly.'

*

Dr Selby arrived after the worst of the attack had passed. He examined Dr Soames and, after much muttering, prescribed a bloodletting to be done once Dr Soames was in bed. He would come back in half an hour. He gave her detailed instructions in his slow voice. Keeping her eyes firmly on the ground, she nodded politely, desperately trying to be the quiet and composed upper servant he no doubt thought she should be. As she escorted him to the door, she seethed silently: she knew him well now, the apothecary turned general practitioner who did not even trouble to understand the inadequate treatments he used; the uncaring pedlar of the latest fashionable pills and potions. But Dr Middlemass in Alnmouth was bedridden with gout, so there was no one else.

She helped Peter to carry Dr Soames up the stairs. He was drowsy after the large dose of laudanum she had given him, and they undressed his long, flaccid body with difficulty. They propped him up carefully on pillows and waited for Dr Selby to return. He arrived promptly and looked round the room before he turned to Dr Soames, ready to find fault. The letting bowl was on the table with a selection of lancets and a fleam, all laid out on a starched white cloth.

'I thought it would be easier to use Dr Soames's own lancets,' Mrs Sharp murmured, head modestly lowered.

Dr Selby made a low snorting sound in response, but he did use one of the clean lancets, much to her relief.

Afterwards she sat with Dr Soames in the quiet room, watching him sleep. This was his second episode of severe chest pain in a week, and she knew from how rapidly the bottle of his own prescription tincture was emptying that he must have had other attacks. She was endlessly grateful to him, but she had to decide what to do.

Dr Soames's daughter, Mrs Thorpe, neither liked nor trusted her and would eject her from the house as soon as decently possible after her father died. Dr Selby certainly would not tolerate her doing any work in Alnwick once she was no longer protected by the reputation and good nature of Dr Soames. But she could not leave him whilst he was ill and, being sure that his daughter would not make any provision for the servants, she would be abandoning them too. And where could she go?

Much later, long after she had heard Peter lock up, she woke suddenly from a dream, perhaps of the other place, to Dr Soames's soft snores. He was sleeping deeply but his pulse was still irregular, faint and fluttering under her fingers as she leaned over him.

She sat, trying to recall the dream, then walked over to the large chest. She hesitated, then took out a shirt and cravat and placed them on the chair. Now detached, trance-like, she turned to the press and lifted out trousers and a waistcoat. She removed her dress and underskirts and unlaced her stays and, with her hair pulled tight against her head, she studied herself in the long mirror. Her face was white in the flickering candlelight. Images of the other place crowded behind her in the glass, whispering ghosts gathering. She shook her head angrily, forcing herself to concentrate on the now, on this task. She moved more quickly, pulling on the trousers and shirt, fingers fumbling with the heavy fastenings on the waistcoat. She looked again in the mirror. Then stepped back, surprised.

Habituated now to seeing a woman in voluminous skirts, she saw instead a pale man staring back at her, frowning.

She changed back, putting on Mrs Sharp again. Mrs Sharp went over to Dr Soames and checked his pulse, still weak and irregular, and then sat down beside him.

The next evening, while Mrs Godwin was sitting upstairs with Dr Soames, she went into his study and looked through his papers. She was searching for his last assistant's certificates. The credentials of the young doctor who had died of consumption two years ago. She found them easily, two elegant parchments fastened in a leather folder, his name embossed on the front. She took out a clean sheet of paper to write a letter of recommendation from Dr Soames about this Dr Borthwick. About a dead man.

She was still writing when Peter came for her: Arthur Black was in the kitchen and he was asking to see her. She blotted the page and folded it away.

Arthur was standing by the stove, taking his weight on his good leg but otherwise radiating health. His curls were tipped with frost, standing round his face like a halo, and snow was falling off his boots.

'I hear as Dr Soames is very poorly,' he said.

She nodded. 'His heart is failing badly.'

'Will he get better?'

'I don't think so. No. It won't be long. A few weeks at most.'

'Dr Selby's talking of him as dead already and telling folk as they should see him now.'

'I know. Old Mr Jameson wouldn't see me today.'

'What'll you do?'

She looked away, out of the window at the moonlit sky.

'Stay and nurse him for now. Try to make sure Peter and Jenny are provided for. Then leave before Mrs Thorpe has a chance to throw me out.' She looked at him again, frowning. 'I'll not give her the pleasure.'

He leaned forward and patted her hand. 'You know that there's a place for you with me and Alice for as long as you want.'

'Thank you, Arthur. But I need to work. Dr Selby will drive me out.'

'Aye, he would that. Man's fool enough. What about going up to Edlingham, setting up as midwife for the villages.'

She shook her head.

'Thomas Weddell's a good man. He'll be needing a new wife soon enough,' he said.

A fleeting thought of that strong body, but she would never risk pregnancy in this place. Not the ignorance and incompetence. Not the pain. Never. She managed to smile as she shook her head again. 'He needs someone younger than me. He'll have no difficulty finding a wife.'

Arthur looked at her, his gaze steady. 'Alice said as you wouldn't stay. I've brought you money. It's not much but'll keep you for a few weeks in food and lodgings.'

'I can't take it. You've done enough for me, you and Alice.'

He laughed then and put a small parcel on the table. 'Alice and Mother'll do for me if you don't take it.'

He put his hands on her shoulders and gave her his bright smile and then he kissed her very gently on each cheek. 'From Alice and me. God's speed wherever you go. But come see us afore you leave.'

She managed to smile back. 'I will. Thank you. For . . .' She shrugged. Words were not enough. 'For being like a brother, and Alice a sister. For being my family.'

He nodded and then he was gone, and the room felt cold and empty.

Over the next few days she appropriated three sets of under- wear, shirts, trousers and waistcoats. She altered them in order both to fit and to conceal her body, stitching quietly in the evenings as she sat by Dr Soames's bed and he slept. Hat and topcoat would have to wait until the last minute, as would boots. His boots were too big, but she had tried them and could walk in them with thick socks.

The days passed as she nursed Dr Soames gently, lovingly, helping him each afternoon to sit out of bed for an hour or so and talk of when he would be back at work. She amused him with stories of those patients who would still see her, their foibles and fussing, and always took care to seek his advice.

Dr Soames had many visitors: Dr Selby, of course, who made less and less effort to conceal his disdain for her as his patient weakened; Reverend MacPherson who prayed intently with Dr Soames every day, genuinely distressed by his obvious decline; his friends, who were saddened, and then others of the gentry who stayed just long enough to say they had been. Mrs Thorpe had arrived in the first week, in a flurry of exclam- ations and anxieties. She stayed just long enough to be sure the will was in order, Mr Sealy visiting twice for that purpose.

The main outpouring of concern, however, came from his patients. At each house Mrs Sharp visited there were questions and often tears. Each day Mrs Godwin opened the kitchen door to find their gifts: jars of jam and fruit and pickles on the step, a skinned rabbit tied up on the gate, even a live chicken in a wooden box. She would call Mrs Sharp to see, for these were precious gifts: food was very scarce now after the long and bitter winter. The hardest to bear was the single hen's egg wrapped very carefully in a pad of wispy sheep's wool. They both knew that someone with so little would go hungry for the giving.

Mrs Sharp tried to be at home when Reverend MacPherson called and would ask him to take coffee or tea or even sometimes dinner. She knew she was almost redeemed in his eyes, and Mrs Godwin was always pleased to sustain a member of the clergy. Every time she saw him, Mrs Sharp studied Reverend MacPherson carefully: how he walked; his tone of voice and the phrases he used; how he took his tea and stood from sitting; everything that seemed male and particular to a man of education and modest means. Each night, when Peter or Mrs Godwin were sitting with Dr Soames, she practised in her room.

Two weeks after his collapse, Doctor Soames asked her to sit with him a while longer, late into the evening. Leaning forward from the heaped pillows, he took her hand, his fingers cold and swollen against hers.

'Mrs Sharp, when I was taken ill you called me my dear. I heard it and I welcomed it. For you are very dear to me.' His head dropped back as he struggled for breath.

She moved closer to the bed, so he could see her face. So she could see his. He smiled and squeezed her hand gently.

'You have been as a daughter to me and brought me great happiness.'

'And you have been such a good father to me,' she managed as her throat tightened and tears welled.

'My dear, we both are aware that I am extremely ill, that my heart is failing, so forgive me for being frank. My plan was to leave you a reasonable allowance in my will, but my daughter and lawyer have persuaded me that I can only leave you the same amount as the servants. To avoid gossip and scandal. Indeed, they wish to protect your reputation even if that leads you to penury.' Pausing for breath he squeezed her hand to stop her speaking.

'You know where the money is kept. I want you to go now and take all but ten pounds. That's how much they think is there, but there is a very great deal more, over three hundred, enough to live respectably for a year or two. Take it. There is money enough in the bank for my daughter and the servants. I have provided well for them. Take the money and whatever else you need. Anything. Leave here as soon as you can.' He collapsed back on to the pillows, lips blue with effort.

She held his hand until his breathing began to settle and then leaned over and kissed his forehead. 'You are the best of men and you have saved me again. I owe you my life certainly, and probably my soul. I'll stay with you until you no longer need me. I'll not leave until the end.' She stopped as the tears ran down her cheeks.

Then, for a long moment they looked at each other, acknowledging all the unsaid words.

*

Three days later Dr Albert Soames died in his sleep in the darkest hour of the night with Mrs Sharp holding his hand.

She sat beside him in the new silence after the last rattling gasp had faded and waited a while, then closed his eyes and pulled the sheet across him, folded to the chin. She trimmed the lamp, leaving it to burn low, and looked at him, no longer listening for the laboured breathing, no longer feeling for the weak pulse, no longer able to help him. Just one more task to do.

She went downstairs and through the kitchen and out across the yard to Peter's room, the candle steady in her hand. He answered on her first knock and opened the door, fully dressed. When she tried to speak, no words came so Peter said them for her.

'Dr Soames is dead.'

She nodded and swallowed down the gasping, aching sob.

'You'll be leaving then?'

She nodded.

'You'll be missed. But Mrs Thorpe's a hard and grasping woman. Best you go.'

She spoke then, voice shaking and the pain in her throat worsening.

'I'll get the morning coach. I don't want anyone else to know.' She paused as he nodded, grave and quiet.

'Before, though, will you help me . . .' She stopped, throat closed again, then whispered, 'Will you help me to lay him out? It's the last thing we can do for him.'

*

The Midwife

Four hours later, as the first grey light appeared, a well-dressed gentleman caught the first coach to Newcastle, his large bags causing some delay as they were hauled up and strapped on to the roof. He spoke very little, other than to apologize to his fellow passengers for his bags in a hoarse voice. That, and the heavy muffler round his throat and chin, suggested a recent cold, so they left him to sleep.

22

London, March 1842

Dr Borthwick wiped his pen and blotted the last page of the letter, then lined it up with the others. All his London life summarized in a pile of correspondence: to the Swans, to Eleanor and to Charles; to his patients and Dr John Atkins; to Lady Burnsfield; to Mrs Bates, hers with a parcel of books.

And beside them the letter from Alice Black.

Everything he was taking with him was packed now in the locked trunk in the hall and here in the bags beside him. He just needed to call in Mr and Mrs Hayward and explain that the rent and their wages were covered for three more months; to tell Betty that she was to go to Lady Burnsfield's household; to leave, knowing all was in order. He almost laughed, knowing he was on the edge of a precipice, that nothing had ever been in order. But he had done what he could. Some consolation in that, he thought.

He picked up Alice's letter, delivered yesterday by the evening post, addressed as always to Mrs Sharp, care of Dr Borthwick. The handwriting was Alice's neat schoolgirl script, but the words were Arthur's, straightforward, a warning. A clerk from a Newcastle lawyer was in Alnwick asking questions about Dr Borthwick, about how long ago he had died. Peter, working for Reverend MacPherson now, had seen the clerk in the cemetery looking at the headstone.

Dr Borthwick folded the letter and put it in his pocket. He had been making plans for weeks now since Dr Preston saw him with Dr Mackay. It was time to leave London.

He heard the bell and then the sound of the front door opening. He stood up, mouth drying, and waited. Betty knocked and rushed straight in before stopping, face flushing.

He kept his voice level. 'What is it?'

'There's Mr Darrow with that lady in the hall. They said as you must be interrupted at once though I said as you were not receiving visitors.' She looked at her feet.

'Thank you, Betty. Please show them in. But listen carefully now. If there are any other callers you *must* say that I have gone out. Call Cook if there is any difficulty.'

He had expected Mrs Swan to be with Charles, but it was Eleanor. Eleanor. Why?

Charles spoke immediately, eschewing all manners. 'Dr Preston has started another rumour. It's very serious.'

'What more can he say? Pederasty, perhaps, to add to lasciviousness with my patients? Well, those few I have not let die by my incompetence? How do I have the time?' Dr Borthwick meant to sound lighter, but he could taste the bitterness on his tongue and feel the colour rising in his cheeks.

Eleanor moved towards him with a sound of distress as Charles responded.

'Worse. He's claiming he has evidence that you're not Dr

Borthwick. Nor even a doctor. That you're a fraud and a trickster. He's said to be going to the magistrate this morning, now.'

Charles looked at him and he watched Charles's expres-
sion change as the silence lengthened, as the expected denial
wasn't made.

Eleanor reached out and took Dr Borthwick's hand.

He spoke directly to her. 'Dr Borthwick is real. Was real.
He was a young doctor working in a small town in the north.
But he died of consumption about four years ago. I never met
him but I took his name and his certificates. Dr Preston is
correct. I am an imposter.'

'But you are a doctor,' Eleanor said, her face still calm.

'I know what my mentor taught me and much more
besides. I consider myself a doctor. But I have no certificates
of my own.'

'I don't understand,' said Charles. 'You did so much for my
cousin. You're well spoken of. But . . .' He turned away and sat
down heavily in a chair by the fire, staring at the flames.

'Why?' said Eleanor, taking Dr Borthwick's other hand as
she moved in front of him, her eyes on his.

'I wanted to live a useful life. To help,' he said. And then,
'Because I knew how to.'

He watched the tears well up and then brim over and run
down her white cheeks. Her fingers were tight on his, but her
body was held slightly away, different from the last time. Did
she know?

'You could have been safe with me in Winchester. Dr Preston would have left you alone there,' she said.

'It would have involved you in the deception.'

'You could still marry me. I am very well provided for. We can move far away. Go abroad.'

Charles pushed back his chair and turned to face him again, leaning forwards. They were both watching him intently now, two people he respected, perhaps loved, but never as lovers. The urge to tell the truth, to tell his story, was growing now, tangible in his gut and chest. But when he spoke, his voice was calm.

'You would do that, knowing I'm a sham?' he said to Eleanor.

She looked at him, her face very still, and nodded.

He smiled then, and moved his hands to her shoulders, holding them gently. 'Thank you, my dear Eleanor. But I must leave London alone. Today.'

She lifted her hands to his face and ran her fingers over his cheeks and chin and then across his lips; then she lifted her mouth to him. She kissed him softly, her lips barely touching his.

'Who are you?' she said, leaning back but still watching his face.

He looked back at her, at the slight frown, the hazel eyes, the tears still pooled on her lower lids. 'I don't know,' he said. 'I don't know and that is the truth before God.' He turned away, throat aching, trying to hold down the sobs.

'Who were you then, before Dr Borthwick?' Charles's voice now, very quiet.

Dr Borthwick turned back to face them both. He gave in, gave in to the tide, let it engulf him. 'Before I came to London I was Mrs Sharp, a nurse and midwife. I was, I am, a woman.'

And then *she* wept.

*

It was Eleanor who took control. She went out into the hall and called for Betty to bring some tea as Dr Borthwick was feeling slightly unwell. By the time Betty brought in the tray they were sitting discussing the weather, so cold and dark with spring seeming still so far away. Dr Borthwick was able to thank Betty as usual, in a calm voice.

Dr Borthwick did not even try to resist Eleanor's plan to take her back with them in the Swans' carriage to the Swans' house. She listened, disconnected, as Charles said that the magistrate might summons Dr Borthwick that afternoon, might even send a constable, so they must leave now. Passively she watched as her trunk and bags were taken out to the carriage. Then, in her final act as Dr Borthwick, she said goodbye to the servants. Betty cried.

In the end it was all too quick.

No one spoke as the carriage moved slowly along the cobbled streets through the freshly falling snow. Dr Borthwick closed her eyes, seeing instead the early morning sun over the sea and the fields hard-frosted as she travelled from Alnwick towards Newcastle. Three years ago. Escaping then, as she was now.

It had taken her six days to reach London: the morning stagecoach from Alnwick, then stopping every two or three hours to change horses, and nights at the coaching inns in Durham then Doncaster then Stamford, Peterborough and St Albans. Endless bone-jarring miles.

Peter had warned her about the porters; about being overcharged for food, for drink, for a room; about bags being stolen. At each stop she got out and checked her luggage, watching it carefully as other trunks and packages were removed and the horses were changed, only then going for food and to use the privy.

That first night she sat on the surprisingly clean bed, her trunk pushed against the door of the small room. She rested her small mirror against the lamp and inspected her chin and cheeks. Both were already reddened and dry. She took a jar from her opened bag and poured a little of the mixture of coarse sand and salt into her palm. She rubbed it across her face, where the beard should be, the face in the mirror scowling slightly at the sting and at the short curls hanging on to the forehead. Cutting off her hair and then watching it burn had been Mrs Sharp's final act.

The young man's face looked back at her.

She could do this.

Her confidence grew as the miles passed and she shed Mrs Sharp and became Dr Borthwick, the young country doctor travelling to London to increase his skills, perhaps make his fortune.

He started to converse with his fellow passengers, apologizing for his hoarse voice, the result of a severe cold, a final present from one of his patients. And they would regale him with their tales of ailments and journeys and families to be seen and daughters to be married. He realized that a young doctor was for them the ideal travelling companion, there to listen to long tales of sickness, to be told secrets in whispered asides. He did not need to speak; just to be attentive and nod gravely from time to time.

*

They arrived at the Swans' house and now Charles was helping her down from the carriage. Helping her, no longer him.

Mrs Swan leapt to her feet as they were shown into the morning room. 'Dr Borthwick. I'm so pleased you are here. But you look so tired. Please come here and sit by the fire.'

'Dr Borthwick is unwell. I'll take him upstairs whilst Charles explains,' Eleanor said. She reached out and touched Mrs Swan's arm briefly. 'Then, Abigail, please come up to my room.'

Mr Swan started to speak but Charles shook his head.

Eleanor took Dr Borthwick's arm, still in control, and they walked slowly upstairs to Eleanor's room. She sat Dr Borthwick in a chair by the window. Dr Borthwick leaned back and watched, numb and unthinking, as Eleanor started to pull clothes out of a chest by the bed.

After a few minutes Mrs Swan came in, closing the door behind her and then leaning against it. She was pale. 'Is it true?' she asked, looking at Dr Borthwick.

'Yes.'

'What will you do?'

Dr Borthwick shook her head.

Eleanor looked up, shaking out a full-length black mourning veil.

'Abigail, we need to be quick. The magistrate might already be at Dr Borthwick's house. He'll be here next.'

'But what? What can we do?' Mrs Swan said.

'My mourning black will be too tight and short, but we could put the bodice unlaced over your evening black and drop the shirts down. The veil will cover it.'

Mrs Swan looked at Dr Borthwick, uncertain.

Dr Borthwick smiled, a small sad smile. 'I am to be a woman again?' she asked Eleanor.

'It's the safest for now. We must leave London. We'll go to Winchester, to my house and then you—' She stopped and took a deep breath. 'Then you can decide what you want to do.'

Eleanor turned to Mrs Swan. 'Please, Abigail. Help us.'

They waited as Dr Borthwick undressed, Eleanor folding her jacket and neckcloth. Dr Borthwick turned away and took off her shirt and then unwrapped the binding cloth from her breasts with practised ease, rolling it neatly. When she had finished she turned back to face them.

Eleanor handed her a long robe.

'I'll find you some undergarments,' said Mrs Swan, her cheeks flushed now.

Dr Borthwick pulled on the robe and then turned away again to undo her trouser buttons.

'Do you have padding in the trousers?' said Eleanor. 'I thought, I thought, well, I felt . . .'

Dr Borthwick heard Mrs Swan's gasp. She took off her trousers and, robe carefully fastened, faced them both. 'Yes,' she said, holding the trousers out to Eleanor who was blushing darker now than Mrs Swan.

Eleanor took the trousers and then felt the front and found the sewn-in pouch. She pulled out the stuffed linen shape and held it out on her palm. She gasped and dropped it and all three of them looked at it, lying palely on the dark rug. There was a moment of silence and then Dr Borthwick felt a terrible urge to laugh. She gave in and felt the first snort, and put her hands to her mouth. Eleanor reached out for her and the three women sat on the bed and laughed. Then Eleanor held her as she wept again.

They dressed Dr Borthwick in the hastily pinned-together dress. Mrs Swan brushed back her short hair and fastened it under a black lace cap and then clipped on a false front with side ringlets. Dr Borthwick sat, a doll.

Eleanor stood in front of her with the veil draped over her arms. 'Who was Mrs Sharp?' she said gently.

Dr Borthwick looked up at her, the cap and hairpiece feeling unreal. 'Me. Just me. For a while. Arthur Black was my first patient in Alnwick and he named me. But I'm not her now.'

'Before her?' Eleanor said.

'I don't know. I have no memory of life before I woke on a farm on Alnwick Moor.'

'So, what will we call you? You need a name just for now.'

'I don't know.'

She could feel them exchanging glances.

'You must have a name,' Mrs Swan said.

Dr Borthwick shook her head. The tears filled her eyes again. She closed them.

Her hands were taken hold of very gently and she heard Mrs Swan's voice.

'Think of this as giving birth. There are things that must be done, painful things. Come and look at yourself in the mirror. Find out who you are now.'

Dr Borthwick looked in the mirror. No ghosts, just a tall woman in a black silk dress, and frilled cap with ringlets framing her pale face. Then the answer came easily, as if she had always known. 'I would like to be called Elizabeth. Mrs Elizabeth Mackay née Soames. The widow of a Dr Mackay. Dr Soames's daughter as she might have been. As I might have been.'

Mr and Mrs Swan were taking tea with their guests in the drawing room when the footman came in and spoke quietly to Mr Swan. Mr Swan left the door ajar as he went out into the hall and Mrs Elizabeth Mackay could hear the magistrate introduce himself, his constable and Dr Preston. She watched the colour drain from Eleanor's face. Mrs Swan turned towards her. 'As I was saying, Mrs Mackay, our gardener swears by tea leaves as a tonic for roses and indeed Charles has told me there is a scientific basis for—' She stopped and raised her eyebrows charmingly as her husband entered the room.

'Sir Jeremy, Dr Preston, may I introduce my wife, Mrs Swan, her friends Mrs Eleanor Johnson and Mrs Elizabeth Mackay, and our cousin Mr Charles Darrow,' he said.

Charles rose and bowed, the ladies remaining seated.

'Charles, Sir Jeremy Gasgoine is magistrate in this borough and he is asking about your and Mrs Johnson's meeting with Dr Borthwick this morning,' Mr Swan continued.

'I hope no accident has befallen our dear friend Dr Borthwick?' Charles said.

'Indeed not. I am just keen to know his whereabouts,' Sir Jeremy said. 'His servants stated he left with you this morning seemingly with no intention to return.'

Elizabeth Mackay watched through her heavy black veil.

She saw Dr Preston's eyes slide over her and then away. She was of no importance, a widow in deep mourning, of little possible interest to him.

'Dr Borthwick had made no secret of his plans to his friends,' Charles said, frowning at Dr Preston. He looked back to Sir Jeremy. 'By prior arrangement, Mrs Johnson and I visited him this morning to say our farewells and to take him to the Golden Cross. Mr Swan had kindly given us use of his carriage, better to convey Dr Borthwick and all of his luggage. He is travelling today to France for a period of study with Professor Villeneuve, an *accoucheur* of great renown. He feels there is nothing more he can learn from London doctors. Indeed, some of them do not welcome him as a colleague.'

'Thank you for that explanation, Mr Darrow. I do not need to trouble you or Mr and Mrs Swan any further.'

'I assume this can be confirmed by your coachman, Mr Swan?' Dr Preston said, interrupting Sir Jeremy.

There was a silence as Sir Jeremy looked deliberately round the room, his gaze resting for a moment on Mrs Mackay. She thought she saw the briefest of smiles as he turned and then bowed politely to Mr Swan.

'There is of course no need to trouble your servants or further incommode your guests. Clearly, even if regrettably, Dr Borthwick has left London. Mrs Swan, my apologies again for disturbing you. Ladies, gentlemen, good day.'

Elizabeth Mackay watched Dr Preston start to speak and then be silenced by the magistrate taking his arm firmly. She heard the whispered aside.

The Midwife

'No more, Dr Preston. You've got what you wanted,' Sir Jeremy said.

Which, of course, he had. Dr Borthwick was gone for ever.

Late that afternoon, the recently widowed Mrs Elizabeth Mackay set off for Winchester with her dear friend Mrs Eleanor Johnson. She was to live for a while with Mrs Johnson, who was herself not long out of mourning and returning home after a long visit to London. The widow, swathed in a long veil over her black mourning dress, leaned heavily on the arm of Mr Charles Darrow as he helped her into the carriage. Mr Darrow was to be their escort on the journey.

Part Three

23

Winchester, June 1842

This is who I am now: Mrs Elizabeth Mackay, widow of Dr Mackay and daughter of Dr Soames. This is how I am introduced to the ladies of Winchester when they call to view me. Their voices are hushed as they talk with Eleanor, letting their eyes slide towards me only when etiquette permits them to address me. I respond, with a small and modest nod of my veiled head, that Dr Mackay was indeed a well-respected physician in Edinburgh with a great interest in nervous disorders. A man most committed to the established Church and to his charitable work. At this point I let my eyes fill with tears and lift my veil just enough to dab at them with a lace-edged handkerchief. Eleanor, watching me, picks up the story of how dear Dr Mackay and her own beloved Reverend Johnson had known each other for many years and indeed that is how we met and became friends and now, alas, widows together.

I listen, the tears continuing to flow easily for all my dead: for Jane and Dr Soames, for the lost women and their lost babies, for the children in the alleys and courts. Easier still to weep for my dead selves, the ones I made and the ones I didn't, the ghosts in the mirror. To weep for the man whose face I never see, even in my dreams.

I am, I know, more than a little mad and I watch Eleanor watching me as the long days pass.

Charles Darrow left last week, the end of his final visit before he sails to Rio de Janeiro. I almost felt awake whilst he was here.

He asked me to marry him, the day before he left. Eleanor must have known: she made us take our morning walk without her, making some excuse about needing to agree menus with Cook. Charles and I walked through the cathedral close and then on down to the river and he spoke with enthusiasm of the cathedral, so grand; the sky, so blue; and then the willows, such a tender green. He tried hard to show me the bright world as he saw it.

We stopped at the mill, still working although the city has grown all around it, and he spoke with the miller, complimenting this and that. But the questions he asked were sensible and his interest genuine. That is his charm: his enthusiasm for life is real and he sees people kindly. It is also what puts him at risk.

On the way back, when he suggested that we sit for a moment and view the cathedral, I was already well prepared.

'Will you miss me when I'm gone on my travels?' he asked, with a smile.

'But of course. Your visits are a source of pleasure and diversion to Eleanor and to me. You know this.' I kept my voice light.

'But you are unhappy still,' he said.

'Less now, I think. Time will pass.'

'What will you do?'

'Survive. As I have done before.'

'You need more.'

I nodded, not looking at him. The tears lurked, ever ready to fall.

'Come with me.' His voice was gentle.

'Charles, you know I can't.' I looked down at Mrs Elizabeth Mackay's hands in the black lace gloves, fingers plucking at the seams, and I stilled them.

'You can. We still have time to marry and then sail together. We can work together. You had . . .' He paused. 'You have a great interest in plants.'

Had. Dr Borthwick had a great interest in plants. The visits to Kew. Those botanical drawings. Charles was talking to him, to Dr Borthwick, not to me.

But who am I? This woman swaddled in black crêpe and lace? The thoughts whirled and some sort of escape beckoned. It was attractive, to run away again. Again. But it would be wrong, for both of us. Where had my courage gone?

I tried to summon Mrs Sharp.

'Marriage is not for you, Charles,' I said, looking directly at him, still veiled.

'We are good friends. We can live as friends. With shared interests. I know men who are married who . . .'

I let the pause lengthen. Now was the time to end this. 'A sham marriage then, without consummation,' I said.

I could see the brown eyes, wide with sincerity, and the tiniest tug of amusement on the lips moving beneath the dark moustache. I could feel the flush across my neck. Then for a moment, he was there, his hand beside mine, and the salt smell of the sea. Then gone, and Charles's voice:

'Your frankness is always a joy. But it would not be a sham, not where there is genuine respect and affection. It would be more honest than most marriages.'

I pushed up my veil. 'Then let me be frank again. I find you intelligent and sincere, kind and charming. But you loved Dr Borthwick, and he is gone, dead. You know you cannot love me, as I am now, as I might want. In the end it will not be enough, not for you or for me. And there is Eleanor.'

He looked away for a while and I dropped my veil back over my face.

He stood up and held out his hand to me. 'Then you must be my sisters, you and Eleanor, and I will be your devoted brother,' he said.

The next day he said goodbye to us both. He held Eleanor's hands and kissed her gently on the cheek. Then he turned to me and I moved close to him and took his face in my hands and touched my lips to his. He closed his eyes and I knew he was kissing Dr Borthwick. I kissed a ghost.

Each morning I sit and read by the window, looking down over the garden. Eleanor has given me her best bedroom, large and airy with pale green walls, furniture of light-coloured wood and rugs patterned with yellows and greens. After we arrived she asked me to choose some pictures for the walls but I couldn't decide so she hung some watercolours of trees and flowers, things she perhaps thought would cheer me. They are overpainted and insipid, certainly not done by her. She is shy about her painting talent.

The Midwife

Today it is already warm and there is almost no movement in the air, the scent of early roses filling the room through the open window. The garden is both decorative and productive; Eleanor would have it no other way.

She knocks and marches in. I know her well now; she can walk into my room sympathetically or firmly or briskly or matter-of-factly. But marching in means she has something unpleasant to say. I pre-empt her. 'Good morning, Eleanor. Such a lovely day. I can already smell the roses.'

'Good morning, Elizabeth. Mrs Brown says you sent your breakfast tray down untouched.'

'Well, that is not the case. I ate some toast.'

'One half of one slice.' She emphasizes each word. 'It's not enough. Your new dresses are already hanging loose.'

'I'm sorry. I'll eat a good lunch.' Meekness is my only weapon. I have no energy to fight.

She comes across the bright room and sits opposite me at the small, round table. A fat, furry bee flies in and lands between us. Its legs are already heavy with balls of pollen and it moves sluggishly in the patch of sunlight. Then I am back watching Mrs Sharp's hands as they turn the material of the white cuffs and re-stitch them, fresh side out, as frugal Alice Black has taught her. Alice laughs at something, sitting at the wide table in the Blacks' kitchen, in the sunlight. She is stitching too, a long seam on rose-pink cotton cloth, a new dress to wear at the fair. But when Alice speaks I cannot hear her.

Eleanor is watching me, waiting until I stop daydreaming. When I look at her she smiles, a small, worried smile. I remember how much Dr Borthwick admired her courage.

'What do you want to do?' she says.

'Today?'

'Today, tomorrow, next month.'

'Charles spoke to you?'

She nods.

'You think I should have gone with him?' I ask.

For a moment her voice is scathing: 'No, of course not.' She pauses and leans towards me, intent now. 'I knew you would refuse, but better perhaps that than nothing each day.'

'Do you want me to leave?'

'No, never.'

So, now I must deal with this. I must find the energy. Again, I try to find Mrs Sharp. Never Dr Borthwick, not him, not with Eleanor.

'I will have to leave some time, you know that,' I say.

'No, this is your home now.'

'Eleanor, you need to marry, a good man who shares your interests, your religion, whom you can love.'

She looks out of the window for a moment and turns back, the little frown in place, her voice very quiet.

'I know what you are saying. But I have you. As Charles said, we can be sisters.'

She is, I know, innocent – perhaps even ignorant of many things. She does not really understand about Charles and his life. Religion is one of her foundations, and her God is unforgiving. I choose my words very carefully, making sure my voice is Elizabeth's voice, lighter than Dr Borthwick's was, gentler than Mrs Sharp's.

'What Dr Borthwick felt for you was very real, I can remember it. The words he said were true. But it is me now. He is gone and I am someone else.'

The Midwife

She is watching my face, my eyes, my mouth. Looking for him still.

I continue, saying what must be said, laying his ghost. 'You have helped me, cared for me, and you will always have my affection, my love as a sister. But you must let him go. Dr Borthwick is gone for ever. In bitter truth he died of consumption many years ago.'

We sit silent for a while and this time I am watching her, watching the uncovered brown hair and feeling that it is true, I am ready to be her sister. That this is love too, a possibility of hope.

She looks up at me, seeing me, a woman, seeing her tears reflected in mine.

'But he did love me?'

The right words come to me then, and I realize that they are mine. Not those of Mrs Sharp, not Dr Borthwick, not Elizabeth Mackay. Me. Whoever I may be. 'Yes, he loved you. As Mr Johnson did. Because you should be loved.'

She looks down, blinking back the tears.

'I don't understand Dr Borthwick and you,' she says.

'He was a choice I made. There was no other way for me to survive.'

She reaches out and squeezes my hand and then she lets go and walks silently away.

I eat lunch, a slice of raised cold pie, to please her and then I realize that I'm enjoying it. I take a second piece and smile at her.

'Are you out this afternoon?'

'Yes, I'm calling on the bishop's wife, Mrs Sumner. I want

the bishop's support for reading and writing classes for working women.'

'Would it be acceptable for me to accompany you?'

She looks at me in surprise and then looks at me again, more intently. 'Yes. But only if you put on your new gown and let Agnes sort your hair. Mrs Sumner will expect you to lift back your veil while you are in the house.'

Without thinking, I start to push the escaped hair under my black lace cap. A woman's gesture.

The bishop's wife is dressed with precision in grey bombazine, every hair properly fixed beneath a white lace cap which has been starched into immobility. She is, however, professionally kind, enquiring after my health and commiserating on the sad loss of Dr Mackay, even offering to include him in her prayers after being reassured that no friend of dear Reverend Johnson could be a nonconformist. I glance at Eleanor, concerned about the lies she tells for me, but she is already deep into the case for the education of working women. Mrs Sumner requires some convincing but Eleanor works hard.

'And what is your view, Mrs Mackay?' Mrs Sumner asks.

I feel a surge of energy, a certainty about what to say which I thought had gone. I modulate my voice carefully, though I rarely slip into Dr Borthwick's deeper tones now. 'I am not as knowledgeable as Mrs Johnson but I cannot help but agree with her. If nothing else we can give these women the ability to read improving works, their prayer books, sermons and the like.'

Mrs Sumner nods at me. She agrees to seek the bishop's support and suggests other ladies who might help. Then, after a moment of obvious thought, she volunteers, subject, of course, to the bishop's agreement, to be a member of a committee to oversee the work. Eleanor expresses considerable thanks.

On the walk home we are stopped by Eleanor's neighbour, who is, as she explains at great length, taking the air with her daughter. Mrs and Miss Butterworth are both wearing poke bonnets of enormous size and I find myself having to stoop and lean backwards and forwards to see their faces. Eleanor, shorter than me, is doing a side-to-side dance. After the usual politeness, she and I walk on in silence for a while. She speaks first, her voice quiet, almost a whisper.

'They were the biggest bonnets I have ever seen,' she says.
'Indeed and obviously new and very extravagantly trimmed.'
'And all those flowers . . .'
'And feathers.'
'Yes, the feathers.'
'And ribbons. Such a bright shade of pink.'

She does not reply and I see that she is laughing, and I feel my throat and mouth move and I am laughing too. The shadows retreat.

It is still light and warm, so we sit in the garden after supper. Eleanor is sketching the fruit trees, which are espaliered against the high brick wall. She is concentrating, the small frown in place as she looks up and then back down to the paper. I am meant to be reading Mr Dickens's newest serial, but the words blur on the page. And then I am watching Dr Soames, sitting in his study, as he turns the pages of his notebook, checking over the visits for the next day. The low sun makes the dust motes dance. And I am somewhere else, his hand on mine, his long fingers stroking mine.

Eleanor is looking at me. 'What do you want to do?'

I am slightly dizzy, perhaps with the sunlight. 'Now? Are you cold, should we go in?'

She smiles sadly, and stands up, gathering her pencils together. 'Yes, perhaps we should.'

I owe her more than this. But I do not know where to start or end. We go inside.

It is hotter each day and the nights are airless. I drowse fitfully somewhere between sleep and awakening and the ghosts gather, some never quite remembered, but I know they are there.

My window is open and I hear the first heavy raindrops, splashing against the sill. A new wind moves the open curtain and blows over my sweat-damp shift. I lie there in the blessed cool and see the lightning, so bright that it blinds me, and I screw my eyes closed. The thunder is immense, the crash reverberating. I am deaf and blind and somehow consumed.

It takes a moment to separate the sound of the scream from the echo of thunder but I know it is Eleanor and feel my way to the door and to her room. The after-image of whiteness still fills my eyes but then I start to see her pale figure huddled on her bed, hands over her ears, rocking. I get to her just in time as the next flash fills her window. I hold her tight and count out loud for the thunder: one, two, three.

'Close but not too close,' I say, loud and confident.

She shakes her head against me.

I try again. 'Isn't it wonderful? All that fury. And the rain is pounding down.'

Agnes appears through the open door, a candle shaking in her hand. 'Cook is hysterical. I can do nothing with her,' she says, voice quivering.

I give Eleanor's shoulders a tight hug and then stand up and take the candle from Agnes and light Eleanor's bedside candelabra. 'Agnes, take Mrs Johnson to the kitchen and make tea for us all. And cut some cake. I'll go and deal with Cook.'

An hour later and we are all sitting in the kitchen, drinking more tea. I have a dress pulled on over my shift, but Eleanor, Agnes and Cook are still in nightclothes and shawls.

Cook had some reason for her hysterics. She was wakened to the thunder and the screams of the cat, who sleeps on her bed. As she pushed the cat away, she was scratched and bitten. I cleaned and dressed the wounds and then went across the yard to check on the coachman and horses. The rain was still pouring from the sky and water running ankle-deep across the yard.

Now, I'm soaking wet, dripping by the stove, and eating cake. I realize that I'm happy.

Breakfast is late to give us all time to dress. It is still howling and raining and barely light enough to see, though it is nine o'clock. Eleanor is quiet as we eat, speaking little until the plates are cleared. I give my attention to Mr Dickens and find him easier to read today.

'Thank you for last night,' Eleanor says. 'I'm afraid I wasn't very brave. I have always hated thunder.'

269

'And I've never minded it.'

She smiles then and after a pause speaks again, slowly. 'It was the first time I have seen you properly awake since we came here. You seem . . . I'm not sure. Better? Stronger?'

'Yes, I do feel better.' It's true. Some of the energy of the storm still fills me.

'So, can I ask you now? Again. What do you want to do?'

I feel the weight appear and settle across my neck and shoulders, a real physical burden.

'I don't know. What can I do?'

'You have such skills. To know what to do to heal, to console, to make the rest of us braver. Can't you use them here?'

'That is closed to me.'

'But why?'

'I cannot live as a man again. To be a lie every day.'

'Then as a midwife again, like Mrs Sharp?'

'Alongside an incompetent doctor who knows less than me?'

Eleanor reaches forward and takes my hand. 'All that passion, that knowledge. It is a gift from God. It can be used. It must.'

'How? My dear Eleanor, how?' I struggle to hold Elizabeth's voice calm.

'We can educate girls. Properly. Set up a school. I have money enough.'

For a moment I see a way, but the tears come too soon and too fast and I am trapped again in the storm.

Eleanor stands up and walks around the table and kneels beside my chair. She is still for a moment and I think she must be praying. Then she takes a breath and looks up at me. 'Tell me,' she says and it is said gently but it is still a command.

'The ghosts are gathering.'

'Your past?'

'They were quiet when I was Dr Borthwick, I thought I had banished them. But since . . . since I've been Elizabeth they are often here.'

'Do you see them?' Her voice is still calm but there is fear in the hazel eyes.

'No, I'm not that mad. Not yet. But sometimes I think madness is waiting for me.' I close my eyes for a moment, trying to find the words to explain. 'When the storm was wild, it was me, the real me who doesn't mind thunder, who dressed Cook's wounds. When I've dealt with women in child-birth, other sickness, there is a certainty sometimes that I know is from the other place. That it is from me. That I am myself.'

She looks up at me with a frown, concentrating hard.

'Is it real? The place.'

'Yes.'

'But you don't know where?'

I shake my head and look for the words, because I don't think I'm mad yet and I need her to understand.

'I am a woman in that place, and I love a man, but I am also free. Free to live, to work, to travel.'

Eleanor sits back on her heels and closes her eyes. This time I am sure she is praying. Her God is close to her, accessible in a way I can't understand. She opens her eyes and looks directly at me.

'Well then, we must find it.'

I am surprised by her conviction. And it is not Elizabeth;

somehow it is me, a woman accountable only to herself, who replies.

'Eleanor, my sister, this is not your journey.'

'But it is. I choose it to be.'

24

Winchester, July 1842

Eleanor is busy making our plans to travel, each day spent consulting maps and almanacs, new books delivered every week. They are opened out on the dining table, the small print well lit by the afternoon sun. She has already decided that we must go to India and I easily acquiesce because I cannot believe that we will.

I try to concentrate on the map I am meant to be studying but it is strange to me. She looks up at me, knowing my attention is wandering.

'Do you recognize the names?'

'Yes, some. But I think only because Dr Soames spoke to me about India and I have read about it since.' I pause.

She looks at me, calm and contained. 'Dr Borthwick would speak of India sometimes, that he lived there as a child but could remember only the heat and the smell of the food and sometimes the scent of the plants.'

I always avoid speaking about him though sometimes Eleanor will mention him now, almost in passing, as a friend moved away to France.

'I can see only those two pictures: the bright white sun and the sea, a ship with a man's hand next to mine. But I can feel the heat on my skin and yes, the smells. But I don't know it was India. That was Dr Soames's idea – for Mrs Sharp to be the widow of a silk merchant from Calcutta. Then I made up the other stories, when I was in London,' I reply.

Eleanor turns away, back to her notes and lists.

Our relationship is changing as the weeks pass, as we talk in the long, warm evenings. I have told her about Mrs Sharp and her life in Alnwick and even a little about the farm, about Joanna. She listens carefully and asks more about the people she has now come to know, agreeing that Dr Soames must have been, in her words, 'a most kind and true gentleman'. Which he was.

More, though, is what I have learned about her life, about this intelligent and loving woman, constrained by duty and expectation. I understand now that her marriage was no sham. When Dr Borthwick first met her, he thought that Eleanor had married the Reverend Johnson, close friend of her recently deceased father, as an escape from spinsterhood. That she had exchanged caring for her frail widowed father for another father figure. But when she describes him to me, she paints a vivid and heroic picture of a man of God but also a revolutionary. I begin to see him as she does, battling the established Church in his powerful championing of the anti-slavery movement, in his support of the poor and in his tolerance of nonconformists. She speaks of him with a fierce and proud love. And, to my surprise, with a memory of real physical passion.

We speak of it just once, late one evening in the garden, both part concealed in the shadows.

274

'Were you ever with child?' I ask.

'No.' Eleanor hesitates.

The scent of jasmine fills the still air.

'No, alas, no. Reverend Johnson—' She stops and I can just see her sad smile. 'Nicholas, my husband, became ill a few months after we married. When we were told he was consumptive, he left my bed, fearing that I might take the illness.'

I lean forward, about to speak, to spare her embarrassment, but her words tumble out now, safer said in the deepening darkness.

'I missed him. I missed what was done as husband and wife. He was older but strong. And gentle. And, well, I enjoyed . . .'

She stops and I know she will be scarlet-cheeked and I am very careful to keep my voice steady. To ignore the flush in my own face. 'As you will when we find you another husband. An intelligent, sensible man who loves his wife for being equally intelligent and sensible. Like Mr Swan.'

'Yes,' she says, calm again. 'Like Mr Swan.'

As I know she had wanted Dr Borthwick to be. 'It is almost dark. Shall we go in?' I ask.

As I stand up she says, still seated, 'Elizabeth, have you been with child?'

I shake my head in the darkness and go inside.

As the days go by it is harder and harder to show enthusiasm for the journey, for where we will start and end. Lethargy claims me again and Eleanor starts to watch me as I drift away, back to the only memories I have.

'Where are you?' she asks, as I sit in the chair in Dr Soames's study, Dr Mackay's watch twisting on its chain in front of me. I come back to the sunlight on the map of France.

'Near Paris,' I say lightly, pointing to the city.

'Do you think you have been there?'

I shrug.

'Oh, Elizabeth. You must concentrate, help me to plan.'

I hear the anxiety in her voice but I am submerged elsewhere.

'Tell me, tell me what you were thinking of?'

'Of Dr Mackay in Alnwick when he mesmerized me,' I say.

'Should we seek a doctor here? Try mesmerism again?' she says, looking at me with her small frown.

That has perhaps the desired effect.

'No, absolutely not.'

She smiles a little at the energy of my response.

'I will take a turn round the garden. The fresh air will help me concentrate,' I say. I leave her and go outside to sit with my ghosts.

Eleanor has arranged a series of calls and social events, perhaps as a distraction. She is right, the activity of fending off the solicitous questions, of telling just enough truth, is an art form and requires me to pay attention.

Today we are to visit Monsieur Lafayette's atelier to be fitted for clothes for our travels. He is a not very genuine Parisian who has become the darling of the Winchester ladies. We are welcomed by the man himself, svelte, oiled and lightly scented, who escorts us to an over-furnished but well-lit room. Our neighbour, Miss Butterworth, is already seated and tells us that her mama is trying on a new dress. A starched maid provides coffee and I listen to the murmur of Eleanor's voice as I drift away: Dr Soames's study again and the watch glinting in the candlelight.

Eleanor touches my arm and I am back, and here is Mrs Butterworth encased in a dress with an enormous skirt and tight fitted bodice and sleeves; her body imprisoned within a corset and layers of petticoats, and yards and yards of viciously bright orange silk.

'Such a summer colour. What is it called?' I hear Eleanor say as she leans forward and touches the silk gently.

'Monsieur Lafayette calls it "*ombre brulée*",' Mrs Butter-worth says, prolonging the consonants and turning towards him.

He is all Gallic charm, prancing around her. 'A colour, may I say, which is very of the moment. And a style which I hope will interest you, dear Mrs Johnson and Mrs Mackay.'

As he looks at me I feel the vomit rise up at the thought of his tweaking fingers and then the corsets binding me, the silk encasing me tighter and tighter. I swallow hard as the room starts to spin and I am lost in blinding light, and then momentary darkness.

Eleanor helps me into the carriage through the fluttering voices. She takes hold of my hand. 'What happened?'

'Just the heat, and the smell of Monsieur's hair oil,' I say and turn and smile at her.

She smiles back, so much wanting me to be well. 'Ah, I thought it might have been horror at the dress.'

'Those huge skirts. Impossible to sit down.'

'And the colour.'

'The brightest possible orange. So bright that I needed . . .'
I stop. Needed what? What word has just floated away? What
did I see?

'Elizabeth?' Eleanor says.

'I almost remembered something. But it is gone.'

After lunch we sit in the shaded end of the garden but there
is little relief from the heat.

'Will it be hot like this in India?' Eleanor says.

'Yes. Indeed, much hotter, I think.'

'We will need muslin dresses, very lightweight.'

I nod, uninterested because I know I cannot go. I must tell
her, but I am too tired.

'Elizabeth, please, we must get ready if we are to leave next
month.'

I look at my hands: Joanna's hands covered in Arthur's
blood; Mrs Sharp's hands holding a dying child; Dr Borthwick's hands examining a dead woman and her dead baby.
None of them are mine.

Eleanor touches my arm and then the words start pouring
from my mouth, unstoppable.

'I cannot do this, always pretend, always be trapped. All
the questions. All the lies. For a life of what? Nothing but
useless idleness. This is not me. This is not who I am.'

I rage on and on through the long afternoon. My only lifeline is Eleanor, holding me as I shout and weep. Later she
helps me to my room and takes off my dress and sponges my
face and hands with cool water.

*

The Midwife

I wake drenched in sweat from a dream I can't remember, and I don't know where this place is. For a moment I'm dizzy and I lie very still, listening, watching. There is a light showing in the gap between the curtains and the door of my room is open; my room at Eleanor's house. I go over to the window and look down at her garden, etched in the moonlight. I am thinned, even transparent, all the anger temporarily drained.

It is time to find the pictures which Dr Borthwick shut away.

It is already hard to remember how I was both him and hidden. Hidden behind a coat and trousers, a voice, a manner, a binding cloth, and always a locked door. But with the freedom to stride out; to ride a horse through the streets at night; to be unescorted in a public place; to be both unremarkable and fully present. To be of use.

I know it was my choice then to be other. I was only him, and he was ruthless about Mrs Sharp, about ending her. Just one letter each quarter day to Alice, as Mrs Sharp had promised, and always one letter back from Alice to Mrs Sharp, care of Dr Borthwick. Mrs Hayward brought in those letters, not Betty; perhaps she thought that Mrs Sharp was Dr Borthwick's mistress. I can remember his amusement and I feel my lips smile as his did. Alice's last letter saved him. No, he is gone now. The letter saved me.

I lean my cheek against the cool glass.

The smell of the London fog and then its taste, and his three fellow passengers pulling scarves over their faces; those were his first memories of London.

'Is the fog always so bad?' Dr Borthwick started to cough.

'Often bad in the winter. It sometimes lasts for days if there's no wind,' the lawyer said.

'But better, most certainly, than the smell of the river in summer,' the clergyman said with a small smile.

'So, Dr Borthwick, are you still of a mind to live in London?' the factory owner asked, but with a certainty that London was the best place to be.

Dr Borthwick nodded to his companions as he pulled his scarf further across his mouth. All London men, they had been helpful in telling him where he could find decent lodgings and where he might later find a house to put up his plate. The lawyer told him where he must definitely not live or work, which seemed to be most areas and certainly all those close to the river.

For four weeks he stayed in a quiet and clean lodging house, recommended by the clergyman. He spent the brief winter days walking the city to get his bearings and to find an apothecary who met Dr Soames's criteria of being both properly licensed and not too enamoured of his own potions. He moved after that to be near Gower Street and the new University College Hospital and started attending the public lectures there.

After three months he rented a house, found two servants, and bought a brougham carriage and a horse: the signs of a man with several hundred pounds. Dr Soames had been very generous.

Dr Borthwick lived his story: the young doctor who had studied in Edinburgh, worked in a northern country town and now come south to make his mark as an *accoucheur*. He made his rules and kept them: never state a fact unless certain where it came from; never engage unprepared in conversations on specific topics; always avoid wider conversation about individuals.

He stopped questioning how he knew, how Mrs Sharp had known, the way to deliver a breech baby, the need for forceps to be a different shape and how to use them. He stopped questioning how, in his head, he could see the fleeting images of twins lying in the womb. In time he just accepted the knowledge, valued it for the care he could give, for making his life bearable, for making him real.

The past was banned; the doors were closed; the ghosts were almost subdued. Months would go by without a dream of the other place, without another pale face in the mirror.

Eleanor wakes me, bringing in my breakfast tray herself.

'Good morning. I thought you might be ready to eat.' She glances at me briefly and then away, putting down the tray, pouring the tea.

I sit up in bed and watch her, watch her hand shaking slightly as she passes me the cup, see her fear for me, or even of me.

'My dear Eleanor, I am so sorry for yesterday. I was—' I stop and hold her gaze. 'I was lost, despairing, hopeless, angry. You were so very kind. My lifeline. I must have seemed mad. Perhaps I was, but I am calmer now.'

She sits down on the edge of the bed, her eyes red-rimmed and shadowed.

'I know where I need to go. Have to go. Back to where my memories were strongest,' I say.

'To Alnwick?' She is calm.

'Yes.'

She nods. 'I know it is what you think of, speak of most now, all that happened there.'

I can't say that it's because I try never to speak of Dr Borthwick. Never to be him. Not here with Eleanor.

I speak slowly, wanting her to understand. 'It is where I was found. In truth, Alnwick is the closest I have to a home, a birthplace. I was made there. But I am not sure how to go back, who I will be.'

She smiles. 'Mrs Elizabeth Mackay, of course. Mrs Sharp came to London to work as a midwife and married Dr Mackay and is now a rich widow. She wishes to visit old friends.'

'But Dr Mackay has been in Alnwick. He is known to be an Edinburgh doctor.'

She shrugs this aside. 'His brother then, also a doctor. You said Dr Mackay had a sister living in London so he could have a brother there too.'

I look at Eleanor's face, animated now. This sober and God-fearing woman. She will be mortified if I call these lies.

'Eleanor, you are better than Miss Austen at the stories you tell,' I say, squeezing her fingers gently and then letting go.

We are taking tea again with the bishop's wife who is graciously concerning herself with our plan to travel north. She has a great number of items to cover and I can easily interpret Eleanor's rapt attention. Eleanor will, within reason, do as she wishes, but she will listen to Mrs Sumner's advice and usually comply, or at least appear to.

They are engaged in a long debate on whether we can properly travel with just one lady's maid or require a second, or perhaps an under maid. When Mrs Sumner kindly asks my opinion, I defer to Eleanor's view, to her wider experience of travel with Reverend Johnson, going so far distant as Venice. I watch Eleanor lean forward ready to interrupt if I deviate from what is proper, and then her small smile as she realizes that I am being unusually tactful.

'Well, I think it may be possible to travel with only one maid if you have a manservant as well as your escort,' says Mrs Sumner finally, settling back in her chair.

'Indeed, we will have Edward with us,' says Eleanor. 'He was Mr Johnson's manservant and coachman for many years and has given me excellent service since then. We are most grateful for your kind advice.'

'And who is to be your escort?' says Mrs Sumner.

Eleanor glances rapidly at me and gives a slight shake of her head. I remain silent.

'We are not yet certain. I have written to my dear friend Mr Swan who advises me on such matters,' she says, looking gravely at Mrs Sumner.

'There is no family member, no older male relative, perhaps?'

'Alas, no. Mrs Mackay and I are sadly without close family other than Dr Mackay's brother, who is also a physician, but lives in Edinburgh.'

Eleanor stops and looks at me firmly.

I say nothing.

'My dear Mrs Johnson, leave this with me. I may have a solution.' Mrs Sumner rises majestically from her chair.

*

We leave soon afterwards and I manage to remain silent until we have crossed the cathedral close.

'A maid, a manservant and an escort? Surely not enough. We need at least two maids, a cook, a gardener. Oh, and a dog. And a boy to watch the dog.' I stop, feeling her arm tighten on mine.

I manage a smile. 'I apologize. I am being childish. But an escort?'

'We are planning for our travel north and back to take several weeks. Even in England, we must be escorted. By a gentleman. Perhaps if we call him a secretary you will approve?' Eleanor's tone is gently chiding.

'So, Mrs Sumner is going to find us a decrepit old man, a retired cleric or the like, to defend our virtue.' I try hard to keep the rising anger from my voice. My stomach starts to churn.

'We will be travelling for much of the way in public, on the stagecoaches. It is not proper to be without a gentleman's protection.'

'Protection. We are grown women. And you are a woman of substance and status,' I say, my voice shaking as I try to be calm.

She puts her other hand on my arm and we walk on in silence for a few minutes, then she turns to me, frowning. 'We could travel with just a maid and a manservant but it would not be enough, not when we arrive in Alnwick.'

'But in Alnwick of all places I need no protection,' I say, hiding behind my veil.

'Forgive me, but I must say this. In the north you were Mrs Sharp, a midwife without family. Not in truth much more than an upper servant. You must be seen now as changed, as a woman of status in society.'

There is so much I want to say and I know that some of it she would understand, but not all. How could she? I nod in acquiescence.

The following week, Mr Maunoir, younger son of Mrs Sumner's brother, is brought to me for inspection: he has recently completed his studies at Cambridge and is to be ordained next year. To be called Eleanor's secretary, he will make arrangements for us as we travel, and escort us on our visits to the cathedrals and monuments which we will see on our way north. He will stay with his own relatives in London while we visit the Swans, and then join us. He is an earnest boy, only moderately pompous. I give in gracefully.

The Great North Road, August 1842

Early on a bright morning at the end of July, we leave London from the White Horse Inn on Fetter Lane. This is the start of our real journey, travelling by stagecoach along the Great North Road.

Mr Maunoir is there, waiting for us by the coach, to help us mount the two steps. He fusses over Eleanor, holding her reticule as she climbs in, and then turns to me. I resist the urge to push past and, with a polite nod of my veiled head, I hold his outstretched hand lightly as I gather in my skirts with my other hand. Eleanor takes my over-full reticule from me as I try to arrange myself on the narrow seat. She is almost laughing.

Our protector follows us into the small space and sits opposite, checking again that we are properly settled. 'I am told that the coach will be full. I may have to sit above. I hope you will not be discommoded,' he says in a serious tone.

'Thank you. I am used to travelling by stagecoach. Mr Johnson was in favour of it. But I do hope you will be comfortable on the outside,' says Eleanor.

'Do not concern yourself, Mrs Johnson. The weather is

good and I often travelled home from Cambridge on top,' he says and smiles, a boy's open smile.

He seems about to say more but stops, resumes his usual solemn look and opens his prayer book. For a moment I think he is going to read us a sermon, and perhaps he would have, but there are other voices at the open door of the coach. An older man is trying to get in: he is stout and has a palsied arm. Mr Maunoir helps him without fuss on to the seat by the door and opposite me.

'Thank you for your kindness, sir. Could I ask that you assist my daughter?'

'My pleasure, sir,' Mr Maunoir replies.

Mr Maunoir, bent double, squeezes his way between me and the old gentleman, twisting sideways, I realize, to avoid any contact with my bombazine-covered legs. The daughter is fortunately short and slender and I move closer to Eleanor so she can sit opposite her father. She seems both surprised and over-grateful.

The coach rocks as feet move across its top and boxes are fastened in place. I hear Edward, Eleanor's manservant, and Agnes the maid speaking quietly as they climb up the ladder.

'How many sit on top?' I ask Mr Maunoir.

'It varies, but no more than six are usually allowed,' he replies.

'Pray do not worry, madam, the coaches are very stable,' the old gentleman adds politely. 'The weight on top will not over-balance us. We are quite safe in here.'

I nod in return, not saying that my concern was for Agnes and Edward, and lean back against the seat, behind my veil. The five of us are to be in very close proximity for several hours, best just to watch and listen as Eleanor leans slightly forward to introduce us.

The coach judders as it starts to move and slowly gathers speed. At first, the ride is surprisingly comfortable, not as smooth as the Swans' carriage but better than I remember from my journey south. Not mine. Dr Borthwick's journey south, not to be spoken of here, not by Elizabeth Mackay, not when my body is wedged against Eleanor, thigh against thigh.

Eleanor has engaged the old man, a Mr Grey, in a detailed conversation about the growing of apples. The initial skirmishes established her as the well-to-do widow of a clergyman and him as the owner of a small estate in Kent where his tenants grow apples for the London markets, and they are deep in discussion of the preferred varieties for baking or bottling as sauce. I realize that this is something I do not know about, perhaps never have. The old man speaks well and pleasantly and occasionally defers to his daughter for comment. She otherwise seems happy enough to listen and smile agreement. Is that her life, simply to reflect him, as the Winchester women did their husbands and fathers? To live constrained by clothes and etiquette? I feel the anger start to rise again and try to concentrate on Eleanor's voice.

At the first stop, we have very little time to eat and use the privy before we are all five back in the coach. The daughter, Miss Grey, offers to take the middle place but I decline. With some polite hesitation she says she has noticed that I am carrying a book by Mr Dickens, *Oliver Twist*.

'My father and I are keen readers of his works and awaited each instalment of *Barnaby Rudge* with great excitement. Indeed, it kept us entertained in the coldest months. We were very happy to light the candles and start our evening pages,' she says.

'I did much the same,' I say. I try to keep the smile in my voice but it was him, not me. Dr Borthwick saved the instalments like a miser, saved them to read in the long, dark evenings of last winter.

'Which of Mr Dickens's books do you prefer?' Miss Grey asks.

'Oh, *Oliver Twist*, because it paints such a true picture.'

'Is it so, the paupers, in London? He does not exaggerate?'

'It is, if anything, worse.'

My answer is too authoritative, even passionate, and Eleanor, Mr Maunoir and Mr Grey are all now listening.

'I know this from my sadly departed husband, Dr Mackay, and of course Mrs Johnson who visited the most desperate areas to give succour to the women and children,' I say, quickly deferring to Eleanor.

She picks up at once and the conversation moves on to how to improve the lot of the poor. I realize that I am interested in what the Greys say, what they understand. When the conversation flags again, Mr Maunoir returning to his prayer book and Mr Grey snoring quietly in the corner, Eleanor leans across me and seeks Miss Grey's views on the education of women living in the villages.

I lift up my veil and smile at Eleanor.

Day by day, we travel north, and Mr Maunoir continues to take his duties very seriously. He is at his best when giving us the benefit of his considerable knowledge of each cathedral as we visit, but less so when trying to help us in and out of the coaches and worrying over the luggage. Agnes and Edward, who have everything in place, tolerate him benignly and I try my best not to tease him. He is so very young.

Each day of the journey we have a pattern. Eleanor and I rise early and put on our travelling clothes: for her a sprigged muslin overdress, expensively full-skirted, over a crisp cotton blouse; for me still an all-black dress but in thin cotton, its expense demonstrated by the pin tucks and jet buttons on the bodice. It has been too hot for the last week to wear bombazine. Then we take breakfast which is always eggs and often fat bacon. I have started avoiding the bacon: the hot, swaying coach and the grease are not compatible.

We travel three stages, sometimes only two, but never more in a day. I usually last only the first stage inside the coach, escaping at the change of horses to sit on top with Mr Maunoir. He was initially overly concerned that a lady in mourning should be seen outside the coach but was slightly mollified by my longest black veil and parasol. And then, I think, by the realization that he now has a very good excuse to escape the stifling coach in escorting me on the roof seats. Eleanor joins us on the two very hottest days: Agnes and Edward are expressionless, and perch uncomfortably, trying not to look at her.

I like to stay in the coach for the first stage so that I can watch Eleanor as she skilfully, but always kindly, interrogates our fellow travellers. The inside passengers are a whole section of society that I rarely met in London: small landowners, clergymen, lawyers; sometimes even women without a male escort, a mother travelling with her adult daughters to visit relatives, two sisters travelling to their brother's house in the next county. I realize that these are people like the Alnwick gentry, families who have two or three servants but do not keep a carriage. The outside passengers are, apart from on the hottest days, the not-quite gentry, the craftsmen and tenant farmers, plus the servants of those inside.

'You are enjoying this,' Eleanor says one evening, as she plaits her hair ready for bed.

We have travelled three stages on a cloudy and blessedly cool day. For two of the stages a gentleman farmer and a lawyer were having a discussion about land leases which drove even Eleanor to sleep.

'I am indeed. The people we meet are so interesting. Apart from this morning, perhaps.'

Eleanor laughs and then mimics the farmer's accent: 'Aye, but the drains should be kept up by landlord, is plain to see.'

'But you slept through the main drainage ditch. All of a quarter-hour about one ditch!'

'I closed my eyes a little while. But it is a joy to have conversation without the formality of London or Winchester,' she says.

'Is that why we didn't travel in your carriage? We could have hired horses at each stage. Mr Maunoir told me.'

'Yes, but Mr Johnson enjoyed the stagecoach so much. The chance to talk to people in all walks of life.'

'Eleanor, are we perhaps being a little revolutionary in travelling by stagecoach? We two apparently wealthy women.'

'A little, perhaps.' She smiles and picks up her book, leaning towards the lamp.

The next few days pass quietly, and I rarely remember any dreams. I am adrift, waiting.

At the start of our third week Eleanor engages in a long conversation with a young engineer who is to work on the next phase of the ever-extending railway north of York. He enthuses at considerable length about the new engines and carriages, all moving at such speed as could barely be imagined. He is sure it will one day be possible to travel from London to Edinburgh by the railway in less than two days.

I watch Eleanor become more and more animated.

'Mrs Mackay –' she turns to me – 'do you think we should try this new form of conveyance?'

'Yes, I would find it most interesting.'

'Sir, please forgive me for interrupting, but is it safe?' Mr Maunoir asks the engineer.

'I can assure you so. I have travelled extensively on the tracks,' the engineer replies.

Mr Maunoir blushes slightly and leans forward. 'I mean, is it safe for the ladies? Them being more delicate. Might such speed affect their constitution?' The final word is almost whispered.

I watch the two men, boys really, discussing us. I hide behind my veil. Eleanor listens passively.

'My dear sir, please be reassured. Ladies –' and the engineer manages a contorted half-bow in the confines of the coach – 'ladies, the Queen herself has taken a trip on a railway and reported it as most exhilarating.'

Our protector is vanquished.

The following morning, we set off from the coaching inn and travel by hired carriage to the railway station, as the engineer calls it, in a village south of York. There is a newly built stone building and the young engineer escorts us to the ladies' waiting room which smells of fresh varnish. I stand at the door and watch Mr Maunoir hurry away to purchase tickets while Agnes drags a heavy trunk across the platform. My body starts to move to help her, but I stop, enchained, a rich widow. Mrs Sharp would have helped. Dr Borthwick too. But the movement was my other self. Whoever she was. Edward rushes past me and takes the trunk from Agnes. I see the smile between them: how had I not noticed before that they are lovers? Or have they just become so, more private at the inns than in Eleanor's house under the watchful eyes of the cook?

The young engineer stands beside me.

'Isn't it magnificent!' he shouts.

'Indeed!' I shout back as the brakes squeal and the huge black engine halts. The thick black smoke drops down over us.

'We need to go aboard,' he says, taking my arm.

The air clears a little as we walk along by the engine, past the metal wheels almost as tall as we are, past an open wooden carriage, past two closed ones, until we reach a bright yellow coach, similar to the stagecoaches but shiny new.

Mr Maunoir is there, holding the door for Eleanor, and then he rushes away – to check the luggage, he says. The engineer takes my arm as I climb up into what he calls the first-class carriage and then follows me in.

I smile at Eleanor who has soot on her face and give her my handkerchief.

'My dear sir,' I say to the engineer, 'you did not warn us about the smoke.'

As he apologizes, I know that the taste of the smoke reminds me only of the burning of damp coal in household fires and of the London fog, nothing more.

The carriage jolts rhythmically on the track but sways much less than the stagecoach. I look out of the window at the stubble in the fields, at the walls and hedges passing by. The speed starts to increase, and I feel Eleanor's hand on mine. I turn to her and she points at the far window. A man is galloping his horse alongside the train, racing us. He keeps up at first, then falls behind. Eleanor looks at me, her eyes wide.

'This is so fast. Is it not astonishing?'

'Yes, it is.'

Then the world shifts and I feel cold sweat on my neck. I have travelled faster. Faster with the wind in my hair. Faster still with my body pressed back in a seat. Faster. But there are no words or pictures. I sit back, behind my veil. The carriage tilts slightly and I'm thrown against Eleanor, who laughs.

I'm dreaming of running along a corridor, somewhere, when I hear Eleanor's voice.

'Elizabeth, it is time to take breakfast.' Eleanor and an echo, another voice, fading: 'Elizabeth.'

Eleanor is over by the window, already dressed, and we are in the new hotel by the railway station in York.

The Midwife

It is over one hundred miles from York to Alnwick, but we cover them quickly, travelling three stages most days. Eleanor seems to share my new impatience and we stay for a second night only in Durham, to have time to visit the cathedral and castle, now part of the new university as Mr Maunoir tells us at some length over breakfast. He does his best inside the cathedral, but I can't concentrate as he talks of the history, of St Cuthbert and the monks of Lindisfarne.

Yet for a moment as I stand in the nave and look upwards, I feel that I know the space around me, the air enclosed within the walls. Not a fleeting word or picture, but a calm acceptance that stays with me as we walk out across the quiet close. And then it is gone as we turn down the steep cobbled road into a crowd of noisy young men in their black academic gowns.

That night I dream of running again. I see the corridor stretching out in front of me, doors open on each side and slamming shut as I reach them, door after door closing. I run faster and faster and then the dream changes. For the first time, far ahead, I see a door at the very end, and I run and run until I awaken, gasping for breath.

The following day passes with a treacle slowness. I am very tired when we arrive in Newcastle and passively follow Eleanor's instructions to eat and then go early to bed. I dream the running dream, over and over, never reaching the final door.

We set off early, even before the first stagecoach, to travel the last leg of our journey in a private hired carriage. It is gleaming black and red, with four matched black horses and surprisingly comfortable seats. At Eleanor's request, I am back in voluminous bombazine and I settle my skirts neatly round me; Eleanor in elegant navy silk sits opposite, Mr Maunoir beside her; Agnes, in her best sprigged cotton, beside me. Fortunately it is a cool day.

So, we arrive in Alnwick, two London-smart widows with a secretary, a lady's maid, a manservant, and all their trunks and boxes. A sight to impress.

26

Alnwick, August 1842

We take the best rooms at the White Swan in Alnwick, though they look quite shabby. I have become too used to southern ways.

After breakfast, sitting by the window in the over-furnished ladies' sitting room, I write a note to Alice Black. I struggle with the words. In the end I pen a brief formal note, which, when the boy has gone with it, I regret as being too obviously from a rich widow.

Across the room, Eleanor is telling the story, the new version of my truth, to the innkeeper. I didn't recognize him: he is new, an incomer from Alnmouth. She almost whispers the sad tale of the widow, Mrs Sharp, who was midwife here three years ago, before she went to London. There she had the good fortune to marry a most eminent London physician, Dr Mackay. But he died in the winter just gone and left Mrs Mackay widowed twice at quite a young age. So tragic.

I listen in, hidden behind my half-veil, impressed by Eleanor's careful hints at my propriety and wealth, at how she establishes my changed status. I am gentry now.

The boy comes back quickly with Alice's reply, very brief

and verbal. Yes, she is at home this morning for visitors. I give him the promised ha'penny and he stands watching me as I walk over to Eleanor in a rustle of black silk and lace.

Eleanor and I process together along Bondgate, Agnes a pace behind. I leave them at the market square and go on alone, my feet remembering the way. My pulse starts to race.

Alice opens the door and looks at the lace veil and then slowly down at my London finery. She nods, unsmiling, stepping back to let me in. As I walk past her along a passage which is so much narrower and darker than I remember, I see that she is heavily pregnant.

Without thinking I walk across to the far side of the kitchen table, to the place I always used to sit when we spent the evenings stitching, she and I opposite each other, old Mrs Black in the chair by the fire. Still standing, I lift back my veil and wait.

'Sit yoursen down then,' she says brusquely and her accent is thicker and her voice rougher than it has been in my head.

Then a well-remembered voice, unchanged, interrupts our silent appraisal.

'Alice. Alice. Who's come by?' Old Mrs Black shouts from upstairs.

Alice raises her eyebrows and now is herself. I feel myself smile.

'She's had an apoplexy. Can barely sit up in bed but still has her voice,' she says.

'I'm sorry. May I go up and pay my respects?'

Alice nods.

'Best take off that fancy bonnet first or she'll think the duchess is come,' she says.

It's all that's left of old Mrs Black, the sharp voice. She is shrunken and wasted, slumped on the pillow, her left arm fixed tight against her side, elbow bent and fingers clawed.

'Good day, Mrs Black. I am sorry to see you unwell.'

She looks at me then smiles, her face pulling across, the palsy more obvious.

'Heard from Reverend MacPherson this morn as you were back and mighty fine. Not seen so much good black silk here in a while.' She pauses to catch her breath and carries on. 'It be true then that you buried another husband?'

I look straight at her: I will not pretend grief here.

'Mrs Mackay now. I was only married a twelvemonth.'

'A doctor?'

'Yes,' I say, smiling, remembering the inquisitions from the past.

'And a rich one?'

'Yes.'

'Aye. That's a sad loss even so.'

She turns away, trying to moisten her lips. And then it is easy. Without thinking I pick up the cup by the bed and put my arm under her head and give her a drink slowly, stopping to wipe her mouth as she swallows. Alice moves round the bed and together, unspeaking, we lift old Mrs Black forwards, arrange the pillows and settle her back down. Her eyes are closed but she speaks again and I lean forward to hear.

'I prayed to Him to send you back. Alice is near her time.'

I look up at Alice and her mouth is tight closed, her face expressionless.

We leave the old woman drowsing and go back to the kitchen. Alice makes tea and then pours it out, mine in the pale blue cup I always used there, the one from Jane.

I wait now, knowing there is more Alice needs to say.

'Were you married again?' she asks.

'No. Just another story. Mrs Mackay is no more real than Mrs Sharp.'

She shakes her head.

'You still don't know. About before. Before here.'

'No. But I'm going to search now. It's time.'

She looks down at her cup and then back at me, frowning.

'Peter said as you might be in trouble. When the man was looking for Dr Borthwick. Peter said as you left here in man's clothes.'

'Yes. I was Dr Borthwick in London.'

'All the time?'

'Yes, I lived as a man, worked as a doctor. A good one. And I paid my own way.'

She almost smiles and then leans forward and looks at me closely, critically.

'False ringlets then?'

'Yes. My hair is growing out again.'

She smiles fully, almost laughs, but there is something else there which I thought at first was sadness, but it is more like fear.

Time passes and we talk easily but there is a secret

between us which is hers, not mine, and she is not ready yet to tell me.

Instead she talks about Reverend MacPherson, married and widowed in the time I have been away, and Farmer Turnbull lost to gangrene and a terrible fever after cutting his hand when shearing, and a maidservant run off with the undertaker's boy. When I ask about Blacksmith Weddell she tells me about his baby, her god-daughter Jane, but barely mentions his new wife Enid, whom she seems to dislike. I tell her about London fashions and the ever-wider skirts.

It is only when I hear Arthur's voice that I realize she has never mentioned him at all.

He comes in bright and smiling, walks up to me and takes my hand politely, and then shrugs and takes my shoulders and kisses me soundly on the cheek.

'Well. No idea who you be today but is a great joy to see you. Been a lot of talk about you gone up in the world. Bit disappointed there's not more lace and ribbons and such.'

He is laughing and I see his energy and joy reflected in Alice's smile but then the fear is back. But not of him.

Surely not of him.

Then I know.

Arthur walks back with me to the White Swan, telling me that I need to be escorted now that I'm a rich widow, proper gentry. He smiles, speaking to me as he did to Mrs Sharp, matter-of-fact, no edge to what he says.

'Will you take me to see Mary?' I ask.

He looks at me, his gaze level. 'It's worse there now. John drinks all the money he gets. Mary's not well. She's in a right shabby way.' He looks past me, taking my arm as we cross the road. 'Reverend MacPherson tried to get her into town. Had a place for her in the new workhouse but she wouldn't come. Have been better there, though. Women are at least fed and clothed.'

'You mean she's not. And what about the children?' I look down at my silk skirt, at the tips of my soft leather shoes. I had abandoned Mary: Dr Borthwick had shut her out, but that was no excuse.

'No one goes up there now except Blacksmith Weddell. John spat on him last time. We send food but—' He stops and shrugs.

'I must go. Even if I can't help them.'

He looks at me slowly, and then nods.

'Aye. I'll take you then. Sunday, after church. We'll call on blacksmith to see his wife and new baby as well. You'll like Enid.'

'Is she like Jane?'

'No, but she does well enough.'

The next day Eleanor and I walk in the morning sun to call on Reverend MacPherson. I am in my finest mourning clothes: my silk dress all pleated and tucked, heavy jet beads, and a modest black-varnished straw bonnet with a token veil of gossamer black lace. Eleanor is resplendent in pale lilac in the latest London style, with white lace at her neck and elbows and her bonnet trimmed with silk flowers and long lace ribbons. The clothes are not for the reverend but for those we might meet on the way.

As we pass the apothecary's shop, I look away, but Eleanor

takes my elbow and almost pushes me in. The assistant is new, I think; I certainly don't recognize him. He rushes forward from behind the counter and offers his assistance.

Eleanor speaks in her polite company voice, but glass-edged and a little louder than usual. 'We have been travelling for some weeks and I am in need of a calmative. The innkeeper recommended we consult the apothecary here.'

'Dr Selby's on a visit, ma'am. But due back soon. He could call on you later. I can send him a note now?' The boy's words tumble out. He'll be blamed if he fails to land such a rich patient.

'Elizabeth, dear. What would you advise?' She turns to me and I see the tiny smile which in Eleanor denotes a ploy.

I look slowly at the familiar rows of white jars and blue bottles.

'Do you have camomile and also valerian root, dried and coarse ground?' This in my new light and carefully modulated voice, more elegant, certainly, than Mrs Sharp's.

He looks at me in surprise.

'We have Dr Selby's calmative draught for ladies. He recommends it highly,' he says, reaching for a nearby blue bottle.

'Laudanum?' I ask.

He nods.

'I think not.'

I watch as he makes up the powder, measuring the quantities I request with a slightly shaking hand. I take pity on him then: it can be no pleasure working for Dr Selby. So, I buy some rosewater and soft soap as well as the powder and listen politely to his instructions on how to make an infusion.

*

We see Dr Selby walking towards us, as we turn on to Bailiff-gate. He starts to smile; a professional, interested smile, head slightly to one side; a response to our moneyed clothes. Then he recognizes me, but too late to stop speaking.

'Good morning, ladies,' he says, bowing low.

'Mrs Johnson, this is Dr Selby, the apothecary,' I say, turning away from him to her.

'Ah,' she replies, and walks past him with the briefest of nods, her wide skirts forcing him to step into the road. I follow her, not acknowledging him at all.

Eleanor takes my arm and we walk on together. The sun seems even brighter as we make our way to the parsonage.

Peter opens the door and I reach out and take his hand, smiling, before I remember myself. I squeeze his fingers as I let go and turn to Eleanor.

'Eleanor, this is Peter of whom I've spoken. He was Dr Soames's assistant and coachman. Peter, this is my dear friend Mrs Johnson.'

Eleanor smiles. 'Peter, it is a pleasure to meet you. Mrs Mackay has told me of your great service to her and to Dr Soames.'

Peter has his hands firmly behind him so she may avoid the embarrassment of shaking his hand. He is, after all, only a servant. Only my friend. I feel a wave of anger but then I see his wry smile, so I follow Eleanor quietly through the hall.

Reverend MacPherson comes out to greet us, bowing his head politely to us both before he speaks. 'Mrs Mackay, it is a great pleasure to see you again. Please accept my condolences on the loss of your husband.'

'Thank you. May I introduce my dear friend, Mrs Johnson.'

He ushers us through to the morning room and coffee is served efficiently by a neatly dressed maid as we discuss the weather and the roads.

I lift my veil and look at him. 'Mrs Black has told me that you too have been bereaved. I was deeply saddened to hear it.'

'Thank you. I lost dear Caroline after only a short time together.'

There is pain in the tightened lips. I reach out my hand and take his for a moment as Mrs Sharp would have done, then turn to Eleanor.

'Reverend MacPherson and I were often together when visiting the sick. Most especially in the early winter of '39 when there was diphtheritis in the town.' I stop, realizing my mistake, realizing I have summoned Dr Borthwick. Three of me in the room now. But Eleanor is looking at the reverend, not me.

'The late Reverend Johnson, my husband, felt very strongly about the duty of the clergyman to the sick and the poor. It seems that you must share his view and indeed his actions,' she says.

I watch as they converse, see her leaning slightly forward, the increase in her breathing; see her look at him as she looked at Dr Borthwick, at me. I feel something like regret and then a deeper relief.

Reverend MacPherson turns to me.

'You were sorely missed when you left us. Dr Middlemass came regularly from Alnmouth. He did his best. And Dr Selby too, of course. But they could not replace Dr Soames and you.

It was a full year before we had another sensible midwife.' His tone is not accusatory, but the words still hurt.

'I couldn't stay. Dr Selby made it clear I would be unwanted,' I say, my voice level and quiet.

'Indeed. Please do not misunderstand me. Arthur Black explained very well why you had left us. I meant only that your skills, and may I say your kindness, were greatly missed.'

Reverend MacPherson is very earnest, and I smile and nod. Then I feel a sudden coldness. Did his wife die in childbirth? Without proper care? Eleanor fills the silence.

'Mrs Mackay has such a range of knowledge. We are considering establishing a school for girls with teaching of mathematics and so on. What are your views?' The hazel eyes are fixed on his again.

Reverend MacPherson insists on escorting us back to the White Swan. I am intrigued by how often Eleanor appears to need help walking on the cobbles, and how attentively he offers his arm. I follow behind, my veil firmly back in place.

Alice's skivvy answers the door: a clean and well-fed girl who is vaguely familiar. She drops a sketchy curtsey and I look at her again as she holds open the door. One of the tanner's brood, probably, from the colour of her hair. I give her a penny and tell her to buy some ribbons at the market. She smiles then and I recognize the girl who carried in the water to bathe her new brother, one of my last Alnwick babies.

Alice is chopping onions and the kitchen is already hot, a huge pan on the open range. She looks up as I walk in and pushes the sweaty hair from her forehead with the back of her hand. Her cheeks are bright red.

'Arthur's at work.'

'It isn't Arthur who needs a midwife.'

'I'm too busy. He's bleeding the pigs. Need the onion and oatmeal ready for the blood puddings.'

'We'll do that first then,' I say, taking off my hat and veil then pulling my lace cap tighter over my hair. I reach up to pull an apron down from the line above the range.

'But you're not dressed for—' She stops, looking at my dress.

'Black cotton today. I've just changed out of the silk and lace. There was a lot of it. You should have seen Dr Selby's face.'

She doesn't smile.

I take the knife from her hand.

'Go outside for some air. It's still cool in the shade. I'll do these.'

Mrs Sharp knows how to do this, I think: she has chopped a basket full of onions and added them to the boiling oatmeal mash before. The puddings have to be made quickly in the summer, but heavily salted and hung to dry they'll keep in the butcher's cellar for weeks. So, I carry on chopping and I don't enjoy it any more than the last time. The onions are fresh, picked with some green still in the leaves, and very strong: my eyes stream and I have to sniff constantly. But fresh blood pudding will be good for Alice.

She comes back in, looking cooler, carrying an armful of herbs from her garden. She chops those as I finish the onions and then she stirs the lot into the mash. We don't speak.

I take the wooden board and knives to the scullery, wash them down and scrub at my reeking fingers.

'Thank you,' she says as she comes through from the kitchen. 'Thought kitchen work would be beneath you now.' She passes me a clean rag.

I raise my eyebrows as I dry off my hands.

'Come on outside, I've fresh raspberries to pick if you want a few,' she says.

We sit for a while shaded by the garden wall and I wait, looking at Alice's carefully tended herbs. Nothing grown that can't be eaten except for her roses. When I turn back, the tears are running down her cheeks.

I take her hand.

'What is it?'

'The baby, it isn't Arthur's.'

Expected, but still a shock to hear her say it. And partly at least my fault.

'Whose then?'

She shakes her head.

'Does Arthur know?'

'No. I don't think so.' She shakes her head again. Then she takes a deep sobbing breath and the words spill out.

'Everyone was having babies and I remembered that day when you said it's not always the woman who be barren. That sometimes a woman might go to another man and be lucky. So that's what I did.'

'Oh, Alice, I'm sorry.'

Then to my amazement she laughs through the tears. 'It's not your doing!'

I know then who the father is. I think for a moment and then look at her.

'Blacksmith Weddell?' I say, not really a question.

'But it were not his fault. Don't judge him. I made him do it.'

I raise my eyebrows. She is a strong woman but less than half his weight and I've seen him lift barn doors.

'He came to the house not long after Enid had the baby to bring hooks for Arthur, but Arthur was up Howick. It was cold and wet, so I asked him in and gave him soup. Mother Black was at church. So, I explained about needing a baby and I asked him to . . . to . . .'

She stops to take a deep breath. I am unable to speak and struggle to keep my face impassive.

'Well, he's a good man and he said no, of course. So, I pushed myself against him and kissed him and the like. Well . . .'

She stops again and buries her face in her hands.

I can see it, and more I can feel it. His big strong body. I feel the flush rising up my neck and cheeks as I struggle for the words to take away her guilt.

'Just the once?' I say, keeping my voice calm and even.

'Yes. Of course.' She looks at me in horror.

'Then I don't see that it was so wrong,' I say very firmly.

She reaches out and takes my hand and sobs again.

'No, it was wrong, so wrong.'

'The reason was right. You wanted a baby for Arthur, for his mother, not just for you.'

'But I enjoyed it. I enjoyed it. And so did he.' She covers her face with her hands again.

The words come easily then and they are from me, from all my selves, from here and from the other place.

'Good. It's better that the baby was conceived in pleasure,

as it would have been with Arthur. Now you must think only of Arthur and the baby and just forget what you have told me.'

'But . . .'

'No. Trust me, I'm an expert on this. Live for now. For the good you can do now. Love this baby and love the man who will be his true father – Arthur. Just do it, Alice. That is your duty now.'

She looks at me, nose running, tears pouring, and manages to smile.

We hold each other tight, and I am myself again.

The knock at our door comes late in the night: I know what it will be. I walk across the room in my shift and open the door a little. The innkeeper is barely visible behind his candle but his bulbous drinker's nose casts a huge, swaying shadow on the wall beside him. For just a moment the memories flutter in the darkness but I push them away.

He is pleasant enough and tells me the butcher has sent word that I am needed for his wife, that the baby is coming. He seems surprised, though, at my nod of agreement.

Eleanor is already out of bed, the candles lit, and pulling a dress from my trunk. 'Here. Your clean black cotton.' She puts the dress on the bed and pulls on her peignoir. 'I'll go and waken Mr Maunoir to escort you.'

'There's no need.'

'You're Mrs Mackay now. You need an escort. And wear a bonnet and veil.'

'Thank you,' I say and leave all the rest unsaid.

*

The Midwife

We arrive at the butcher's house within a quarter-hour. Mrs Sharp would have walked there alone, even in the night, but I make my thanks to Mr Maunoir, promising to send for him for the return journey. The skivvy opens the door. I remember now that she is called Pearl, the second child of the tanner's wife, and I delivered her fourth brother, baby number ten for his mother.

'Hello, Pearl. Is she upstairs?'

She nods.

I look with approval at the pans boiling on the stove and the pile of white linen warming beside them.

'Did you put those on?'

'Yes. Young Mrs Black, 'er had told me what to do.'

I smile: even now Alice is efficient.

'That's well done. I'll go upstairs. I want you to keep a check on old Mrs Black and then bring up the water and linen when I call.'

'Yes'm,' she says solemnly, eyes wide.

Alice is walking round the bed, leaning against Arthur. He looks straight at me, almost as pale as the first time I spoke to him, when he lay bleeding.

'Alice, love, Mrs Sharp is here.'

And I know he is trying to joke and that he is scared.

'Aye. My ears are still working,' Alice says.

She turns and manages a smile and then starts to groan and stands still, holding his arms.

'When did it start?' I ask Arthur.

'She woke me just after midnight but had been going about two hours then. Wouldn't let me send for you 'til now.'

*

The day comes early with sunlight through the window. Alice is as strong and brave as I had expected her to be, but Arthur is unexpectedly distraught at her pain and I send him away to get his mother's breakfast.

We talk between her pains: the butcher's wife who works hard fourteen hours every day but the Sabbath and the woman who has taken off all her veils. For I am certain of my skills: my hands are Mrs Sharp's and Dr Borthwick's and my other self's as I examine Alice again.

I call to Pearl, asleep in the chair by the bed, and tell her to bring Alice water and sit by her, and I leave them and go along the corridor for Arthur. He is sitting with his mother, reading her the morning prayers. She manages her palsied smile when I say Alice is nearly ready. I ask him if he wants to come in and be with her and he shakes his head. But as I leave the room, he follows me.

Alice squats on the floor on all fours with Arthur kneeling in front of her, mopping her face, and with characteristic stoicism she pushes and breathes and I do no more than take hold of her daughter and wrap her in a towel. And then we help Alice on to the bed and she and Arthur hold their child, while I weep just a little, and then Alice and I deal with the afterbirth.

Later, after I have washed the mother and her baby and Arthur has carried the soiled linen away, we all sit together and drink tea, brought up by a bleary-eyed Pearl.

'We already decided what to call her. No choice,' says Arthur. The curls are halo bright again and the smile is back.

Please not, I think, after old Mrs Black whom Alice once confided in me was called Eglantine.

Alice looks up. 'Elizabeth, of course. Your name. Suits you better than Joanna,' she says.

'Thank you,' I say, and I am very happy.

'Aye and she'll be Jane too. For Jane Weddell, a good friend to us both,' Arthur says.

I look at Alice, but she is serene, smiling down at Elizabeth Jane. I catch Arthur watching me and he smiles the full generous smile he gave me that day when he first looked up at the dirty wretched woman sitting on the cart.

He knows, of course. And it will never be spoken of.

27

Alnwick Moor, August 1842

Arthur arrives for me on Sunday morning, prompt as always, and hands me up on to the trap in front of the long-suffering Mr Maunoir. As Arthur walks round by the horse, Eleanor runs out of the inn and climbs up on the step beside me. She pushes a parcel into my hand.

'For Mary,' she says aloud and then whispers, 'I understand.' She kisses my cheek quickly and gets down.

I look back as the trap pulls away and she is watching with that slight frown. I wave and she waves back. I know there are tears in her eyes as there are in mine.

We argued last night. Eleanor wanted to come with me to the farm and she was bemused at first by my refusal and then became angry at what she called my stubbornness. We were sitting at the small table by the window, both meant to be reading in the last of the evening light, but she kept restarting the conversation I didn't want to have.

'I know that the place is not clean, that they are very poor. But it cannot be worse than Duck Lane.'

'No, but you don't need to see it,' I replied, quiet and calm.

'I want to be there in case you are upset.'

'It is better not. Arthur will be with me.'

'I cannot understand why you are so stubborn about this. Why you do not want my company as well.'

'You do not think Arthur is good enough to support me, to be my friend?'

She stood up, bright colour flushing her neck and cheeks. 'Elizabeth. That is unfair.'

It was. I looked down at my hands but said nothing. She moved round the room, tidying away her books, and I struggled for words that were honest as I looked up at her. 'Eleanor, please forgive me. You have shown nothing but politeness and respect to my friends here.'

'As I would show respect to Mary and John, no matter what their station . . .'

She stopped and I saw the frown of concentration. Then the compassion for which Dr Borthwick had admired her. She walked back round the bed and sat down again at the table and took my hand. 'What happened there?'

I closed my eyes at the image of John Elliott, slowly, so slowly fastening up his breeches with the hands that had forced my thighs apart. And banished him, again.

I looked at Eleanor, my friend, my sister. 'You know that I was lost and ill and they took me in, and Mary cared for me as well as she could. I owe her for that. But they are poor, destitute, and I am ashamed. Not for me, not now, but for them. John Elliott is not a good man. He is a drunkard. He blasphemes and curses.'

She watched me, squeezing my fingers.

315

'I want to protect you from that. From the foul things he will say,' I said, which was the truth. But not the whole truth.

She nodded and smiled, a small, uncertain smile. 'Let us take some tea and then go to bed. You have an early start tomorrow,' she said.

Arthur says nothing until we are away from the cobbles. As we turn west, out of the town, the breeze is full in our faces and I reach up to tie my bonnet ribbons tighter. No veil today.

'Bad weather coming over from west,' he says.

I look up at the blue sky streaked with white.

'Looks fine to me.' I turn to him. 'How do you know?'

'Them high clouds and the breeze from west. There'll be a big storm by evening. Need to get back afore it.'

'Well, you'll want to be home in good time, anyway – a father now! How are Alice and baby Elizabeth today?'

I can feel his smile.

'Both beautiful as the day. Oh, and Alice said as well to tell you her milk is full in and babe is sucking well,' he says, without any embarrassment.

'Good. I'll see them this evening, but I'll want to wash and change my dress before. I'm assuming Mary and the children will be lousy.'

He turns to me, his hands light on the reins.

'It's right bad at the farm, worse than afore. A lot worse.'

I look down at the horse, and then at the road ahead. The hips and haws are set early in this hot summer, the hedgerows dotted with orange and purple, and here and there the elders are already heavy with dark berries. The small fields near the road glow golden with barley and oats. Further away the moor rises up, sheep dotting the green, and furthest of all the dark bulk of the Cheviots.

I know this place.

I don't want to ask about the farm, but I have to. I turn to Arthur.

'How bad?'

'James died last summer.' He hesitates. 'There was measles in the town.'

'And the baby girl?'

'Sickly from born. Died that winter. Alice, aye and me too, we thought as no need for you to know. Not in a letter. Nowt you could do.'

No, I think but I do not say. No, nothing Dr Borthwick could do when he let himself forget. I am ashamed.

I can feel Arthur's discomfort as I sit beside him on the gently swaying cart, the sun warm. I realize that he has always treated me as if I was, I am, an equal; that he has always been honest. A rare gift given with generosity.

'You were right, Arthur, and you know I trust your judgement. And Alice's. Well, Alice is always right. We both know it.'

And we manage to smile.

It is all joy, though, seeing Blacksmith Weddell and Enid and baby Jane. He lifts me down from the trap and hugs me before standing back, blushing, but she, just a young girl, almost bobs a curtsey. I go and take her hand.

'Such a pleasure to meet you, Mrs Weddell, and I am so looking forward to seeing your baby.'

The kitchen is different, messier, and filled with the

sweet-sour smell of the baby. Jane is gone, but there are pink roses in the blue vase that was always on the dresser.

Enid puts the warm milky baby into my arms, another Jane but this one plump and healthy, and it is a real pleasure to hold her and chat with her mother, who is shy at first but has a ready laugh. She is round and rosy-cheeked with dark curls. Filled with life.

As we are leaving, I say quietly to Thomas that I would like to visit Jane's grave, up the hill by the little church. He says he will come with me. Enid, busy showing Arthur the iron swinging frame which Thomas has made for the cradle, looks up. She goes to the dresser and takes the bunch of roses, the stems already neatly tied with string.

'Thomas said as you would likely want to visit her, so I cut these for you to take. Her favourite.'

I thank her and say goodbye.

The sun is still warm, but the breeze is stronger, full in our faces now, as the horse makes slower time up the hill.

Arthur tries to fill the silence, but I make it hard work for him.

'Blacksmith said as he'll make us a frame for Elizabeth's cradle. What do you think?'

'Yes, it looked good and strong.'

'Aye, he makes nothing flimsy.'

I nod.

'Enid's a good girl,' he tries again.

'Yes. They will do well together, Enid and the blacksmith.'

'And the babe looks fine and sturdy.'

'Yes.'

Arthur turns his head and gives me one quick smile. 'Mind, Enid keeps pigs in the yard at back. Rosie gave her two weaners.'

I nod.

Jane's yard and primroses, the first time I as Joanna was there. I can see the starving woman washing her head under the pump, trying to wash away her despair. And then I see Joanna's bone-thin face, the hollow eyes and dirty lank hair reflected in the small square mirror in Jane's scullery. And then a fleeting image of my other face. Gone again.

But I can feel the ghosts as they come crowding in.

Arthur reins in the horse, then gets down and pulls on the wheel brake. The gate to the home field is hanging off its hinges. I start to move and then stop as the acid fills my mouth and I feel the sweat cold on my neck. I swallow the bile and the world spins. I bend forward.

Arthur's warm hand is on mine as he climbs on to the step. I lean against him and the blackness slowly recedes.

'There's no need for you to go in. I'll go and take the food and money. You best stay here.'

I push against him. 'No. I have to.'

He waits patiently and then helps me down. He picks up the basket and I walk beside him to the door, clutching Eleanor's parcel.

Arthur knocks and calls and pushes open the door. The smell of unwashed bodies is the same, the same here as in Duck Lane, but there is also the pungent smell of damp wool, of sheep. The smells I once awakened to. I swallow hard and breathe slowly through my mouth.

Mary is sitting by the empty hearth: no fire, no stockpot, no pile of wood or peat. I walk over and she turns and looks at me, face blank. I kneel in front of her.

'Hello, Mary. It's me, Mrs Sharp, Joanna.'

There is no response at all. Face thin and pale, no longer reddened by the wind, she reeks of urine and faeces and rancid sweat. Pity washes over me as my stomach heaves again.

'Oh, Mary. When did you last eat?'

Nothing. Just the blank stare.

The door swings open and she flinches as John comes in. He sees Arthur.

'I told ee to keep out,' he shouts, slamming the door behind him.

He moves across the room, fists raised, and then sees me beside Mary and stops, swaying. He is thin and filthy, but worse, his left cheek is eaten away, just an oozing hole.

'You . . .' He looks me up and down. 'Must have made good money whoring.' His voice slurs. 'Back fucking the butcher now, I bet.'

I look directly at him, breathing slowly, holding my back straight. I say nothing.

'Have you brought money? You owe me,' he says. As he speaks, air bubbles through the ruined flesh at the side of his mouth.

Part of my mind says syphilitic gumma, too late for help now, as I nod towards the table where Arthur has put the food and parcels.

'Bugger off then. Both of ee.'

Mary stands up and moves uncertainly towards the table. She is pregnant and her left arm is bent and scarred.

Arthur takes my silk-gloved hand and leads me to the door.

We sit silent in the cart until we are down the hill and the wind is hard on our backs. I realize that even Arthur, the indomitable, is shocked.

'He has syphilis, the great pox,' I say in Mrs Sharp's voice.

'Aye, that's what Peter told us. Seen a lot in the Navy, he said. But was just a sore then. Not a hole. Not seen the like afore. Hope I don't again,' says Arthur.

'Mary will have it from him. The baby too if it lives to be born. Perhaps that's what killed the little girl.' Or John Elliott murdered her, murdered them both, the girl and James. But I don't say it.

'It is part of the illness, to go mad, in the end.' I use Mrs Sharp's voice again.

'Good,' says Arthur.

I know that he is angry and I am not. But I should be.

My mind drifts as the wind strengthens and the sky darkens above us. The ghosts line the road now. I cannot see them, but they are there. I know this place, know it better than Mrs Sharp did.

I was here before.

I am in the corridor, running and running but I am getting nearer now to the door at the end. Slowly, slowly it starts to close. I try to run faster but my legs are so heavy and so slow. I reach forward through the thickening air so very slow, now barely moving, and my fingers touch the handle and it is ice cold and . . .

Light dazzles me and I blink and shake my head. Far away, beyond the storm clouds, is a brilliant stripe of aquamarine below a cerulean sky: the sea, too bright, too shining. I have seen this before, before a storm.

And I am other, seeing through her eyes.

My eyes.

'Arthur, stop. Stop!'

I hold on to the seat as he pulls up the horse, the trap swaying. He reaches for me, but I am already climbing down.

'I must go up on to the moor. To where I was found.'

He grabs my hand and holds it tight, shaking his head.

'I must go now. Now. Before it's too late.' I am shouting.

'I'll come with you. The storm is near upon us.'

He is still holding my hand.

'Please. Let me go.'

He looks at me, the man whose life I held in my hands and who in turn gave me a name. And he lets go.

28

Alnwick Moor

The woman walks fast up the moorside, her breath coming quicker. She reaches the first rocks and stops, bending to gather up her skirts in one hand, and then clambers over to the steeper slope above. She strides out, leaning into the rising wind. Her bonnet blows back from her head and she struggles to unfasten it, the wind whipping the ribbons across her face. She turns, and far below she can see the man. He is waving his arms, perhaps shouting.

The ribbons loosen and she holds the bonnet for a moment, then lets it go and watches it blow away across the heather. She waves once to the man and takes hold of her skirts again and climbs upwards.

She is crying.

The first flash of lightning is far away, and her lips move, counting until the distant roll of thunder. She walks up and up until she reaches the shoulder of the hill and stops, looking down, breathing heavily. The first large drops of rain are blown hard against her back and uncovered head. The world bleaches white and she throws back her head, shouting the numbers, 'One, two.' Then the thunder rolls through her, so loud she covers her ears. She bends forward and starts to run as the rain drenches her.

Up and up, and then the arcing light again and she stops as the rumbling builds and breaks and smashes. She stands, waiting, the wind wrapping her soaked skirts around her, water running down her neck.

This time the brilliance and the noise are the same and the air burns.

The sky shatters. Then darkness.

Alnwick Moor

The woman lay unmoving, curled in the heather, white face beaded with rain.

Her eyelids fluttered, then opened. Time passed and she moved, pushing up on one elbow, and paused, breathing slowly, before sitting up. She looked down at her sodden clothes, then ran her fingers over her face and through her wet, curling hair. Slowly, she stood.

She started to walk down the valley and then stopped and turned back, northwards, away from the town.

The broken memories crowded in.

30

An Ending

Oregon,
27ᵗʰ July 1851

My dear Eleanor, my friend, my sister,

   I write to ask for your forgiveness, in hope for what I do not deserve. I should have written before now, but I told myself that I feared to hurt you again. In truth I feared the pain of trying to explain.

   I correspond with Dr Mackay and, in each of his letters, he writes of all that he knows of you, though our correspondence is about events long past by the time the other reads it. Now, I must write because he has told me that you have a daughter, and you have named her Elizabeth.

   This is what happened on the day I disappeared, and what I have since remembered.

   I ran up on to the moor in the storm to escape from all the fragments of my past, or perhaps to find them. An act of despair. Arthur tried to stop me. All I can truly remember is lightning bleaching my eyes, crackling around me, and the crash and vibration of thunder. I must have fallen unconscious.

The Midwife

*When I awoke the pain in my head was terrible and at first
I could hear nothing, though I could feel the gale blowing. I
waited there in the violent silence, waiting I think for death.
I could not live any longer with all the people in my head,
those I had made and those made for me, and those that I
could only glimpse in mirrors, those that were lost to me.*

*But death did not take me, only the start of shivering so
much that my teeth were rattling. I got up and started down
the hill to the road and then so very clearly heard a voice
behind me calling Elizabeth. I was certain then that it was my
true name. I turned, knowing that he could not be there and
knowing that this finally was madness. I went northwards,
away from Alnwick, from you, from all my lives.*

I ran away, leaving you. I am so deeply sorry.

*The next day, or perhaps later, a shepherd gave me milk to
drink and showed me to the north road. I do not know when I
decided to go to Edinburgh, to seek Dr Mackay's help, though
it became my purpose. I remember little of the journey but it
took many days. I lived on the money I had in my purse and
the kindness of strangers to a wretched woman in distress. Dr
Mackay took me in, gave me sanctuary. I was very ill for weeks.
Slowly, with his help, I found more of myself again. We pieced
together a story which seemed to fit. I do not know how much
of this is the truth, but it makes sense to me now.*

*I lived in India, I think as a young girl, though I can
remember playing in snow as a small child. I married an Indian
man, a doctor and scholar. I must have learned medicine from
him. I have a very clear memory of women in silk face coverings
and then caring for them as they gave birth, unveiled. We
travelled together overland and by ship and I can remember*

huge, tiled palaces and eating pomegranate. Dr Mackay thought that our marriage would have caused controversy and perhaps we had to travel, even to escape. I do not know.

I do, though, know for certain that I have been with my husband in hot countries and on a long voyage across warm seas and I have walked with him by the side of crashing waves in icy cold winds. I know he is lost to me but at least now I can remember him. I can feel him holding me, his face above mine, his brown eyes, his mouth with the dark moustache, his voice saying Elizabeth.

I do not know how I came to Alnwick Moor that first time, though it is not so very far from the sea and I have walked much further.

As I became stronger I realized that I could not come back to you, could not be all those different selves, and that you needed to be free from me. I decided to travel to America, to a new world. Dr Mackay wanted me to write to you then, to say that I was safe, but I couldn't. I should have. By the time I arrived here at my journey's end, I knew you were married and had a child. It seemed too late.

I am one person now. My name is still Mrs Elizabeth Mackay, a doctor's widow. Here, in this new town on the Willamette River, I am doctor, nurse and midwife. I was accepted, reluctantly at first, because I was needed. Now I am respected; even, I think, liked by some. I am training two girls as midwives and another as my apprentice. My new frame-house is solid and my garden productive. Best of all, my daughter is two years old. I found her, a newborn baby, on my porch. I do not describe her as abandoned but as a precious gift, left there because her mother knew that she would be cared for. I hope she will grow to be brave and strong enough to change the world, as you are. She is Eleanor, named for you.

I will never properly know my life before, but I can see the face of the man I loved, and I can see your face and remember that love too. I am at peace and this is my home.

If you can, then please find it in your heart to forgive me.

Your loving friend and sister,
Elizabeth Mackay

Epilogue

Extract from Durham Victorian History Society Newsletter, April 2019

For those of you who couldn't attend, here is the text of Dr Emily Dickinson's *International Woman's Day Public Lecture* which she gave at St Julian's College on 8 March 2019.

Dr Dickinson is a Durham graduate and was resident at St Julian's whist undertaking her doctoral research. Her best-selling biography of Eleanor MacPherson is based on her final thesis. Signed copies of *Education, A Woman's Right: A biography of Eleanor MacPherson (1810–1890)* are available at the University book shop.

A strange coincidence

In researching Eleanor MacPherson, I came across the fact that she met her second husband in Alnwick, a town in Northumberland, and was intrigued about why she was there. That led me to the story of the woman who went missing on Alnwick Moor in 1842. What I hadn't expected at all was the contemporary link – the strange coincidence that is the title of my talk this evening.

For those of you who are not as obsessed with Eleanor as I, it might help to set the scene with the well-known details of this amazing woman's life, most of which relate to her time in Newcastle and Durham after she married the Reverend Angus MacPherson in 1843. It is often assumed that Eleanor met Angus through some link with her first husband, Stephen Johnson, also a clergyman though best remembered now as a leading abolitionist. But that is not the case.

After Stephen's death in 1840, the widowed Mrs Eleanor Johnson spent the winter in London with her friend, Abigail Snow. The women remained close friends until Eleanor's death in 1890. It was Abigail's daughter, also Eleanor, named for her Godmother and mother's friend, who wrote the first biography of Eleanor MacPherson, published in 1894. That biography was partly based on the considerable correspondence between Eleanor and Abigail, but the correspondence itself was later lost in the Blitz when the Snow family home in London was destroyed. The biography describes Eleanor's two marriages, both to remarkable men, but, unusually for a Victorian text, focuses mainly on Eleanor's achievements as an educator, an abolitionist and latterly as a women's suffragist. As you may know, Eleanor established the Newcastle School for Girls in 1848 and the Durham School for Girls in 1856, after her husband was made Vicar of St Julian's. She was the primary mover in establishing St Julian's College for women in 1858 and was on the Board of the College for over 30 years. She was the driver of the widening of the curriculum beyond teacher training to include BA and BSc degrees.

Sadly, she died before graduates of St Julian's became the first female graduates from Durham University in 1898.

From the 1894 biography and all other sources, it appears that both of Eleanor's marriages were happy. There were no children from her first marriage but three survived to adulthood from her second: Angus, Elizabeth and Stephen. Elizabeth MacPherson was one of the first students at the London School of Medicine for Women in 1874 and continued working as a doctor at the Hospital for Women until her death in 1910. She never married. However, Stephen, her younger brother, a clergyman, had a large family. I will come back to his descendants.

All of that is on Wikipedia. What isn't, is where the widowed Eleanor Johnson met Reverend MacPherson. Well, as I discovered, it was in Alnwick, in 1842. We know this because both are mentioned as giving evidence in relation to the disappearance of a Mrs Elizabeth Mackay, also referred to as Mrs Sharp, on Alnwick Moor on Sunday, 28th August 1842. What took some time to unearth was that Eleanor Johnson and Elizabeth Mackay were friends who had travelled together from Winchester to Alnwick, where Elizabeth Mackay had previously lived and worked as the midwife, Mrs Sharp, prior to her second marriage. I can find no entry in relation to that marriage, which appears to have taken place in London, in the national archive, but registration of marriages was still incomplete in the 1840s. Reverend MacPherson's diaries mention Mrs Sharp's 'compassion and care' during the diphtheria epidemic of 1839 in Alnwick and there is a detailed account of him seeing her (now Mrs Elizabeth Mackay) and Mrs

Eleanor Johnson in Alnwick on 25th August 1842, just three days before Elizabeth Mackay's disappearance on the Moor.

There is scanty information about Elizabeth Mackay's actual disappearance. It was reported by Mr Arthur Black who appears to have been a highly respected citizen, later becoming Mayor of Alnwick and owner of considerable property in Alnwick and Morpeth. There was certainly a search of the high Moor, but this was delayed by a storm: there was severe flooding and the road from Alnwick was impassable for several days. The cause of death was reported as lightning strike, but the body was never found.

The strange, perhaps unsettling, coincidence relates to a more recent tragedy and one which is, I know, still of concern here in the north. Professor Elizabeth Wilson, an obstetrician in Newcastle, disappeared during a storm on Alnwick Moor on 21st January 2018. She was walking with her husband, Dr Ravi Chakrabarti, and two friends along the footpath close to the military installation on the top of the Moor. They had turned back due to the worsening weather when the thunder and lightning started. Elizabeth was walking in front. The three survivors all described the same events: a brilliant white lightning flash and huge rolling thunder; Ravi shouting out to lie down; all being momentarily blinded and deafened. When they stood up again Elizabeth was not there. She has not been found, despite extensive searches, nor any trace of her. Nothing, nothing at all.

Professor Elizabeth Wilson was, is, the great, great-granddaughter of Eleanor's son, Stephen.

Just a coincidence, I know, but I realized the link sitting in a dark room in the Durham archive and I definitely had that coldness-on-the-neck and goosebumps feeling. I do again standing here now.

So, best I think to end this talk in Eleanor MacPherson's own words, quoted in the 1894 biography, from a letter to her daughter, Elizabeth, on the day she was accepted on to the medical register:

'I named you for my friend Mrs Elizabeth Mackay who sadly died before you were born. She was a woman of exceptional intelligence combined with great skill and compassion. She saved many mothers in childbirth. The times were not kind to her and she was not able to study medicine as you have so bravely done. You have more than honoured her name. I am so very proud of you, my beloved daughter.'

Acknowledgements

In the depths of the first national lockdown, our first grand-child was born, 350 miles away. It was such a joy that both mother and baby were well, alongside the real pain of not knowing when we would be able to see them. Three days later, Debbie Taylor phoned to tell me that I had won the *Mslexia* Novel Competition. Too much good news in such a strange and difficult time seemed to be tempting fate, but it was still quite a week.

So, my first thanks are to Debbie, the *Mslexia* team and the competition judges. One of the judges was Charlotte Robertson, of Robertson Murray, who has since been a brilliant agent and guide through this totally unknown territory, for me, of fiction publishing. She knows how grateful I am. Thanks too to the excellent editorial and publishing team at Pan Macmillan: Caroline Hogg, Rebecca Needes, Mary Chamberlain and Gillian Green among many.

I came late to fiction writing, having spent a lot of my professional life writing reports and papers which had to be technical, accurate and very dry. There was a real pleasure in making up a story but also, for me, the risk of an easy escape into too much research. At one point I drove along the road between Alnwick and Rothbury, struggling with the position of Alnwick Moor and Edlingham village in terms of two of the scenes in the almost-completed novel. I then realized I could be a little wanton with the geography as this is a work of fiction. My apologies, though, to local residents.

I have tried to be accurate with the description of the early Victorian society in which the novel is set: the poverty and the affluence, the restricted life of women, and the terrible burden of disease. My main source of background medical history was the Wellcome Collection library (Euston Road), which is an amazing free resource with extremely helpful library staff and easily accessible online material. In Alnwick, the volunteer-run Bailiffgate Museum was a valuable local history resource.

In terms of learning to write fiction, I thank tutors and fellow students on the MA Creative Writing course 2015–17 at Newcastle University. I loved being a student again, though learning to be a beginner was initially a challenge. Most of all, my thanks go to Margaret Wilkinson, a brilliant teacher, tutor and mentor. No adverb was left unchallenged, and I owe her a focus on uncluttered dialogue. I also benefitted from seminars and two Spring Schools organised by the Newcastle Centre for the Literary Arts (NCLA); a Writers & Artists course led by William Ryan; and the inaugural Mslexicon Writing Weekend in 2019. Last, but absolutely not least, my thanks to my 'writing buddy' Lesley Turner, who read large sections of the text at various stages and whose comments were always useful, positive and challenging. The gossip over coffee was good too.

The Midwife

And the thanks from the heart. My mum and dad gave me the great gift of loving to read, and a voracious appetite for fiction of all types. Money was tight in my early childhood but there were always books. Thanks above all to my immediate family: to Hugh for our many shared years and to our adult children for being themselves. They read a near-final version of the novel and were kind in their comments. They were the critics who mattered most.

Finally, my thanks to the welfare state and society as it was in the 1970s and early '80s. I had the uncountable benefit of growing up in that period of true social mobility. I was the first person in my extended family to go to university and the state fully supported me financially to go to medical school. I was never in debt. This is how it should be.

Tricia Cresswell
June 2021